Shattered Trust

Shattered Trust

LESLIE
ESDAILE BANKS

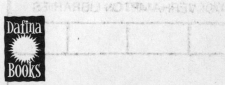

KENSINGTON PUBLISHING CORP.
http://www.kensingtonbooks.com

DAFINA BOOKS are published by

Kensington Publishing Corp.
850 Third Avenue
New York, NY 10022

All Kensington titles, imprints and distributed lines are available at special quantity discounts for bulk purchases for sales promotion, premiums, fund-raising, educational or institutional use.

Special book excerpts or customized printings can also be created to fit specific needs. For details, write or phone the office of the Kensington Special Sales Manager: Kensington Publishing Corp., 850 Third Avenue, New York, NY 10022. Attn. Special Sales Department. Phone: 1-800-221-2647.

Dafina Books and the Dafina logo Reg. U.S. Pat. & TM Off.

ISBN 0-7582-1331-X

First Kensington Trade Paperback Printing: September 2006
10 9 8 7 6 5 4 3 2 1

Printed in the United States of America

This is for my daughter, Helena . . .
my best friend, giggle-buddy, warm hugger,
and the light of my heart.
I am proud of you in every way. May the
good guys win in the end your whole life long!
Love, Mom

Acknowledgments

Thanks to: Manie Barron, my agent, who always finds the best projects; Karen Thomas, for her willingness to let me test my hand at creating many different heroines; Nicole Bruce, for her steadfast support . . . and my daughter, Helena, who is my best girlfriend.

Chapter
1

Villa on Grand Cayman, Present Day

James Carter's skin was like dark, bittersweet chocolate. Smooth, a confection that had slowly melted in her mouth all night long, a flavor that she could still savor hours later on the back of her tongue.

Laura stood in the kitchen of their newly rebuilt house, her hands besotted with mango nectar, as she meticulously peeled the skin away from the fruit and watched dawn burn the dew from the hibiscus that nearly covered her kitchen windows with their bright-hued wash of color. Heaven on earth.

After the terrible storms that had decimated the property over a year ago, only her battered memory of the disaster remained. There was no physical evidence left of the destruction. So why were their souls restless after more than a year of hiatus from the hectic, insane urban reality of Philly? she wondered. All those who'd hunted them had been either imprisoned or permanently neutralized by death. Her family was no longer at risk, nor was she in peril. The money was righteous; she'd come out holding financial aces worth millions once she was done. Therefore, the quiet, nagging feeling of unrest made no sense.

Her wild and crazy cousin, Najira, was safe and sound and living not far from their house on the island with James's partner, Steve, and her brother Jamal. Their father, her Uncle Akhan, had healed nicely, and was back in his old home in North Philly, safe. Her sisters and their children were stateside, well provided for, and going on about their normal lives without interruption. So why the case of nerves?

The only thing she could chalk it up to was memories . . . gruesome, visceral memories of treacherous games, dangerous liaisons, and heavy losses. Like the angry storms that had swept through Florida and the Caribbean, she'd swept through Philadelphia's black elite and had served a harsh blow of justice like a force of nature. Yet, by all accounts, it seemed as though the landscape had healed over, things had gone back to normal, and all evidence of her wrath was invisible to the naked eye.

But that didn't mean it hadn't happened. It had. Infrastructure had been rebuilt, just like it had been in paradise. Power, literally and figuratively, had been restored. Roads, water sources, homes, and buildings had been newly constructed and replaced. However, no one forgot what had taken place not so long ago. Every time it rained hard, people were wary. Human nature. Every time folks probably heard her name in Philly, she was also aware that they most likely whispered about Hurricane Laura in hushed, reverent tones. So be it.

What was there to do? She and Najira finally accepted the reality that her fund-raising business was dead from it all; it had died on the vine from foundations, politicians, and grant sources too wary of her capacity to inflict destruction to accept proposals. Thus, like some of the facilities in the Caribbean that would never come back after the storms, she'd ultimately shut down Rainmakers, Inc., and had given all loyal employees a hefty severance with glowing recommendations. Rest in peace. She and her small inner circle could live off the residuals of millions. Whatever. Maybe it was finally just time to meld into the obscure and become a private citizen again.

Laura rinsed her hands and reached up into the cabinet for

the coffee to begin a fresh pot. Carefully opening the vacuum-sealed mason jar of fresh beans, she breathed in deeply before dumping some into the small grinder. Her new husband was like black coffee, too. . . . James always filled up a room without saying a word and eclipsed all vacancies within it, silently, mysteriously, and lingered in her subconscious with his wonderful aroma. In a very quiet way, he'd filled up her spirit like that as well, a gentle force that created an urge, a hankering that could rarely be ignored.

He poured over her senses still, hours later. The pungent scent of their lovemaking clung to her skin beneath her dampened robe. Remnants of his sticky essence made the flesh of her thighs fuse together as she made coffee and a small plate of fruit. She stared at the huge diamond on her hand, allowing the natural sunlight to bathe it and sparkle in the facets. More than a year of rapture, and her soul was now restless. Why?

For all his slow, calm delivery of words and actions, she could feel something palpable constantly roiling just beneath the surface of James's skin. He seemed to be at peace, but wasn't . . . like her. In fact, as she turned the dilemma over and over in her mind, Najira and Steve also had a quiet desperation in their eyes when they all got together. The only one who was being honest was Jamal. He'd flat out admitted that for all the glory of paradise, he was bored.

Laura pressed the top of the Cuisinart grinder and the aroma of freshly ground coffee entered her nose. The slight hum in the kitchen connected to her spinal column and she lifted her hand; the noise seemed out of place in the early morning silence. This hour required reverence, stillness. The atrocities of the world seemed so far away, yet she knew they were also close enough to breathe against her ear until the hair at the nape of her neck stood up.

"Hey," a quiet male voice whispered from the kitchen doorway.

She didn't turn around or start. "Hey," she said calmly. "I was making coffee and some fruit. You want some?"

Laura glanced over her shoulder. James leaned against the doorframe and raked his hair, but didn't sit down.

They both just looked at each other for a moment.

"I know," she said quietly, and then went back to the task of finding a filter for the pot.

He nodded. "You feeling it, too?"

"Yeah," she said just above a whisper and added water to the coffeemaker. "How long have you?"

"Couple of months," he admitted and entered the kitchen. "Something's nagging my gut."

"It isn't over, is it?" She stopped making coffee and stared at him. "Your gut is never wrong, James. Neither is mine."

He slowly sat down in a chair, closed his eyes, and leaned his head back against the wall. "I know, baby. I know."

James let his breath out in an audible sigh. She turned on the coffeemaker and came to the table to sit across from him.

"You first," she said with a half smile.

He opened his eyes and ran his palms down his face and gave her a sheepish grin. "That's not what you said last night."

She chuckled. "Yeah, I know. But you're avoiding the subject. So, since I got mine multiple times last night—you first, this morning."

He nodded and chuckled with her, leaning on his forearms on the table as he sat forward to stare at her. "I'm not trying to blow the groove, Laura, but I've got this weird feeling like . . . like it's too quiet. I keep telling myself that it's just because I'm not used to a life without drama that I'm feeling like the other shoe is about to drop. Does that make sense?"

She leaned forward and clasped his hands within hers. "Yeah, I know exactly how you feel. I've been reading the newspapers from back home online."

He chuckled, squeezed her hands gently, and then sat back. "I thought we were gonna banish the States for a while?"

She smiled and stood. "How about that coffee?"

He watched her move to the counter, loving the way her shapely body flowed beneath the peach silk of her robe. Her cinnamon brown skin looked like it sucked up the color of the fabric and reflected it back out through her pores. Her short, dark, velvety hair was a mussed profusion of curls on top of her head, evidence of the torrid night before. "Coffee, huh?" he said, trying to keep his nature at bay as he watched her fix their morning brew. "Isn't that how this all got started a long time ago?"

She laughed and glimpsed him over her shoulder. He loved the way her dark, smoldering eyes glistened with mischief in the privacy of their kitchen . . . and the way her lush mouth pouted as she devised a comeback line. He waited patiently for her and the coffee, wondering why he was trying to ruin paradise. It made no sense.

He had all that any man could want. Screw the fledgling detective agency. He and Steve could open a small water sports business by the resorts and live out the rest of their lives in peace. What better way for two ex-cops to retire? They had both made it out alive, whatever gunshot wounds they'd sustained had earned them citations, they'd healed, had gotten out of the system with a solid pension, and they'd even scored a nice profit from their one and only job. There was no need to stir the pot with unfounded worries. But his gut was never wrong.

Laura brought two mugs of coffee to the table with a fruit plate and slid into a padded wicker chair. "Your coffee," she announced, and then sipped her java with a sly smile.

"And the Internet says what?" he said, taking a slow sip and then picking up a piece of mango from the plate, his eyes never leaving hers.

"The good senator resigned office and got off with a spurious plea bargain. He's been acquitted. All charges against him have been focused on the doctor, Senator Scott's errant son, and dead people."

James nodded and put the piece of mango in his mouth, half chewing, half sucking the flavor of the sweetness, and allowing his tongue to enjoy it before answering her. "Figured as much," he said, casually sucking the juice off his fingers. "If he went down, a lot of other very high-ranking politicians all the way to D.C. would have also gone down, baby. You know how this goes."

She sighed and took a piece of fruit up from the plate, stared at it for a moment, and then popped it into her mouth. "Uhmm, hmmm," she mumbled, chewing. "It's a viper's nest all the way to the top. That's why I shut down Rainmakers."

He smiled and slurped his coffee. "So, if you're out of the grant-making and political fund-raising business, then why are you following the stateside news like a hawk?

"I'm not, really." Her gaze slid away from his with a smile.

"My Scorpio wife is such a gorgeous liar," he said, leaning his head back and dangling another piece of fruit above his mouth, and then allowing it to drop in.

She laughed. "It's not a lie. It's—"

"An evasion. Talk to me, Laura." He smiled and leaned forward, taking up his coffee again. "What are you up to?"

"Nothing," she said sheepishly, sipping her brew and staring at him over the rim of her mug. She set it down with precision. "I'm just watching our backs."

He slurped his brew with a half smile. "You've got serious trust issues, baby." He set his mug down calmly. "But I can't talk too bad about you, because so do I."

"You've been online, too, I take it?"

He chuckled. "You know me well."

"You're worried, too?"

His smile faded. "We did a lot of damage. People with an axe to grind are out in the world again—temporarily gone, but not forgotten."

Her grip tightened around her mug, although her facial expression remained serene. "You think I need to get Akhan out of Philly?"

"Might not hurt to bring him in close with the family down here for a while, until our guts ain't in a knot."

They both stared at each other for a moment.

"You know my uncle loves his community and won't leave Philly."

"I know," James said quietly. "He's one of those old-school warriors that will be there until the bitter end with a shotgun at his door, talkin' about ain't no revenuers coming on his property."

Laura sighed and smiled. "You've talked to him."

James smiled and nodded. "So have Najira and Jamal. Repeatedly."

"I see," Laura said, taking up her coffee again. "Glad to know I'm not the only one with secrets."

He laughed and shook his head, his hand sliding under the table to stroke her thigh. "Nope. But it was all with good intent."

The heat of his hand there made her relax, just as much as his words had. It was oddly comforting to know that he was also on alert and that she was not alone in her wariness.

"Now that I'm fully awake," he said in a low murmur, "and I've had some Joe . . . I have other intentions that are *real* good, too."

"Hmmm . . . sounds like an attempt to distract me."

"No, more like an attempt to relax you and to get that big brain of yours to let go of what we can't do anything about until it happens."

"I like to be prepared for the worst-case scenario," she said, closing her eyes as his hand stroked warmth into the flesh of her leg.

"Me, too," he said quietly, still caressing her thigh. "We'll get Akhan to visit, for an extended stay. I can beef up security here and I know Steve is on the same page."

She opened her eyes. "You're not worried about an actual physical hit, are you? I was more thinking in terms of some financial attack, something to screw us business-wise, or to shut down our contacts to entrepreneurial ventures back home."

James pulled back his hand and leaned forward to clasp hers. This was exactly what he didn't want her to think about. Truthfully, it was exactly what he didn't want to consider, but had to, especially now that the subject had been broached.

"Laura, listen to me. The man's son will be behind bars until the end of time. His niece was killed, shot by her own husband—whom I'm sure they all know by now that you had a hand in bringing down, even if they'll never be sure how. All his cronies and contracts were fucked. The man's reputation was so badly damaged that he can't even get a job in a 7-Eleven back home.

All his allies have distanced themselves from him. The casino boys won't even jeopardize their construction contracts to help him out, given that the big eye in the sky, the media, has been all over this thing like white on rice. To my mind that leaves an old man with nothing to lose, a lot of time and energy to focus on vengeance . . . which you and I both know can fuel the craziest of things in a person for years, baby."

She squeezed his hands tightly and let her gaze drift out of the window toward the horizon. James slipped his hands out of her grasp and stood, rounding the table to stand behind her and caress her shoulders.

"I didn't want to worry you," he murmured, bending to land a kiss on the top of her head.

"I'm all right. Just thinking."

His hands slid down her shoulders in a slow, comforting rub back and forth. "No you're not. But that's OK. I got this, baby. Maybe that's why you married a cop."

She forced herself to smile. "You still have your Peacekeeper?"

He leaned down and nuzzled her neck. "Yep, plus a shotgun, a rifle, two nines, and plenty of shells."

He felt her body tense and gently pulled her up from the chair to embrace her. "I told Mr. and Mrs. Melville the situation a few weeks ago. The man is coming this week to install a security alarm system in here that should have been a part of the rebuild while construction was going on, anyway. Plus security cameras . . . and I've alerted the island authorities of any potential issues. Steve's getting his house wired, too, with a monitor in his office that links to ours—plus panic buttons."

Laura laid her head on his shoulder, her hands caressing his back. "You're really worried, aren't you?"

His answer was a tender kiss. "No . . . I just have trust issues." He forced himself to smile for her sake, and knew she had done the same for him.

She looked into her new husband's intense, dark eyes and saw an old fear flicker within them. She understood it well, and knew the same was frozen within hers.

Without more conversation, she surrendered to his method of banishing reality as his hands untied the sash of her robe. Yes, she understood his need to touch skin, to keep himself rooted in the present. That had also become her need.

His mouth took hers in a slow opening of lips, a gentle duet of tongues, and she understood that their minds no longer had amnesty from the past, now that the dread had been admitted and named. Paradise had been compromised, but coffee-sweetened mango still tasted so good first thing in the morning. Their hiatus had been a placebo; they knew that. Caresses and passionate days and nights were just anesthesia . . . an endorphin rush, like morphine, to chase away the adrenaline tension of bad nerves. That didn't matter right now.

She helped him shed his burgundy silk boxers, and allowed him to lead her back to the kitchen chair. She totally understood James's way of saying, "Baby, I'm worried." That was her way of banishing fear, too.

It was all in his eyes, the way he took her mouth again ever so gently as she carefully straddled his lap. It was all in his touch, the way it grazed over the surface of her skin like she was fragile glass. It had been so obvious in his newfound interest in opening a small sporting goods shop with Steve . . . the way they'd both talked in rapid-fire sentences about the most mundane of things; serving burgers and light fare, frozen drinks, Najira doing the books, Jamal working the registers, her marketing the concept to the resorts.

She understood that James's way was an easy slide into the present that kept him anchored, the same way he'd just slid into her. His motions were steady, not rushed, like his planning. Methodical to the point of crazy-making was his trademark, unraveling her resistance to let go of the past and the tension, one slow stroke at a time . . . his unspoken signature making her keep her eyes on him, her eyes on the present not the past, a gentling of her spirit, the way one would calm a frightened thoroughbred. Just don't look down and come to me, his touch beckoned, hands gliding over the now too-sensitive tips of her breasts, causing her soft gasp, which he swallowed.

"I got this," he whispered into her mouth.

She swallowed his promise with a slight shudder. "I know," she murmured against his neck, allowing her fingers to revel in his short-cropped hair, the slight waves within it teasing her fingertips. Her husband knew her very, very well, just like she knew him and could tell that he needed her to stay in the here and now.

Releasing the threat of tomorrow, she bore down on him harder, gently rotating her hips in a slow, undulating circle that finally drew a quiet gasp from him and made him close his eyes.

God yes, his wife knew him so very, very well, and the disturbing conversation began to ebb and flow like her hips, pushing itself into the far recesses of his mind. His hands found her tight, fleshy backside as her hands rested gently against his shoulders. Thoughts of possible hit men embedded in their future seemed so remote as he became more deeply embedded within her, their thigh muscles working in unison, in partnership to keep their slow, steady rhythm, the flow of agonizing movements unbroken.

He loved the way coffee and mango lingered in her sweet kiss . . . the way her tongue explored the inside of his mouth, pulling a moan up from his lungs as her tempo increased ever so slightly. Yeah . . . right now, nothing else mattered, and that was just the way he liked it—easy. Nothing too profound. Her body heating until he could feel a light sheen of perspiration beginning to claim it. Her voice a muffled whimper grazing the soft tissue of his palate, something to savor and allow to hold him hostage, just like her natural scent.

She threw her head back and gave him access to kiss her windpipe, and down to the soft cleft at the base of her throat, her full, pendulous breasts swaying slightly to every rise and fall of her voluptuous body against his—easy. Coffee with her in the morning, have mercy. A slow sip of hard, java-hued nipples between his lips; his most favorite of ways to begin the day.

"Laura." One strangled word, her name, brought her back to him hard, and fast, and hot—scalding . . . making him meet her where she was, close to the edge, as the burn ran down his shaft and imploded in his sac.

She moved against him like a sudden island rain, pelting his groin with intense pleasure, no longer a slow dissolve of his sanity. This morning wasn't a light shower, but had opened up to an unexpected, torrential downpour—an event that would now happen quickly before the clouds parted and allowed in the sun of her smile again.

Humid, wet, she contracted against him, consuming worry, washing it away with a steady beat against his hard ground until he almost lifted them both out of the chair with each upward thrust. The steady sound of the wicker's groan was no comparison to his, her breaths now a chant of urgent compliance—easy was gone, heat surreal. His hands in her hair, not long, needing the feel of her fleshy backside, her hips to anchor and gain leverage until he could barely breathe.

The sound of his voice thundering throughout the kitchen had done her in. *Slow*, what was that? *Tender*, the word had lost meaning. Patience was an impossible concept when she could feel his definition sliding within her . . . the head, the groove of it pulling against her agony-fired canal, lodged so tightly inside her that she could feel the vein pulsing down his engorged shaft to the wide berth of his base each time he drew out again.

Then he'd found that spot like he always did. His tight, muscular legs were pushing them both up and half-out of the chair till she nearly shrieked it felt so good. Every bulge of six-packed abdominal sinew worked like a hard, fast sit-up, his arms steel cable wrapped around her waist—her hands ached to hold his fantastic stone-carved ass, but his massive shoulders were all she had access to.

His touch was now a severe, aggressive sweep of pleasure against every aching place on her skin, leaving her unable to take enough of him into her fast enough, hard enough. Forget about tomorrow, when his name became a non sequitur fused with the Almighty's, "OhmigodJames!"

Head thrown back, mouth open for air, he felt the first lightning strike arch her, and then it immediately sent a crack-whip of motion down her spine that opened him up to a pure holler. Nails in his shoulders, he didn't care, just don't stop the electric current; let it flow. Jags of pleasure sent a convulsing wave through his scrotum that he couldn't hold back if his life depended on it. Her body froze like her gasp had for a second as though she'd been hit with another sudden jolt of lightning, then she released in repeated, jerking shudders that ruined him to thunder her name one more time.

And just as quickly as it had begun, the storm was over. Damp forehead to forehead they stayed in the chair for a long while, breathing hard, clinging to each other, dazed.

When he could finally focus and open his eyes, she peered down at him with a brilliant smile like the island sun had just come out again.

He wiped his brow with the back of his forearm and let out a deep exhale. She dabbed at her cleavage with the heel of her palm, chasing a tiny trickle of sweat that rolled down between her breasts. He watched the perspiration, his eyes following the path of it until she'd blotted it dry, his mouth also going dry in the process. Lord, his woman was fine.

"Good morning to you, too," she said with a soft chuckle and then kissed the bridge of his nose. "Want another cup of coffee?"

"Maybe in an hour," he said, smiling, and dropped his head to her shoulder, beat. "Coffee like this every morning might kill me, woman."

Chapter 2

Steve rolled over with a groan and rubbed his palms down his face. His shoulders still stung from the slight sunburn that had reddened and had begun peeling the tender skin. The floorboards in the house were strumming with bass line from the stereo, which meant Jamal was up, and the sound connected to the mild hangover throb in his temples. It was time to get back into some sort of routine. Never in a million years would he have dreamed that he'd be trying to escape from an extended vacation.

Slowly swinging his legs over the side of the bed, he attempted to gain his bearings. Najira's quiet appearance in the doorway of the bathroom helped considerably. She was wearing only a towel, and he watched the dampness soak into her pretty brown skin. Was he outta his mind? This was *the life*.

"Good morning," she said with a bright smile that lit up her face. "I figured since my brother was cranking the music, it was time to get up."

Steve shook his head and chuckled. "Yeah," he added with a sigh. "But can the man give it a rest—just once?"

She came to him and leaned in closely, whispering in his ear. "You know why he cranks the music, so don't even play."

A sheepish grin slid across Steve's face. "What can I say?"

"Nothing," she giggled, and kissed the top of his head. "Go get a shower, man."

"Thought you might hang out in there with me?"

She rolled her eyes and walked away with a smile, giving him feigned attitude as she sashayed across the room. "I already got mine."

"So you'd just leave a man hanging like that after you already got yours? You're wrong, 'Jira."

They both laughed hard.

"That's why Jamal's got Missy Elliott rockin' the house first thing in the morning—he ain't tryin' to hear you get yours, okaaay?"

"He didn't hear all that," Steve said laughing as he walked into the bathroom. He peered around the doorframe. "Did he?"

She held up her hand and sucked her teeth, trying to appear annoyed.

"That was real early, though," Steve protested. "After smokin' blunts and wearing out the blender with rum drinks, you know Jamal wasn't hardly awake."

One hand went to Najira's hip. "He probably wasn't when you started, but after hollering and—"

"All right, all right," Steve said, holding up both hands and backing into the bathroom with a belly laugh. "Let's go get some breakfast."

Najira shook her head as she listened to the shower go on at the same time the toilet lid slammed up. "Bathroom door all open . . ." she grumbled as she slipped on a thong and began searching in the dresser for a tank top and shorts. How in the world had she found herself hooked up with a cool white boy from Philly, living with her half-gangsta brother, no less, down in paradise with her outrageous cousin around the corner in a villa? No job, more money than she'd dared to dream of, all because they'd pulled a smooth heist that was so sweet it still tasted like cotton candy.

She couldn't make the smile leave her face. Pure contentment settled into her bones as she yanked her dreadlocks up into a ponytail held by a scrunchie, dressed, and left Steve washing up in the shower. What were she and Laura doing messing with two ex-cops and loving every minute of it?

Cool air filtered through the house and put small pebbles of gooseflesh on her skin as she made her way to the kitchen looking for Jamal. The blaring music added extra bounce and rhythm to her step, almost making a giggle bubble up within her as she entered the brightly lit room and saw Jamal hunched over a plate, shoveling food into his mouth.

"Hey," she said, swinging open the refrigerator door.

"Yo," he mumbled through his food. "Don't even look for any fried fish or grits. Gone."

"Dag, Jamal. You ain't leave nothing good for breakfast." Najira extracted the nearly empty carton of orange juice and held it up to the light. "If you were only gonna leave a corner, you might as well have drank it all."

"Hand it here, then," he said smiling. "Got the munchies like *a mother* this morning."

"See . . ." she shook her head and handed him the carton, too done as he turned it up to his mouth.

"That's why y'all need to go on ahead and make some fresh, 'cause you know I done drank out the carton any ole way."

She cut him a glare through a smile and went to the fruit bowl to gather up a few oranges and a small pineapple for the juicer. "You know," she said slowly, peeling the fruit without looking at her brother, "we've gotta get into some sorta routine around here."

"I have a routine," Jamal said, unfazed, wiping his plate with a biscuit and stuffing it into his mouth.

"You know that business idea Steve and James was talking about? Well, it might be good to have something to do every day, other than sitting around here, or—"

"Knocking boots every chance you get."

Jamal gave her a sly smile and went back to his plate, seeming pleased when Najira looked away.

"I'm serious," she finally said, setting the small paring knife down on the counter hard.

"I am, too, boo," Jamal said calmly. "I have to get up and get outta here early every day like I'm in a shelter program or something to keep from hearing—"

"All right, all right, all right," Najira said, becoming peevish as she shoved fruit into the juicer and depressed the top, hoping the sound would drown her brother out. "You get on my nerves, Jamal."

"I love you, too." He winked and stood up, stretching like a lanky cat, his boxers three inches above the waistband of his baggy jean shorts, and then raked his fingers down the exposed, greased parts in his immaculate cornrows. "I ain't hatin'," he said, taking his plate to the sink. "Steve is cool with me; I just don't wanna hear all that, is all I'm saying. I'm still your big brother, feel me?"

She swallowed away a smile, determined to stay annoyed but couldn't. "That's why we've gotta get something productive happening. Just like James said the other night, he and Steve had never done more than ten days off at a stretch, and really hadn't been beyond the Jersey shore, at that. Nobody is trying to travel to any terrorist hot spots, and after you do all the clubs, try all the water sports, take all the tours, and act up at Carnival, other than chill on the beach, golf, or fish, what is there to do?"

Jamal leaned against the refrigerator with a soft thud and folded his arms. His expression became serious as he searched her eyes for answers. "I hear you. Never thought I'd ever say something like that, myself. A year island hopping, seeing all the fine women and chasing booty for days . . . just having stoopid money in my pocket, I gotta do something, 'Jira. I ain't cut out for the quiet life."

Najira nodded, and moved him aside to collect eggs and breakfast sausage out of the fridge. "Laura agrees; we've been laying low for a long time, and everybody is bored. Like, she was a real workaholic, and I've never known her to take any kind of real extended vacation in her life—even on so-called vacations, she was really working, scheming, schmoozing, hooking up a deal, hustling something." Najira looked at Jamal and stared at him for a moment. "I think she's feeling it the most."

"Not necessarily," he said quietly, closing the refrigerator door as Najira balanced her armload of food.

"What do you mean?" Najira waited, and then watched Jamal push away from the appliance to go stare out the window.

"'Jira . . . all my life I've been hustling, scramblin', trying to get here." He turned and looked at her, his expression pained and his tone gentle. "I always wanted to be phat paid, have enough money to never worry about the basics, with extra left over to be able to do whatever I wanted to do. Now I'm here, got that, and . . . I can't explain it, sis. It's like this empty feeling . . . I don't know. Like living on the edge was the razor that kept me sharp, kept me—I don't know."

She set down the eggs carefully, and placed the sausage beside them as a guard so they didn't roll off the counter. "I know. Maybe because we've got Dad in us."

He smiled. "Yeah. The old man was always freedom fighting, always had something to do."

She chuckled sadly and reached down a pan from a hook above the center island range. "Be constructive and productive, right?"

Jamal nodded and let his breath out hard. "Yup. How many times growing up did we hear that?"

"So, what are we doing?" she asked, beginning to prepare breakfast for her and Steve. "Laura got married," Najira added quietly. "But she ain't gonna have no kids, probably."

Jamal froze for a moment and then glanced around the kitchen, dropping his voice. "You pregnant?"

"Huh?"

He closed his eyes and rubbed his palms down his face. "Oh, aw'ight."

"Jamal," she said, both hands on her hips. "Do I look ready for kids and all that, yet?"

"I'm just saying . . ."

"What?"

He glanced around the kitchen again, clearly listening for Steve. "This is the one, ain't it?"

She looked away and began breaking eggs into a small bowl, whipping them hard with a fork. "You got a problem with that?"

"Steve's my boy, I'm just wondering how Pop is gonna take it, long term."

For a moment, neither sibling spoke. The only sound in the kitchen was Najira's frantic destruction of egg yolks.

"Have you really broken it down to Pop how deep this has gotten?" Jamal's question lingered in the kitchen, blending into the sound of a metal fork hitting the side of a Pyrex bowl.

"I didn't think it was necessary to tell him who I was sleeping with, if that's where you're going."

Jamal watched her go back to the refrigerator and extract a stick of butter and several biscuits. She took her time, dropping a pat into the pan and turning the skillet over the heat until the butter melted and coated the bottom of it.

"I'm cool with it, sis," Jamal said in a mercifully quiet tone that finally made her look up at him. "You just need to be sure you're really cool with it before you break it down to Pop. You know you're gonna have to stick to your guns to get him to deal with it. 'Cause you also know he probably had one of the Budweiser king of kings series poster brothers mentally picked out for his baby girl, boo. The gunshot ain't kill him, but, uh . . ."

"I know, don't even say it," she muttered, holding up one hand as she stirred hardening eggs around in the pan with a spatula. She watched the slurry begin to congeal in the skillet.

"You're doing it all backward," Jamal said with a sheepish grin.

"I am not!" Najira practically hollered. "I know what I'm doing. I know how I feel, and—"

"If you don't start the other stuff, first, the eggs are gonna get done before the sausage, is all I'm saying." Jamal reached down a black, cast-iron pan, issuing Najira a sly wink, and began helping her cook. "Timing is everything."

"I know what I'm doing," she said in a testy tone, snatching the pan from him.

"I ain't trying to cook for your man or get in between it," he said grinning. "All I know is, you need to have a real conversation with Pop before he gets down here."

She stopped moving about, nearly paralyzed. "Did he say he was coming?"

"Do it matter?" Jamal said, raising an eyebrow.

"Stop playing," she whispered.

"Aw, girl, no. He didn't say he was coming, just that I know James and cuz are trying to get him down here with the quickness."

Najira let out her breath and turned off the flame beneath the pan. In jerky, halting motions, she flung sausage links into the pan Jamal had reached down, and then spun around to put biscuits in the microwave.

"I don't understand why all of a sudden there's this big rush to get Dad to come down here and whatnot." She opened the refrigerator door and leaned in, hunting for guava jelly, fussing at the shelves. "There's no good reason for the man to be uprooted from his neighborhood and friends, if that's what he doesn't want to do—besides, if he's dead set on staying put, and hates to fly, why can't they leave well enough alone? I mean, Jamal, the man won't halfway take the money we send him, let alone pack his bags for an extended stay." She stood quickly and placed her hands on hips, still staring at the semi-vacant shelves for what no longer existed. "Give me one good reason."

Najira stepped back quickly as the refrigerator door seemed to close on its own and Steve's sudden presence gave her a start.

"For his safety, hon," Steve said carefully.

Najira placed a flat palm on her chest. "Don't *do* that. Lord have mercy, Steve!"

"She's just a little edgy this morning, man," Jamal quipped, and then headed for the door.

"Hold up, J," Najira said. She immediately turned her attention to Steve. "What do you mean, for his safety?"

Jamal shrugged. "Might as well tell her, seeing as how you got enough ammo to go against SWAT in the garage. If it gets hot up in the tip, at least she should know to duck from shells flying before pulling her cute little Jeep in there."

Steve closed his eyes and sighed as Najira blanched.

"What ammo, Steve?"

"Aw, dude . . . c'mon," Steve said, letting his breath out hard and going to fix a pot of coffee. "Not first thing in the morning."

"What ammo, Steve?!" Najira said again, her voice becoming strident.

"And the super security system," Jamal added, nonplussed, taking a swig of juice directly from the juicer.

Najira whirled on him and snatched the container from him, sloshing juice on the floor. "We already have an alarm system."

"Not like the one your boy is getting rigged to work on monitors over at James and Laura's joint."

"Oh, shit . . ." Najira walked away from the stove and sat down in a kitchen chair.

"That was just about the smoothest delivery I've seen in all my life," Steve said sarcastically, glaring at Jamal.

"Just being real, man," Jamal said with a shrug, beginning to sample the cooling eggs in the pan. "The girl needs to know what time it is, just like you need to know that, if Pop decides to come here for a long visit, y'all gonna have to chill while he's under this roof, ya mean? Like, he's old school, even though 'Jira's grown and all, and—"

"J, this is a new millennium," Najira said, dropping her head into her hands. "People can't be judged by—"

"Oh, yeah, I feel you. But did you happen to tell Pop about this being a new millennium? He mighta missed that part, being an old sixties revolutionary cat, and Civil Rights—"

"I know, I know," Steve said, snatching a mug down from the cabinets. "Your old man is like mine in a lot of ways. I'm from Port Richmond, remember—and my folks weren't exactly into the 'we are the world' thing, either. I got it. Not with my daughter. No problem."

"Steve, don't be like that," Najira said, her tone soft.

"Long as you know and don't take it wrong. Me and you cool," Jamal said, offering a fist pound that Steve ignored. "Aw'ight, look, don't be feeling some type of way about what I'm saying."

"I'm not feeling *some type of way* about that," Steve argued. "I'm just pissed about—"

"Talk to me about the ammo and alarm systems," Najira said between her teeth. "Both of you."

Steve and Jamal looked at each other.

"James started the shit, truth be told," Jamal said, opening his arms wide. "Me, I was a bystander."

"Don't blame my partner, man," Steve said, pouring black coffee into his mug and slurping it. "Laura is the one who probably got Jim acting all weird and jumpy about hypotheticals."

"No doubt," Jamal agreed, going to get one of the biscuits from the microwave and tending the sausage in the skillet. "The girl stays paranoid."

"Not without good cause," Najira said quietly. "I would think we'd all have learned that by now."

Steve looked at her and then raked his fingers through his damp blond hair. "Yeah."

"Is that all you've got to say, 'yeah'?" Incredulous, Najira stood up again. "When were you guys gonna tell me there was a problem?"

"A *potential* problem," Steve corrected, sipping his brew with care.

"Might as well sit down, sis. Eat. Chill. And listen. Steve will break it down for you. It ain't rocket science. Me, him, and James are just walking on the safe side, just in case." Jamal crossed the room and headed for the door.

"Where are you going?" Najira said quickly, her gaze darting between her brother and Steve.

"You know when Pop gets here, you are gonna have to go with turkey products and whatnot. He don't do the pork thing, either."

"Yo, man," Steve said, rounding the center island in the kitchen.

"I know you are not going to drop a bomb like that in here, get 'Jira all upset, and then walk."

"Man," Jamal said with a smirk. "You handled your business this morning; I'm gonna go handle mine. There's this *fine* ass sister down at the marina who—"

Jamal stopped talking when the telephone rang. Everyone looked at it, but nobody moved. Finally Steve went to the wall unit and snatched the receiver off the cradle.

"Yeah," Steve said, his tone surly as he glared at Jamal.

"Good afternoon to you, too, man," James said.

Steve glanced up at the clock. "It's eleven in my house, which means it's still morning."

James's laughter boomed through the receiver. "I just called to see if you wanted to head down to the marina, bust a grub, and look at that space we were talking about. But if I caught you at a bad time . . . ?"

The continued laughter made Steve temporarily pull the phone away from his ear. "Something like that," he said once James's chuckles had abated.

"Holla at me later, then. If I had known I was interrupting your groove, I woulda—"

"'Jira knows," Steve said flatly, and turned his back to Najira and Jamal.

James stopped laughing and static filled the receiver.

"Capice?" Steve asked, vindicated by James's stunned silence.

"Roger that," James said, his voice somber. "When?"

"Oh, just freakin' now, dude," Steve said, glaring at Jamal over his shoulder. "We were just talking about it, and since homeboy is all about heading down to the marina, your timing couldn't have been any better."

"Laura and I will be right over."

They sat at the open air restaurant, leaning in, keeping their voices low and speaking in hushed tones, waiting for lunch. Najira took the news with stoic disbelief, like someone in the family had died, as Laura laid out the facts as best she knew them.

Even the shapely young waitress couldn't pull Jamal's attention away from the huddle. James slowly nursed a beer, watching each person's facial expressions. Najira picked at her napkin, her eyes glued to Laura's gaze. Steve casually munched on bread sticks and then chased the dough in his mouth down with an angry swig of beer.

"So much for being bored stupid," Jamal murmured. "You think they'll really come for us or are we trippin'?"

"I don't know, brother," James said evenly, wincing as he swallowed away another sip of beer. "That's the part I don't like, not being sure."

"What if we're getting ourselves all worked up for nothing?" Steve offered. "It's been more than a year, most everybody involved in the first round of cases either died or went to jail for a long time."

"True," Laura said, her voice a quiet, calm murmur. "I'm not worried about the people who went down in round one. All of that led to me, anyway. But the Haines fiasco got the rest of you involved. It won't be long before all of those people who are behind bars, and anyone—like the senator, who got a plea bargain in the second incident—will begin connecting the dots. That's what I'm concerned about."

"We need to figure out how they'll try to come for us, and which one of them is bold enough and still has resources enough to try to drop us," James muttered.

"You know they operate in networks," Steve said, letting his breath out hard. "So, my suggestion is you think in plurals, man. Which *ones*, plural. OK."

James nodded. "Kinda hard to get a bead on things so far from home. No real contacts here. I don't like it. Feels like we're sitting ducks."

"Then maybe we need to go home and bring the noise to them before they bring it to us, and for real squash the bullshit before it even jumps off?" Jamal hailed the waitress for another beer. "To me, *that* seems like a plan."

"Much as I hate to leave paradise," Steve said quietly, halting his words as a beer was set down in front of Jamal.

"But a possible hit?" Najira whispered once the waitress had moved away, leaning in farther to keep her statement confidential. "Isn't that extreme, especially since that's how they all wound up—?"

"Najira," Laura whispered between her teeth. "Those Machiavellian bastards already went there, remember? Now, they are *really* dangerous, because what do they have to lose? Think about it. If we had something they still wanted or needed, that would be one thing. Cheap insurance. But now that they are fairly certain how badly they got screwed out of millions, their reputations and careers destroyed, their families totally disrupted, and—"

"I know," Najira said, slumping back in her chair and briefly closing her eyes. "All they have left is revenge."

"You wrote the book on that one, cuz," Jamal said, clinking his beer bottle against her glass of iced tea.

Laura nodded and sat back, ruffling her hair with her fingers. "Precisely."

Chapter
3

Two detectives stood over the body, shaking their heads as they pulled off their latex gloves and dropped them into a hazmat bag near the scene.

"This poor bastard can't seem to catch a break," the older of the two men said. "First his niece, then his son. This is old-school mob hit type of shit. A wire around the throat while the man was sitting in a chair in his own home eating breakfast. Wife walks in on the body after her morning constitution and freaks out. That old lady doesn't have enough upper body strength to pull off something like this. Don't seem like the type, either." He glanced at the other officers on the scene. "Dust the house for prints, but I don't think you'll find anything out of the norm—this was a pro job."

"I hear you, Joe." The younger detective turned his back on the grisly site and lowered his voice. "Did you hear how they did his son?"

His partner nodded. "I heard he was a real asshole, but to sodomize a man to death . . . geesh. They said the guy died from internal bleeding before the guards even found him—then what the coroner found inside him would make you lose your lunch. The man didn't even have a chance to bury his kid before he got whacked . . . what was it, twenty-four or forty-eight hours ago? Now there'll be no media courtesy to allow the widow to privately grieve. All the gory details will be out. It's a damned travesty, if ever I saw one."

"All this bullshit is giving me the willies," the younger man said, wiping the sheen of anxiety perspiration from his brow with the sleeve of his navy suit. "What do you think he was into that coulda gotten him and his boy handled like this? I mean, given who he was and all."

"Who knows? They all had their hands in the cookie jars, and we just got done with all of that insanity. Maybe some folks got nervous and just decided it was time to clean up the trail, since all roads eventually lead to Rome."

The more seasoned police veteran let out a long sigh then went to the window, motioning to the coroner's black van. "Bag him and tag him," he called out and then turned to his partner. "Get some coffee, kid. It's gonna be a long day. Any time a VIP goes out like this, there'll be a lot of paperwork and Cap is gonna need enough ammo to fend off the media in a statement by the evening news."

James paid the bill and the emotionally weary fivesome stood slowly. Steve's cell phone vibrated on his hip, and he exchanged a glance with James as he took the call.

"Yo," Steve said, alarmed at the number that flashed on his display.

"Yo, Sulli, you should put on cable tonight and watch the news. A bad wind is blowing through Philly, and I'm just giving you a heads up that it wasn't us."

The call disconnected, and Steve stared at his cell phone for a moment.

"Talk to me," James said in a quiet voice. "The color just drained from your face."

"That was Caluzo. He said a bad wind was blowing through Philly, but it wasn't his people. Said to watch the news."

James unhooked his cellular from his waistband and began

dialing a number he knew by heart as the others around him remained mute, staring.

"Yo, Cap," James said the moment the call connected. "Talk to me. I hear there's some crazy shit going on in Philly."

"You're retired," his old captain said. "Stay that way."

"C'mon, man, don't front on me like—"

"I'm serious, Carter," Cap said, his tone low and lethal. "How did you hear about the shit all the way down in the Caribbean when it hasn't even broken yet in the news? *You* need to talk to *me*."

"Can't do that, man. You know I don't work like that."

"Then stay on vacation and stay out of it."

The call abruptly disconnected.

James shot a holding glare around the group. "We take this outside," he said quietly, and began walking.

When they'd all reached the beach and were out of earshot of anyone else, they all began firing questions at him at once.

"James, what the hell was that all about?" Laura said, grabbing his arm.

"Yeah, man. Whassup?" Jamal said, his tone frantic as his gaze shot between Steve and James.

"Cap wasn't giving an inch, I take it," Steve said flatly, raking his hair. "Figured as much."

"What's this all about, Steve?" Najira said, her voice growing strident.

"I don't know," Steve said. "Call your Dad—*now*."

She dug in her purse, ransacking the contents, but kept her eyes on Steve. The moment she found it, Jamal went to her side, and they all patiently waited until the call connected.

"*Hotep*, sweetie," Najira's father said brightly. "To what do I owe the honor of this call from my child so early in the day?"

"Nothing, Dad, just thinking about you and wondering when you might come down for another visit?"

He chuckled. "Let me speak to Laura. Tell her that Akhan knows her methods of persuasion too well by now to be fooled. But I love you anyway. Put her on."

Najira extended the phone toward Laura. "He wants to speak to you."

"Queen Sister, how are you?" he said carefully, going into his usual conspiracy theory ruse of distancing family from him on any electronic device.

"Fine, Brother Akhan," Laura replied, humoring him with good reason. "We were wondering how things were fairing in Philly—how you are doing these days?—and thought a break from the routine might be in order."

"Oh?"

Laura began pacing, the game of double-talk driving her nuts. "Yes. I think that would be a good idea. In fact, *I insist.*"

"Is this a new concept of yours, or something that has been brewing in your head for a while?"

She sighed. "Both, but it has become a nagging thought as of this morning. Please visit, we miss you."

"If you feel so strongly," he said, his tone becoming distant, "I might have to comply."

"There are flights daily, and I'll reimburse you. In fact, if you fly into Miami—which is only like two and a half hours, from there it's about an hour. We could have dinner together. How's that sound?"

The elderly man hesitated. "It sounds rushed."

"It is, because we are so eager to have you in our company."

Silence filled the line.

"I need to pack," he finally said.

"No you don't," Laura replied quickly. "We can go shopping and that would be fun. You have a passport, right?"

"I do."

"Good. Then it's settled. Call my cell, or Najira's, when you get here. We'll pick you up from the airport."

"But I haven't had my tea yet."

She could hear the smile in his voice. "Please," she whispered. "Do it for me."

"Sounding like that, dear child," he said quietly, "how could I refuse?"

"I'll see you soon," Laura said, and then handed the phone to Najira without waiting for the old man's reply.

"I love you, Dad," Najira said softly. "Say hi to Jamal." She passed the phone to Jamal, who kept his line of vision trained on the group.

"Yo, Pop. How you livin'?" Jamal said. "Glad you comin'. Holla at us the minute your flight gets here, aw'ight?"

The group watched Jamal hard.

"OK. Cool," Jamal muttered, and then hung up.

"I gotta ask you all a serious question," Jamal said, keeping his voice so quiet that it could hardly be heard above the surf. "Why you freak the old man out like that over one phone call that didn't tell us squat? I know we've got to be careful and to watch our backs, but it ain't about being so paranoid that—"

"My boy, Caluzo doesn't make long distance calls about bull-shit," Steve said defensively. "He doesn't do 'hi, how's the weather,' chitchat."

James rubbed his palm across his jaw. "Cap was jumpy like a mother, man. That's all I need to know. Think about it. If Caluzo called Sulli, then whatever went down involves people we were tied to during the cases."

"Yeah," Steve affirmed. "He said, quote, 'It wasn't us.' Doesn't that sound like plausible deniability on a hit?"

"Yep," James said, blowing his breath out hard.

"Then who?" Laura asked, looking out toward the turquoise blue sea. "The only reason a guy like Steve's contact would call is if it was a big enough fish to cause a serious tidal wave in a lot of people's lives, meaning potential financial fallout." She turned to hold Najira and Jamal with her gaze. "When your father first answered the telephone, 'Jira, how did he sound?"

"All right," she said quietly. "What are you getting at?"

"He didn't know anything about whatever this thing is Caluzo was referring to, or if I know your dad like I know him, he would have had that real strained sound to his voice when he's sending a coded message. He wasn't sending any tips to me, just being on-guard and cagey."

"So, whatever just went down couldn't have come from his peeps, is what you're saying?" Jamal stared at Laura hard.

"I don't think so, and there's not too much he misses that goes down in the community."

"True dat," Jamal said, kicking at the sand. "Maybe I should make a few calls to my boys stateside to see if anything crazy jumped off in their world?"

"No," James said, placing both hands on his head to stretch the tension out of his back. "I already messed up by calling Cap out of reflex. Any more calls stirring the pot will just turn the big eye in the sky toward us, if it hasn't already started moving in that direction."

Laura and Steve nodded in unison.

"It just kicks my ass that I don't have a clue about what Caluzo was talking about," Steve said, bending down and pitching a seashell. "I hate mobster parables!"

"See, this is why I wanted to go back to Philly for a few," Jamal said, his voice sullen.

"I feel you," Steve said. "I hate being out of the loop."

"All right, people," Laura said, folding her arms over her chest. "We need information. There is one call I can always make that never leaks."

All eyes focused on her as she pushed a speed dial number.

"Rick."

She quietly prayed that his cell wouldn't roll over to voice mail and almost did a jig when Rick's voice filled the receiver.

"Hey, lady," he said in an upbeat tone. "How's my favorite girl?"

"Being nosy, as usual."

Rick laughed. "So life down in paradise hasn't changed you a bit."

"Not at all," she said trying to keep the strain out of her voice. "Sooo . . . what's new?"

He laughed harder. "I thought you shut down Rainmakers, Inc., and had gone into retirement counting our millions on the beach."

She forced a chuckle. "I have."

"So, how's married life treating you? Don't tell me you've already gotten bored with the big lug you married—because if so, I might have to change my domestic condition and fly down there to sweep you off your feet."

"No, and I missed you, too, hon," she said, unable to keep the smile off her face. Even in the worst of times, Rick was a pure trip. "But, seriously, you know I like to always keep my finger on the pulse, so what gives?"

"Now, see, you're in no position to return an information favor like old times," he said, teasing her.

"Who said?" she joked back. "My resources are far and wide, you never know who I might know."

"Hmmm . . . then maybe you might want to help us all figure out who shoved half a utility closet up Howard Scott's ass while he was doing his bid? He didn't make it, but that's off the record. Kid hemorrhaged to death in the laundry room, and we're not releasing details for twenty-four more hours, but you didn't hear that from me—and let me add that I have the drop on it, so don't blow my lead story."

Laura covered her mouth. "Oh my God!"

The group tightened their circle around her.

"Yeah, and shame, too, because his old man just got whacked—strangled with a telephone cord or wire, but, again, that's gotta stay on the down low until the police make a media statement this afternoon. Now, once again, your turn, love of my life. Got any hunches, or you working any angles in this that might be interesting for a guy like me to know?"

"Not yet," Laura said in a stunned murmur, "but if I do, you'll be the first to know, as always."

"Why do I let you always string me along?" He laughed at his own joke.

She couldn't laugh, much less move her mouth to speak.

"I know you know something, or how else would you have the drop on crap going on here all the way down there? Stop teasing me."

"I promise, the minute I have a lead, I'll call you and only you."

"Ahhhh . . . exclusive rights. That's my girl. I love a monogamous woman."

Laura forced a soft chuckle. "I always play straight by you, Rick. You know that . . . but just do me one more favor."

"Name it," he said in a cheery tone.

"Be careful on this one. I don't think it's local."

"Duly noted," he said, all the effervescence gone from his voice. "This is some serious shit, huh? A senator and his son. Very wild."

"Yeah," she said quietly. "Very wild and very dangerous. Thanks for the heads-up. I owe ya."

"As long as you owe me, I'll never go broke," he said, trying to regain his former upbeat responses.

"Yeah," she said flatly. "Just watch your back."

"OK. I can tell from the sound in your voice, you're worried, and I don't like that sound at all. Never heard you like that, Laura. Now I'm concerned. You all right? What are you into this time?"

She paused and ruffled her curls with her fingers, squinting as she peered past the group to the horizon. "That's just the thing, Rick. Nothing."

He sighed. "All right. Tell me anything. Just behave yourself and be careful."

"You, too."

"I love you, kiddo."

"Me, too," she said quietly.

Rick chuckled nervously. "He's standing right there, staring down your throat."

"Yep."

"Oh, so it's like that, now." He laughed, but the sound was strained. "If the big guy is staring you down, then I am worried. Having an old man as an ex-cop doesn't bode well during a call like this. If he's in it—"

"Good-bye, Rick."

"All right. Good-bye. Guess I should just be honored that you're having information phone sex with me."

She laughed and this time it wasn't forced. "Get off the line, man."

"Bye," he said quickly, and hung up.

"Do I dare ask?" James said, shaking his head.

"No, but the call was revealing."

"And?" Jamal said, turning his palms up to the blaring sun.

"Howard Scott, Jr., got waxed in prison," she said slowly. "Went out so foul, I can't even—"

"They probably did him old school," Jamal said. "But you knew that was coming, given how he played everybody around the way." Jamal shook his head and made a face. "The way he did Moon and them, sheeeit. I knew they was laying for him. That's a no-brainer."

"Somebody took out his father, too, Jamal," Laura added carefully. "That wasn't a homeboy hit. Telephone cord or a wire."

"Geez Louise," Steve said raking his hair back with his fingers. "No wonder Mikey called me, because that's old Sicilian signature, if ever I heard it."

"But, if we were worried that the senator would send somebody to come for us, doesn't that sorta take that off our backs?" Najira's gaze darted around the group. "I never, ever, wished anything like that on him or his son, but it just seems like to me that we're in the clear, then."

James shook his head. "Uh, uh. No. I still don't like it."

"I'm feeling my partner on this," Steve said. "Homeboys in prison can get to anybody any time, but a guard paid off to look the other way . . . hey, how do we really know who did Junior?"

"Why do we care?" Najira said, becoming frantic. "That's not our business!"

"Just like homeboys don't do the wire thing, generally," James said, ignoring Najira's outburst.

"And a senatorial hit ain't light fare in these days and times," Steve added. "Not to mention, me and Mike Caluzo are cool and all, but I'm not his priest. Why would he feel it necessary to tell me it wasn't his people, ya know? He's been an enforcer a long time, has done however many jobs that I never wanna know about—so why the big confessional thing now?"

"Because he's *your friend*," Laura said calmly, her tone so serene that it made the group go still. "And friends give friends the heads-up when something really foul is about to go down . . . just so they'll die knowing it wasn't an internal betrayal and their friends weren't involved."

"Old Sicilian code," Steve said quietly, gathering Najira in his arms.

"Sho' you right," James said, and then glanced at Najira. "Now you see why it *is* our business?"

"Part one and two of the job is done," a man with a thick Russian accent said into his cell phone.

A black sedan rolled up next to his in the Washington, D.C., parking lot. The darkened back window rolled down by a crack and an envelope was pushed through it. He reached out and accepted the manila folder.

"Everything you need for the rest of the job is in there," a quiet male voice said. "Make it happen. Your wire transfer is complete, check your account."

Both sets of car windows rolled back up. Both cars leisurely drove away in opposite directions.

"Mrs. Melville," Laura said as calmly as possible into the phone while James drove their Jeep back toward the house, "I'm giving you and your husband a few weeks off with pay. . . . Uhmmm, James and I just need a little bit more honeymooning time alone in the house, you understand."

"Oh, my, yes, I do," Mrs. Melville said with a conspiratorial laugh. "I remember being your age, once. But don't you need me to at least cook, or what about laundry and such things as keeping the place tidy for you, my dear?"

"I'll manage," Laura said, closing her eyes, hating to have to lie to the sweet older woman who had become her right hand. "I'm trying to show my husband that even though I have fantastic help, I can be a bit domestic. I promise not to make too much of a mess during this experiment."

Mrs. Melville chuckled and clucked her tongue softly. "You're sure? And you know, if you need anything, we're at your disposal."

"Yes, and bless you," Laura said quietly. "But this is best for now."

"All right, dear heart. You call if you need us."

"Will do. Bye."

Laura terminated the cell-phone call and slumped in the seat. "This is worse than before, James. I thought we'd put all this crap behind us. I hated having to lie to that dear old woman."

"It's best this way, baby," he said, turning into their driveway. "That's all we'd need is for her or her husband to be in there if something crazy jumps off. This way, we can sleep at night."

"Yeah, but not in our own home." Laura leaned forward and stared at him for a moment.

"I hear you. A hotel room?"

She closed her eyes and ran her palms down her face. "Yeah, maybe. I don't know. Maybe we leave Grand Cayman and go smaller, like Cayman Brac—"

"Smaller means even less security, whatever that is anywhere in the world, these days," James countered.

"All right, how about if we go to a larger island, or maybe—"

"Laura, face it. If someone is hunting us, or simply cleaning up any of the trail from all that Philly madness, then it's only a matter of time before they find us. We have to get to the root of it, figure out why we're in it, what they're searching for—since we can rule out family vengeance at this point, I think."

"Ahkan is on his way . . . what are we gonna tell that man, James?"

"The truth," James said flatly. "Start there. We all get our stuff, quietly check into one of the resorts, and then all sit down and put our heads together. Maybe once he gets here, he might have a take on this, since he was also close to Haines and might know what other bull Haines was into, or who might be sending a clean-up squad. Bottom line is we can't run forever. At this rate, we might as well go back to Philly."

Chapter
4

Akhan took his time moving through the house. These were some strange times. "Ashé," he murmured, acknowledging the ancestors as he gathered up a few essentials and stuffed them in a knapsack. He kept away from the barred windows while going to the one black telephone he owned with a rotary dial. The call was efficient like the universe.

"*Hotep.*"

"Yo."

"Juney, an old man needs to take a discrete ride to the airport, son."

"You got it, Pops. When?"

"Now. Down the street and around the corner."

There was a pause.

"So it's like dat?" Juney asked.

"Yes, it's like that, soldier."

"Cool. I gotchure back. Five minutes."

"Thank you. May the ancestors bless you."

The call disconnected.

Akhan glimpsed around his North Philadelphia home, leaving the radio on, the lights on, and then headed for the back door. He checked his watch, becoming annoyed with himself for being

so predictable. Age had created a routine. A daily walk down to
the park, long, then quiet contemplation on a bench, feeding the
birds. Perhaps a game of chess or dominoes, if a willing player appeared. Waiting for the youngbloods to come out and get schooled,
a chance to interact with others and espouse what they thought
was philosophical rhetoric. He loved the debates. They had much
to learn. Yet he still had much to do.

He slipped out the back door and through the tiny yard. In
April the heat hadn't stirred the air to a humid, dank odor from
waiting garbage cans, nor had larva begun to multiply. That was a
good sign, he mused, passing along the narrow divide of concrete and old wrought iron gates that separated each neighbor's
postage stamp of privacy. The dogs didn't bark. They all knew
him and he fed them daily for just such an occasion, should one
ever arise. Their silent, tail-wagging welcome told him that his
passage was safe as he tossed small bits of lunch meat over each
fence. He considered it a toll worth paying.

At the end of the alley, he hesitated until he saw Juney's ragged
Eldorado roll to a slow stop. He kept his eyes on the window, then
saw the lock pop up—that's when he made his move.

In a quick jog-step he reached Juney's car and got in, closed
the door quietly, and ducked down. Juney immediately pulled
away from the curb, but did so without burning rubber.

Juney looked in the rearview mirror. "*The man* was on a roof
across from your house with a scope, bro' Akhan." He kept his
eyes on the mirror and zigzagged through the streets to be sure
they weren't being followed. "I think it's cool, now, but all that
smack you be talkin' up in the park ain't no joke, old dude. You
know dey got black helicopters and whatnot for us, right. Figured
dey was after you because you be dropping science 'round da
way."

Akhan sat up slowly and peered through the back window.
"There was somebody across the street on a roof?"

"Sniper," Juney said, looking five ways at the intersection. "Had
the full kit, laying low. The moment I got your call, me and my
boyz took a peek up on the flat tops from down my house. Seen

'em, but he ain't seen us. Funny thing was, he wasn't wearing black SWAT gear, feel me?"

"Nationality?" Akhan rubbed his jaw and glimpsed out the back window again.

"White, brother—whatchu think? I said *the man*, not jus' Po Po."

"No uniform." Akhan grunted.

"It ain't the cops, is it?"

"No," Akhan said, leaning back against the seat. "Too dangerous. If he's got a sniper's kit, he's a professional."

"Like we ain't?" Juney scoffed. "All I gotta do is hit my cousin on two-way, and he can bring that Uzi up from the basement. Sheeit, we'll spray the joint and blow his foul ass off a rooftop—you don't be coming up in da hood trying to bring noise to one of the old playas, especially one dat done paid his dues and been like a father to how many of us? Naw, we ain't having it. Way I see it, we all owe you man. Respect. Say the word, and we'll smoke him like a blunt."

"Might need to ask you to do that for an old man one day—but not today. I've always said, be strategic, right?"

Juney let his breath out hard. "Yeah."

"First of all, you spray the roofs, one of the kids or somebody's mom might get shot and killed." Akhan paused, allowing the import of the words to sink into Juney's conscience, but well understood where the young brother was coming from. "If this was an intended hit, scheduled to blow me away in front of my own house—kill the hit man, and whoever sent him will simply hire another one. What I need to know is, who sent him and why."

"Cool. Well, we know he ain't roll up here on SEPTA, so his car is probably somewhere nearby. Want us to tag and open it up—you know we can clean it out like *Gone In Sixty Seconds*, my boyz is all pro, too."

"Now you're being strategic." Akhan rubbed the stubble on his chin. "It'll probably be a rental, nothing flashy, and most likely anything identifying will be in the trunk—not on him, in case something went down. He wouldn't carry anything on him. The car will be in a bogus name, but the tag will help. . . . I know some people that know some people who can run a license plate, get a lock on which car rental agency he got it from, and from there get an alias."

Juney reached over the seat and offered Akhan a fist pound. "Yeah, 'round here we all know some people that know some people."

"Can your boys make it look like a run-of-the-mill crash and sweep?"

"We'll do it lovely, will make it look like junkies got him."

"Then your boys will have to move quick. One needs to watch his position on the roof; the others hit the car, and then be out."

"We got you, Pops, relax."

"You still have that key that I gave you a long time ago? Plus the number I gave you last year?"

"Yeah," Juney said, his tone mellowing with respect.

A silent understanding passed between them, both knowing that it was the glue that had forged their relationship ten years prior, as it had been a confer of the ultimate trust between two men that trusted no one.

"I should be on my way for my morning walk right now. Five minutes, and your target is gone. He'll know that something unusual in my schedule changed." Akhan paused, staring at the young street soldier before him. "Be careful, son."

Juney nodded and extracted a two-way cellular from his baggy jeans pocket. "Like I said. We got this."

"Change of plans," James said evenly as he watched Laura dash around the bedroom trying to stuff as many of their clothes into a suitcase as quickly as possible.

She stopped moving about and stared at him. "Come again?"

"This is insane and a bad plan, Laura. We go to a small hotel, or even a resort, and we have less room to maneuver. Here, we'll have a beefed-up security system installed by the end of the day, can walk the perimeter in shifts with weapons without alerting the authorities, and if it gets ugly, can drop an assassin after ques-

tioning him, if we have to—without the chaos of innocent by-
standers that could get hurt, or worrying about the Royal
Cayman Islands Police."

"What are we gonna do, James? Just sit here?" She wanted to
pull her hair out by the roots.

"We can't keep running, baby," he said quietly, going to her to
try to calm her with an embrace. "Don't you wanna just stop running for once in your life?"

She sighed hard and briefly laid her head on his shoulder.
Weary beyond words, she had to agree with at least that much of
what he'd said. This was supposed to be a sanctuary that she'd
found so many years ago. The Caymans. Peace on earth. A country only one and a half times the size of Washington, D.C., that
was devoted to banking and finance, her forte; a place where the
dollar was still relatively strong and there was no formal taxation
of any kind. No sales tax, no income tax, no capital gains tax, no
property tax, no inheritance tax in a land overrun at one point by
pirates, folks who obviously understood underground economies.

Hell no, she didn't want to leave her idyllic haven that was only
four hundred and eighty short miles from Florida, a hundred
and fifty miles south of Cuba, and northwest of Jamaica, and serviced by all the major airlines. Here, she understood the law—
British common law, the language was English, but the people
her own, with a substantial mixture of every world culture. Beauty,
art, white-sand beaches . . . Laura closed her eyes. A land where
the Silver Thatch Palm reigned supreme, and stood tall next to
wild banana orchids, and allowed Grand Cayman parrots to nest.

"But what are we going to do?" she whispered, half as a question to James, the remainder of the query for herself.

"Do what we've always done so far—bring it to them, before
they bring it to us. Investigate. Find out who has an axe to grind,
and then bust 'em."

She tentatively nodded as he withdrew from the hug.

"You call Najira and tell her to stand down on the packing. I'm
going to the garage and bring in some heat."

She sat down slowly on the edge of the bed and watched him

go to the dresser to pull out his old shoulder harness and Peace-keeper.

Watching him do that didn't make her feel any better.

It was his chance to be initiated, his chance to come up. Juney was *da man*, and more than that, was his big brother. All he had to do was open the safe under Juney's bed, get the key to the old dude's house, do what he was told, and be out.

Ramir looked both ways and slipped out of the house, and then made a quick dash down the alley, trying to stay clear of growling dogs as he leapt over the short fence toward his destination—Brother Akhan's back door.

Sweat made his white T-shirt stick to his back as he worked the locks, cracked open the door, and then dropped to the floor, scrambling across it with agility. He immediately spied the coats on a hook by the front door, and yanked off the hoodie sweatshirt that had been tied around his waist. Moving quickly, he slid up the wall, hugging it like he were a part of it, slipped off the army fatigue jacket that the old man always wore, and then scrambled toward the couch on his belly, using his elbows and knees to propel him.

In swift, jerky motions, he yanked at the worn pillows and crocheted sofa throw, stuffing them into the body of the jacket and hoodie to fill the fabric out. His hands trembled as he worked the fastenings, constantly glancing at the front window and back toward the hall. Finally satisfied, he shimmied on the floor to the kitchen and retrieved a mop, and hastened back to the overstuffed coat on the floor of the living room and stuck the long wooden handle up into the bundle of fabric. Sitting with his back against the wall next to the window, he shut his eyes for a second and mopped at the rivulets of sweat coursing down his temples. Then he pulled out his two-way.

"Ready," he whispered.

"Do it," his cousin ordered.

Using two hands, he raised the coat to his far left, straining to keep the motion fluid but jerky enough to seem like a person had walked to the window from the hall toward the window. He carefully rounded his body with the scarecrow form and brushed the curtain just enough to draw a portion of it back so that the fatigue jacket briefly showed.

Within seconds, two pops shattered the glass, exploding pillow contents from the hoodie where a head should have been and making yarn fibers plume. He instantly dropped the jacket and made a loud crash by kicking over the television. Then he was out.

On hands and knees like he was making a break from a rival gang in a club, he found the back door, stood, and bolted, hurdling the fences, doing a hundred-yard dash that rivaled Olympic records. He hit the back door to his house and entered it, falling forward into the arms of a group of waiting friends. Everybody got down, guns drawn, spines pressed against lower cabinets and sections of the wall, breathing hard.

He moved with calm precision, breaking down his weapons and gathering his equipment in a routine he could have accomplished in his sleep. Job three was completed. The roofs in this godforsaken neighborhood were a cinch to scale. There would be no eyes, no witnesses. These animals preyed upon and killed one another all the time. He released the window bars he was holding, jumped down, and adjusted his knapsack on his back. Two short blocks to his car and he was history.

Blending into the block like a lost Temple University grad student, he in his rumpled corduroy pants and wrinkled college T-shirt fit right into the environment. A few crack addicts and women pulling laundry carts barely considered him as he stepped over two dead dogs in the alleyway that had been silenced for pragmatic reasons and entered the adjacent block.

There was no need to run; a cup of coffee was in his future. It was a clean kill that would no doubt be attributed to a gang drive-by shooting that had gone wrong on an impoverished street. Doing jobs in neighborhoods like this was so easy that he almost felt guilty for taking payments for them . . . almost.

But when he spotted his car, he froze. Pure rage hastened his steps. The trunk was popped open, the passenger's side window had a small hole in it, and the door was ajar. He bit down on his lip to keep from yelling in frustration. Now he'd have to take the bus or the subway in order not to risk a car theft as a getaway. The equipment could be replaced, but the information in his bag could not—at least not immediately, not without questions from his employer, not without the major inconvenience of ditching the old identity for a new one. Fucking junkies. He hated these animals. No morals.

Laura jumped up from the edge of the bed and grabbed her purse, desperately trying to get to her cell phone before it rolled over to voice mail.

She didn't recognize the number, but pressed her ear to the phone regardless.

"Hello."

"You don't know me," a strange male voice said. "But Brother Akhan gave me this number for emergencies. This qualifies, sis."

"What's happened?" Laura breathed out.

"Write down this tag number," the voice replied flatly.

She immediately snatched paper and a pen from her bag and waited.

"You good?" the young male voice asked.

"Yes. Go."

She scribbled down the number she'd been given, along with the state licensure and rental car agency. "Is he all right?" she asked, nearly holding her breath.

"Yeah. He's cool. But he said you'd know what to do with the stash we got. Can't keep it on us."

"What is it?"

"Not on the phone."

Her fingers clutched the small credit-card-sized unit against her cheek. "You have to tell me something," she said through her teeth, "because where I tell you to drop it will depend on what it is."

A long sigh filled the receiver, and then information began to pour into it so fast and so furiously that her jaw went slack.

Laura squeezed her eyes shut tightly. "I know this is the last place you'd trust, but I need you to listen to me carefully. If Akhan trusted you to give you my number, I need you to trust me—then when you're done, clear my number out of your cell for your own safety. Got it?"

"Aw'ight. Lay it on me, sis."

"Go down to the roundhouse and take this to Captain—"

"Po po! What are you, sick?"

"Give the contents to a same-day bicycle courier service in Philly. Use the name James Carter as the sender. Mark the contents 'urgent,' and do as I say. That's all I can tell you right now. I'm going to give you the name of a police captain that we can trust. Just do it."

There was a hesitation. "If this gets fucked up and the old man gets hurt, sis, I'll find your ass and come looking for you myself."

"Thank you," Laura said quietly.

"You better know I ain't playing, and don't thank me for doing this stupid bullshit until I make up my mind that I'ma go there. Hear?"

"I'm not thanking you for the delivery. I'm thanking you for coming after me if Akhan gets hurt. Now I know for sure that you're legit." Laura sent her gaze toward the bedroom door when James came into view. "So, I'll say it again so you'll hear me," she added with emphasis and then gave him the name. "*Thank you.*"

Another hard exhale filled the receiver. "Aw'ight. I hear you. I'm out." Then the call went dead.

"Talk to me, Laura," James said, eyeing her. "What was that all about?"

She stood and began pacing, telling him all that she'd heard as she made a slow, disoriented loop back and forth between the window and the bed.

"That was the thing to tell him, wasn't it?"

James nodded. "It was."

"Fill in Steve and the rest of the crew," she said, not looking at him as she gazed out the window. She waited for James to make the call and to verbally download all that she'd just explained.

"So now we know," she whispered once he'd hung up. "We aren't just paranoid."

"Correction," he muttered. "We're paranoid, but with good reason."

"I thought this was all over," Donald Haines, Jr., said quietly as he sat in his mother's new waterfront condo.

Elizabeth Haines continued to hug her body as she stared out the large picture window. She couldn't even turn around to face him as he sat stunned on the sofa awaiting a response. Her son had aged; his handsome face now hosted lines from the strain. His once brilliant blue eyes now always held a haunted shadow within them, like hers did. She'd never wanted any of the horrors of her or her husband's political lives of intrigue to touch him, but it had. Her dead husband's business affairs and tangled web of political favors and back-scratching had shattered their lives. Donald had left her practically nothing, even the house that they'd built had been bargained out from under her as his last laugh in the will.

But none of the carnage that resulted made any sense. The Mafia had received their pound of flesh; their casino charters and construction contracts for the new gaming houses coming to the state of Pennsylvania had all been preserved. Her ex-lover, a once renowned doctor, was behind bars for a very long time for Donald's actual murder, and her son's ex-lover was also safely put away for his complicit role on the travesty.

A slight shudder passed through her as she remembered how narrowly she'd escaped the same fate. Who would be foolish enough to want to stir up that awful nightmare again? Even for vengeance?

"Mother . . . are you all right?" Donny asked quietly, standing and going to her.

Who would kill the senator and his son? What purpose would that offer?

She embraced him slowly, filling his arms. "No," she whispered, a hundred thoughts attacking her mind at once. "After all of this, how can you or I ever be all right?"

He hugged her tightly and nodded, "I know."

She stroked his back, gleaning as much comfort from him as he gave, and laid her head on his slight shoulder. "Have you spoken to Alan?" she asked in a careful murmur, almost afraid to open the wound that made her dear son bleed.

She felt him tense, and then he drew away from her.

"No. That's finished," Donny said through a thick swallow. "Why would I call or write him in prison after all he did to me . . . to us . . . to our family? That would be like me asking if you've been in contact with—"

"I know, I know," she whispered, closing her eyes. "Don't be cross. I only asked because I'm trying to fathom who we might know that would be ruthless enough to murder someone . . . trying to understand and work it all out in my mind, who might have been in business with the senator and his son, and only those two are likely. That is the only reason I mentioned it, and will never breathe their names again."

She watched her son rake his hair in agitation and then finally sit. "They can't reach us or anyone we know from where they are. I don't think."

They both stared at each other.

"That's just the point, my beloved. And be honest, it ran through your mind like it has run through mine . . . you've thought about it."

He nodded after a moment. Her refined, blue blood stature was disorienting as he thought about the ruthlessness it concealed. Her fit, trim frame ensconced in a chartreuse designer cardigan, a strand of pearls gracing her throat, and her elegant crepe wool winter white slacks covering still shapely legs, made him wonder how she could have done all that she had. Her hair was pulled back in a neat, blond chignon, and yet her exterior beauty would always be marred for him by what he knew her capable of.

"And don't forget, mother dearest," he said, his voice now brittle, "you also were involved in trying to do the same—murder my father. But the fact that you didn't is the only reason you and I are even having a conversation today."

She turned slowly back to the window and stared out at the Delaware River. "I should have known that your visit wasn't to merely check on me, but to look into my eyes while asking if I was involved."

"Then turn around and look me in the eyes and tell me. Were you?"

She glanced at him over her shoulder and set her jaw hard. "No."

Again, they simply stared at each other for a moment.

"You and I are so much alike, and you are your father's spitting image. Donald used to handle me like this." She turned away and continued to gaze out the window. "I suppose once trust is shattered, it's like fine bone china that can never be repaired. I never expected this from my son."

He stood to leave, and picked up his London Fog raincoat, folding it over his arm. "But that I still love you as my mother is something. That is all I have left to give you."

She nodded and fought the tears, but never turned as he walked away. "Right now, that I will cling to. Thank you."

There was no answer, just the gentle close of the door.

Chapter
5

Laura stood inside the small airport with her family waiting for her uncle, her mind whirring. The brightly dressed tourists and returning natives of that land provided stark contrasts within the clean, brightly lit two-story building. Everything around her seemed to be moving in slow motion. Instinctively she knew customs agents would be leisurely stamping documents to admit people to the country. Baggage handlers would take their time in the island heat to throw luggage up on the huge conveyor belts. Mini-vans would take their sweet time to herd tourists into hotel shuttles. Red caps and families would greet weary travelers and usher them to a rented or owned car. Where was Akhan?

When he finally emerged from a new throng of tourists, she hung back to allow Najira and Jamal to rush up to him first. Calmly, she entered the family reunion, so relieved to see the old man that it took her a moment to release James's arm to go to him, lest she keel over.

Wearing only a backpack as his luggage to complement his traditional uniform of African print garb, sandals and socks, a crocheted knit cap, and an exhausted expression, he greeted her warmly with a tired embrace.

"Thank you, Laura," he said just above a whisper. "We should go."

Making cursory acknowledgement of James and Steve, Akhan set his line of vision forward toward the exit, and kept his gaze sweeping as they walked to the parked vehicles. Only once he was safely tucked inside Laura and James's car like a diplomat, did he close his eyes, breathe a sigh of relief, and begin to temporarily relax.

"What happened?" Laura asked, turning to peer at her elderly uncle over the seat.

She glanced at James, who kept his eyes forward on the road, but had glimpsed Akhan in the rearview mirror, like a professional limo driver.

"They're coming for us," Akhan stated flatly.

"Who?" Laura waited, and watched her uncle rub the stubble on his jaw.

"I don't know. There are so many possibilities. The question of 'why,' is moot. We have ruffled a lot of feathers over the years, Laura."

"Then, let's focus on the most likely candidates—namely those who have an unsettled debt and the resources to see that it's collected."

Akhan chuckled. "Again, that would be many."

Laura dragged her fingers through her hair, knowing just how right the old man was. "We follow the money, then."

Akhan's smile broadened. "Again, Laura—"

"I know, I know," she said, growing frustrated. "That's a lot of sources."

"So, you two figured out how you're gonna break this to Pops?" Jamal said, clearly taking delight in Steve and Najira's case of nerves.

Najira spun in her seat, straining the seatbelt while Steve kept his eyes straight ahead on the road, his jaw tight.

"Nooooo, and don't start no signifying mess when we get to Laura's, okay? Dad has been through a lot of drama, he's elderly, exhausted, and ran out of his home to come here like a refugee—so don't start no shit, Jamal."

Jamal raised both hands in front of his chest, laughing. "Yo, I was only asking, because sooner or later he's gonna figure out the deal. Thought it might be best if you hit him with it straight, instead of playing games. You know Pop."

Najira turned around and slumped in her seat without responding.

"If it's gonna be a problem," Steve said quietly, I can maybe go crash at Laura and James's place . . . until this gets sorted out."

"Yeah," Jamal chimed in, uninvited. "Pop beat getting shot, dealt with a mad-crazy flight, and whoever knows what else. No sense in giving him a heart attack now that he's safe."

"Oh, shut up, Jamal," Najira practically yelled. "It's gonna be fine. Besides, there are much more important things to worry about than all of that. Just let it alone."

Steve discreetly reached over and squeezed her hand. "First things first. Let your Dad settle in, get his bearings, calm down, we develop a strategy—then you two can talk . . . only when the time is right. I'm cool with it."

Najira nodded and stared out the passenger window as everyone fell silent for the rest of the ride home.

When both vehicles pulled up into Laura and James's driveway, by instinct James and Steve jumped out first and cased the house. No one had to be informed of the process, it went like clockwork. Each person knew their roles, who would stay, who would get out, and when to move once the coast was called clear.

A nod from James once the house had been swept made Laura climb out and assist her uncle, while Jamal took up his father's backpack. The fivesome trudged into the house like soldiers, and headed for the real meeting room—the kitchen. Akhan sat and the others slowly joined the table with him. Laura found water, fresh juice, and fruit to place before Akhan, already knowing he had to be hungry, tired, and, at his age, in need of immediate attention to his physical being. Once Akhan had begun to refuel his body, Laura turned on the teakettle and waited.

"I have a guest room all ready for you, some fresh towels, and in the nightstand you'll find something to make you feel safe."

Laura glanced at James as Akhan searched her face.

"Glock nine-millimeter," James said flatly. "Clip is in it, safety on. I'll do a quick run-through on how to use it, once you've showered."

"Thank you," Akhan said quietly, and then briefly closed his eyes.

It was in that moment that Laura realized just how shaken her uncle had been. Never a complainer, and always seeming to have a steely handle on all circumstances, her uncle had been terrified for the first time she'd ever witnessed in her life. Just his quiet expulsion of air, the way his shoulders dropped with relief to be in safe company, her house a haven, unnerved her, because what if it wasn't.

All eyes were on him, as though each person in the room had come to the same conclusion at the same moment. New tension filled their expressions, as though it had been silently transferred from Akhan to everyone else in a matter of telepathic seconds.

Najira glimpsed Steve from the corner of her eye, which brought her father's attention first to her, and then it settled on Steve.

"Welcome to the family," Akhan said calmly, taking a slow sip of his juice.

Steve simply stared at him. No one spoke. Akhan didn't smile or avert his eyes, but set his glass down very precisely.

"At my age, one becomes very philosophical," the elderly man said, his tone neutral. "One may be old, but do not assume blindness."

"Dad, see—"

Akhan held up his hand, stopping Najira's words while everyone else held their breath. "No need to explain. I saw it at Laura's wedding." He nodded toward Steve, who gave a quick, nervous nod back. Akhan's gaze slid to James. "He was your partner for years, watched your back, and stood as your best man. I take that as an endorsement from a man whom I respect."

James nodded. "We go back a lotta years, and dude's always been righteous."

Akhan nodded, sighed, and pushed back in his chair, folding his hands over his stomach. He then looked at Jamal. "My son hung with you, has been living with his sister for a year or so now." He kept his penetrating gaze on Jamal. "My son, like me, has good discernment in character—a necessary thing for survival in the streets. There would have been a falling-out, if things were not as they should be. Jamal is still here, therefore I can only assume that things are correct."

"Yeah, Pop," Jamal said quickly, glancing at the others. "It's all good."

Akhan again nodded, and then turned his attention on Laura. "With all that is at stake, and all the unspoken business that must be conducted, I know my dear niece would not have you as a part of her inner circle, if you could not be trusted. Of all those I know, Laura is the shrewdest most skilled strategist."

He let his gaze linger on Laura. Warmth and pride filled her at the most profound compliment her uncle had given her. Yet it also sent a chill through her, as his small speech had the ring of a eulogy to it—someone unburdening his spirit so he could make his peace and go home to glory.

"He's been with us since it all started," Laura said, resting her hand on Akhan's shoulder.

Akhan briefly covered the touch with a rough hewn palm and then both their hands fell away. He fixed his gaze on Najira, who was looking down, until her eyes met his.

"Daughter . . . he makes your eyes smile and also become shy. He has the endorsement of those I most cherish and trust in the world. Why wouldn't you come to me and let me know? Haven't I always taught you that a house united will stand, a house divided will fall?"

She nodded, her eyes glistening with myriad emotions, and that's when Akhan finally smiled.

"Then, given what we have to face, I thought it best to go into the challenges united. We do not have time for old prejudices to divide what has become our house." Akhan looked up at Steve's stricken expression. "Ashé?"

Steve nodded, still seeming unsure.

"You pass inspection," Akhan said with a soft chuckle. "Laura, make some tea. We pour some libations to honor the ancestors and call it a day. I'm tired."

"Just like that, Pop? You cool?" Jamal, incredulous, stood and walked to the stove to make tea, when Laura's legs couldn't push her to stand fast enough.

"At my age, you don't waste time. You observe, accept or decline, and then move on. I accept."

Steve almost toppled Akhan's juice and water glasses, quickly reaching over the table to shake his hand. "I'm not playing games with her, sir, and will do right by her."

Akhan shook Steve's hand and chuckled. "I know, because otherwise I'd have to kill you."

James looked away and swallowed a smile, as his partner sat back very slowly and raked his hair. Laura was on her feet.

"Uhmmm, why don't I show you to the shower, and I'll make some broiled fish and something more substantial for you to eat—the fruit was just to take the edge off."

Akhan stood slowly with a wry smile. "Yes . . . and then James can show me the fine points of how to use his gun."

No one said a word as Akhan and Laura left the room. They just simply stared after them, rendered mute.

"You all right, man?" James said, landing a heavy hand on Steve's shoulders.

Steve rubbed his palms down his face and blew out a long breath. "Oh . . . shit . . ."

"Yeah," Jamal said, fixing a cup of tea to take into the next room. "Pop don't play. But once you're in, you're in, unless you do something to fuck that up." Jamal glanced at Najira. "He means what he says. He will shoot your ass, if you yank my sister around."

Najira grasped Steve's hand and squeezed it hard, glaring at Jamal. "He's not like that, and you know it."

"I feel you. I'm just saying."

"All right, y'all," James said, leaning back in his chair and closing his eyes. "Crisis number two for the day averted. Let the old man sip his tea in his room, eat, get some shut-eye, and then we've gotta make some decisions on how to move forward."

A vibration on James's hip made him open his eyes, sit forward, and bring his cell phone to his ear. All eyes were on him as he took the call.

"Yeah, Cap. Good to hear from you. What's up?"

"Got a delivery of some really interesting equipment, with ID that hit a brick wall when we tried to do a database search on it."

"What kind of brick wall?" James said, cautiously.

"A *federal* brick wall," Cap replied, lowering his voice. "A you-do-not-want-to-fuck-with-this brick wall."

"Then you know that me and Laura ain't in it, right?"

A long silence filled the receiver.

"My hunch as a detective says you're clean," Cap finally replied. "You got anybody local that can do a hack, on the DL?"

"Maybe," Cap said, not committing.

"You already did it, didn't you?"

Nervous laughter filled the receiver.

"Call me curious," Cap muttered. "This guy has an international rap sheet, and did a lot of 'special projects' for the feds. He's Russian. Names too many and too hard to spell to give you on the phone. Suffice to say, this ain't some local, regular vendetta shit. But with a senator dead and a trail leading to an old federal black ops pro, won't be long before I have to give up the evidence and turn this over to higher authorities—you know what I'm saying. It'll be outta my hands. You all just stay safe."

"I hear you," James muttered back. "Thanks for the heads-up, Cap. I owe you."

Cap chuckled. "Yeah, yeah, yeah, that's what they all say."

By the time the call disconnected, Laura had returned to the kitchen. She was greeted by blank stares of pure disbelief.

"What happened?' she asked quietly.

"Got a call," James said, standing. "I'll tell you about it while you fix Akhan's fish."

They all sat around the dining room table, barely picking at the broiled sea bass and steamed vegetables that Laura had prepared in a zombie state. Akhan ate slowly, methodically, as though measuring each bite of food with the slow recount of each witness's words, thinking.

"James and I need to resurface and draw the fire our way," Laura finally said, taking a careful sip of her herbal, mango tea.

"I don't like the sound of that," Steve said, shaking his head. "Splitting up the team is too risky."

"If there's some paperwork, thus money, at the root of this, then most likely it was something I've orchestrated. James is top gun on security. He and I can cover much more ground without risking any family as targets," Laura argued. "As it is, my sisters and their kids are still in the states. If they came for uncle, they'll eventually go for them in an attempt to smoke me out of hiding."

"We do this thing as one family, Laura," Jamal argued.

"Yeah. We're all in this together," Najira contended, standing to go get a bottle of wine.

James and Akhan had remained strangely silent. The dissenters looked at them. Akhan broke the silence first.

"Let's study the pattern," he said, slowly pushing his finished plate away from him so that he could make a tent before him with his fingers. "This all began with a transfer of power by the late Donald Haines, correct? What part of that had federal ties?"

Laura nodded. "Yes. You and I gave him a slate of approved programs that he sanctioned. We set up those programs on abandoned old factory lands earmarked for redevelopment. But it was city- and state-owned land, any federal money was sent down from Washington, hit state coffers, and then trickled down to the city. We got our apportionment from state and city budgets."

"Ah," Akhan said, nodding. "And we have a dead state senator, and a dead son of a state senator."

"All right," James finally said, entering the conversation. "But those boys aren't feds."

"But they used to go back and forth to Washington all the time," Laura added, her gaze never leaving Akhan.

"And our dear friend Donald met an untimely demise . . . which may have unsettled deals he had to repay those federal connections—a scratch-your-back arrangement to make it lucrative for certain monies to be released, so that those who gave up thirty-year land leases at the state level could be renumerated."

Laura closed her eyes and let out a hard breath. "With Senator Scott getting screwed and losing power, who knows who at the federal level didn't get their itch scratched." She opened her eyes to Akhan's wise gaze.

"It's always a very delicate balance, Laura," he said, no emotion or judgment in his tone. "I had oversight, locally, over those program lands—given your shutdown of Rainmaker's, Inc. With Scott gone . . ."

"There's no way for them to wrest back the leases or get a cut off the program funds," she said with a groan.

"Precisely," Akhan said.

She stood and began to pace. "OK, then we have to find out who Scott was dealing with. Who would have stood to benefit in some way in exchange for him funding the city to do the programs?"

"Ashé," Akhan said quietly, taking up his tea again. "Or, what will most likely happen is, you'll witness an erosion of those programs. Good grassroots organizations discredited for fiscal mismanagement, programs not getting funding the following year, thus the land leases voided, somehow, and the monies redirected to new ventures and new so-called priorities."

"Damn, that's some crazy shit," Jamal muttered, shaking his head.

"Indeed, son. Nothing is stable. All of this is built on shifting sands."

"I'll go with the theory," James said. "But why a hit? That part of it is personal. They could shake the programs out from under your or Laura's control, and get back whatever money they felt they were owed. However, when bodies start dropping . . ."

"It's real personal," Steve said. "Sending a message."

Both James and Steve nodded.

"Yeah . . ." Laura said slowly. "That's why I need to get stateside with James, do some on-the-street digging, and find out who has a personal axe to grind in relation to the programs that got transferred to Akhan."

"You may not be able to fix this, Laura," Akhan warned, taking a way-too-calm sip of his tea. "This may be a wake-up call to simply remove you and anyone else associated with you permanently from the equation, given how dangerous you've been to them in the past."

"Then that's all the more reason for me and James to go. If I can find out who's been wronged, I can perhaps shield those program directors locally from a media or fiscal beat down, transfer what can be salvaged to some compromise agencies that can absorb the innocent without too much fallout, and then wait for them to try to off me . . . and have something waiting for them."

"Still the Scorpion, I see, my young queen sister." Akhan set down his tea and smiled a very strained smile. "My concern is that, this time, it may not be that simplistic."

Chapter
6

"We're deeply concerned."

Vladimir Chertoff glanced around at the waning lunchtime political crowd within the Watergate Hotel, and then settled a lethal gaze on the two men before him. The one wearing dark aviator sunglasses with a communications wire discreetly tucked behind his ear troubled him, but not as much as his older contact who kept a blank expression on his alcohol-puffed face as he spoke in a low warning tone.

"There is no cause for worry," Vladimir grumbled. "It was a slight detour, but I will deliver as promised."

"Here's our dilemma," his contact said evenly. "When you lost your bag, local Philadelphia police acquired it."

"I didn't lose my bag. Junkies—"

"You lost your bag," his contact said quietly, leaning forward and cutting off his explanation. "We pay you well not to lose your bag. You've done work for us in some of the worst ghettos in the world, from Bosnia to the Sudan . . . and you've never lost your bag. This concerns those above me who think you may be getting sloppy. A ghetto in North Central Philadelphia cannot be as daunting as those in central Afghanistan, can it?"

Vladimir didn't answer the charge, but simply glared back at the beady blue eyes that challenged his.

"Your target escaped. Period. He knew you were coming, because when the local police got there, a scarecrow had taken your bullet. Which leads us to believe that no mere junkies stole your bag, if someone was prepared to set up a countertrap. It wasn't crackheads, but someone shrewd enough, with enough underground information to set you up. And the local police receiving a gift out of the blue was also a very well-orchestrated move."

His contact pushed back from the table and sipped his coffee slowly. Vladimir could feel perspiration building in his armpits and between his shoulder blades, making the black silk shirt beneath his suit cling to his body.

"I will address it."

Neither his contact nor the silent security beside him spoke.

"I said, I will address it," Vladimir repeated, and then waited for a nod that never came.

He was on his feet in seconds. His contract had been canceled mid-job. The way of his world was very efficient; he was a dead man walking. He tossed down his napkin and rushed out of the restaurant. Bright sunlight blinded him, and he was so momentarily disoriented that he couldn't remember where he'd parked. The humidity of Washington, D.C. was stifling, even at this time of year. Sweat coursed down his temples as he found the open lot where he'd parked away from the hotel, always sure to keep his vehicle separated from him, hidden, lest anyone tamper with it at the scene of the job. Today, he wished it was closer.

He began jogging, relieved to finally see the new rental, and he handed the valet his ticket stub, glancing around quickly. If they'd found it and rigged it, the valet would lose his life—not him.

Without incident, the valet brought his car around and stood for a second, waiting for a tip. Vladimir brushed past him, jumped in his vehicle, and turned the air-conditioner on full blast. Several blocks away, he reached in his breast pocket for a cigarette and carefully placed it between his lips. This was a small job, by comparison. An old man and a woman. Who gave a shit if his contract was canceled? There was plenty of global mercenary work to be done. He had the means to disappear. If they fucked with him, he'd hit his contact and the men that hired him as a go-between. Fucking American slime balls. They could do their own dirty work.

Vladimir grabbed a book of matches that had been stashed in the change holder, cupped his hands around the end of the cigarette to keep the air conditioner from extinguishing the flame, and flicked a match with his thumbnail.

The resulting blast shattered every window in the car.

Cap sat at his desk in the Philadelphia Police headquarters, listening carefully to what his inside man down in Washington told him. It paid to have friends everywhere, especially those who observed a little local courtesy for the men on the street. He nodded to himself as he hung up, and then looked at his cell phone.

James stared at the incoming number on his digital cell phone display. Twice in one day . . . oh, yeah, this thing was heating up. He took Cap's news stoically, and kept his line of vision on the riveted faces around him.

"Might be coming stateside with Laura for a few, man," James said, studying the expressions around him. "Any markers you can call in so I can do some digging, up in Philly and down in D.C., would be most appreciated."

"This is some very foul bullshit," Cap replied. "I'll make a few entrée calls, from there, you're on your own."

James closed his cell phone and looked at Akhan. "The guy who was after you just bought it."

"How?" Akhan said, leaning forward to brace himself against the dining room table.

"Air-conditioning refrigerant had been replaced with the kind that's highly flammable. It was a warm day in D.C., dude was a smoker. Kaboom," James said calmly. "An accident. I hear tell the media will probably do a special on the subject on the nightly news, a Consumer Report segment about the dangers of low-end, Freon-type replacements. This was very, very smooth. No car bombs, no shots fired from traceable ballistics, just a rental car that might have gotten serviced by a bogus can of refrigerant during the normal P.M. cycle. Like I said, a convenient, very clean accident."

"Then, if the dude who was looking for Pops just got his contract canceled, maybe they've called off the dogs, feel me?" Jamal said, glancing around. "I say we all lay low, stay here, and ride out the storm. Maybe your man at The Round House in Philly is on the case, it scared them off, and they decided that the bullshit wasn't worth it. Ain't no need for you and Laura to be going to Philly and D.C., kicking up no dust unnecessarily."

"That's not how it works, dude," Steve said, worry haunting his eyes. "They canceled his contract, permanently, and will get someone to replace him who isn't as sloppy."

"We're out. It's real basic. We have to step to them, before they step to us." James briefly held Jamal's gaze and then looked at Laura.

Akhan simply shook his head and he stood up. "Be safe when you travel," he said, glancing at Laura and James and dismissing Jamal's argument. "I'm going to go lie down for a while and rest."

They were up before dawn, packing under duress. She and James moved around the bedroom in utter silence. It was as though they were doing a quiet, choreographed waltz. The only time they spoke was to say good-bye to the family, who had agreed to stay in Najira's home, since the main targets were Laura and Akhan. But nothing on Grand Cayman was in Akhan's name, especially not real estate.

Try as she might, she couldn't let go of the worry as she and James drove off. The faces of the people who stood in the driveway were the only family she had left in the world, save her sisters and their brood. Laura kept her eyes on them until the vehicle turned the corner, etching every face into her memory, burning it into her psyche like a brand.

"You think they'll be all right?" she finally asked James, already knowing the answer.

"We can only hope so. Got a vet cop in there: Steve. Jamal ain't no slouch. Your uncle is handy with a weapon and doesn't miss much. Najira is as loud as an alarm system. Everybody's got a weapon. That's all we can do."

His statement, though designed to console, didn't. She couldn't blame him, though. What he'd said was the naked truth. James didn't do platitudes or false promises. That was what she loved about him most. The man was brutally honest to a fault.

"I'd feel better if we had a little heat on us," she finally admitted.

"Can't get it through airport security. Gotta pick up what we need when we get to Philly, and then drive it down to D.C. with us."

She knew that. They looked at each other. Her nerves were rubbed so raw, they were showing. James reached over, clasped her hand, and drove with only one of his. That was all that needed to be said.

"Déjà vu," Laura remarked flatly, staring at her unopened suitcase on the floor of the Ritz Carlton.

James poured himself a Chivas from the courtesy bar and sat down hard in the hotel room chair, sipping it neat. "Yep." He let his breath out in an audible, disgusted rush and rubbed the tension away from his neck. "Back in Philly, flying in under radar, no home to go home to—ain't nothing here the same, yet everything is."

"We had a year," she said quietly, making his eyes meet hers. "A good one."

"You talk like it's over, like we're dying."

"Feels like I am," she admitted, and stood to pour herself a rum and coke.

"I've never heard you give up," he said, watching her intently.

"What you hear is fatigue," she said, coming toward him and

absently clinking her glass against his. "I can't even think any-more."

"It's called frustration—that's what's got you in its grip, baby."

She sat across from him and nursed her drink. "How did you come to that conclusion?"

"Am I wrong?"

She smiled for the first time since they'd left Grand Cayman. "I don't know. What's your theory, doctor?"

"I think you're beyond pissed off, because somebody set a ball into motion without you. And, be honest, you spent a lifetime setting up a very clean game, moving the pieces around so you and your family could be safe and old vendettas settled. Then you retired, decided to get out of the game, and somebody ain't finished playing yet. They're forcing your hand, unraveling all that you built lovely. Since you've been disconnected from the inner workings, it's like you're a freshman all over again, and have to learn the new game."

He peered at her as he took a slow sip from his rocks tumbler. "I know my wife that well. It's pissing her off, and being pissed off without a way to vent that energy is wearing her out. Basic math of the way Laura Caldwell's mind works."

Her smile widened as she took a healthy swig from her glass. "*You're* pissing me off."

"Because I'm right," he said, chuckling.

"Yes," she said, and set her glass down hard.

"Good, because I've noticed over the years that, when you're good and angry, you're at your best."

She arched an eyebrow and gave him a nod of respect. "Thank you."

"Much obliged." He grinned and finished his drink. "I also noticed that, after great sex, your mind works wonders, too."

"Really?" She spun the glass on the table and kept her gaze fixed on him.

"Really," he said, his smile sliding to a serious expression.

"Must be a Scorpio thing, and you wouldn't understand."

"How many times have you left my bed, and then gone off to do something crazy?"

She laughed. "A number of times."

"Not this time," he said, no mirth in his tone. "It's too dangerous. Even if you have to wake me up and tell me you're going out, I want to be in communication with you at all times. Understood?"

Her broad smile went to a very sly one. "All right . . . but is that also an offer for some very good sex this afternoon, so I can develop a plan?"

He tilted his head to the side and just stared at her for a moment. "It can be, if you're gonna do it."

She stood up and walked over to the king-size bed without a word, and unbuttoned her winter white, crepe wool jacket. Letting the garment hit the floor as she slid it off her shoulders, she watched James's eyes assess her gold silk blouse, gently tugged it out of her slacks, and then pulled it off over her head.

It was a silent, provocative floor show for a man who'd endured much, but still believed in her . . . a man that, if things went down wrong, she might never see again. It was a final good-bye, as much as it was a reinforcement of all that was good in her life. Time was to be cherished, especially when it was running out. Sand was pouring through the hourglass faster than she could draw her next breath. It was a visceral knowledge, like watching a car accident occur in slow motion before one's eyes, helpless to intervene. The equation was thus very basic; if she was going to die, then this was the last thing about this ugly world she wanted to remember; if he left her widowed, then she never wanted to look back wondering why she didn't take the time to show him how much she loved him.

Laura unfastened the back of her flesh-toned-and-black lace, Victoria's Secret demi-bra with purpose, and watched her husband's eyes go to half-mast. Her eyes never left his as she slowly unzipped her winter white slacks at the side, and stepped out of her brown leather flats. Using two fingers, she pushed the pants down over the swell of her hips, rewarded by his expression of open desire. He was breathing through his mouth by the time her slacks hit the floor, leaving her exposed and wearing only a lacy, flesh-toned thong.

This man needed to know that for all of the drama they'd been through, he meant everything to her. What she couldn't find in words to tell him, she would show him. As she gazed at him, each memory came into focus, made her breath become shallow, and she drew her thumbs to her mouth to wet. Drawing a lazy trail of moisture over her breasts, she watched the effect that had on him through lowered lids, brushing her thumbs across her nipples until he licked his dry lips.

Yes, lover, I will miss you so if you don't make it was the message. *Yes, my dear husband, I know you'll grieve, if I'm gone, as would I for a lifetime without you. My past was pitted with bad deeds,* her hands said, *but I will be as bad as you need me to be this afternoon.* The admission was made with each erotic sweep of her body. Every touch that landed against her skin as she kept watching him watch her across the room expressed the same thing: *James Carter, make the most of these few idle hours,* she said by simply cupping her breast, allowing her head to fall back, and her thighs to part ever so slightly for him. *I'm so sorry that my past caught up with both of us,* her soft moan meant. *This is yours. I'm yours. That's all I can give you right now, since tomorrow isn't promised . . . but you'll never have to wonder about this. That's a promise I can keep.*

He read her silent messages very well, but couldn't find the words to tell her that he did. His line of vision was trained on her smoldering glances, then had slipped down her pretty face to her lush mouth to then fully appreciate her gorgeous body, her breasts, her cinnamon skin, her hands that touched places he craved, her flat belly, and the way her long, shapely legs tensed as she moved. When she opened her thighs framing her swollen mound, he almost stood. He was jealous of her palm as it slid down her torso and of the fingers that circled her navel, scattering light caresses lower until they disappeared beneath the flesh-toned fabric and made her draw a sharp breath.

Unable to move as he watched her hand pulse under the thong, he felt his groin automatically follow that same pulse, the throb in it connected to the same tempo, his inner thighs tensing and releasing just like her hand. If there was one last thing he wanted to remember about what they had, or about this life, Laura chose well. His body had immediately responded to her tender offer. There was no negotiating with that, as he watched her, amazed, at the effect she always had on him. Her timing was impeccable. Her understanding of him, even more so.

Just by the way she peeled her clothes from her luscious body, he knew she wanted him to observe, see the gift unwrapped slowly, to allow him time to burn the memory into his brain. What he wished he could tell her was that it had been branded there from their first encounter.

She used her body well, just like she mastered time management. He wouldn't squander these few hours. His wife was right . . . Cap forewarned him not to fall by the station; otherwise he'd have to haul him in for questioning, which would get messy. Contacts would be off the records, as would a little assist for old time's sake. Unmarked guns had been ordered by way of cellular hook ups, along with their new ID, and a car without a traceable VIN . . . everything they needed would be ready in a few hours for pick-up off-site—he loved the fact that Laura was ready now. This was a much better option than sitting in the room and wringing their hands.

He stood up slowly, unable to continue watching her sensual disrobing at a distance. Time was running out, and he needed to touch her to stop it for just a little while. When she'd hooked her thumbs under her thong, had shimmied it down to the floor, and licked her lips, that had spurred his decision. Her hand glistened when she'd removed it from her panties, and the sight of that sent a shiver down his spine.

In one pull, his cable-knit sweater and T-shirt came off over his head, but there was something in her eyes that slowed his progress.

Her gaze slid down his body and landed on his belt. "Let me do that," she whispered, and eased herself down to kneel.

It was an unspoken offer, one that made him stop breathing for a moment before he could will his legs to walk toward her. What her position promised also made him abandon his shoes as he moved to stand before her and gently caress her face. Her beautiful brown eyes said *I love you,* and that was the last thing he saw as his eyes slid shut at the sensation of her graceful hands tracing the insides of his thighs.

The hot, moist feel of her breath teased his stomach and made it clench as her sensuous touch skipped past the ache that desired it most. A few hours, yet time had slowed to a halt. Pending disaster—but he was in heaven. Listening to his belt being unfastened and the leather of it stripping through the loops on his pants . . . waiting for her lush mouth—sheer agony. But she took her sweet time, pulling at the front clasp of his slacks, and lowering his zipper one tooth at a time.

Just the sensation of the light wool fabric falling open, the rush of cool air, followed by the heat of her breath, dried his throat. Long licks and mind-consuming kisses scored his abdomen and his thighs while her butter-soft caresses melted over his ass and burned through his silk boxers. In a perverse change of perspective, he suddenly wished time would speed up, rather than continue its leisurely pace of driving him insane. Each kiss, each lick, and every touch drew his breath in sharply and tightened muscles that he didn't know he had.

The boxers came down in painful increments, leaving only a long wet drip in their wake. Even the air now burned him; her soft cheek against the angry surface of suddenly exposed skin caused a contraction. But she ignored it, holding his hips steady, and turning her lips against his sac. A hot lash of tongue released a trapped moan, a full suckle of the overly sensitive skin turned the moan into her gasped name. He couldn't help moving to the rhythm of each pull, each slow rotation of her tongue, no more than he could help bending to stroke her hair . . . trying to coax her to rush time and take the most pained part of him into her mouth. He almost outright begged her to suck it.

Cool air covered by tender hands made him look down at her.

Laura's chin was tipped up, her expression stone serious. Their eyes met, he tensed and braced himself as she lowered her mouth, but never let her eyes leave his. The shudder that she produced started at the base of his spine, ripped across his shoulders, and jerked his head back—her tongue a spiral of ecstasy within a hot, deep cavern of pleasure. She knew him so well; too well, so excruciating and exact . . . in tempo, and pressure, and just, right . . . *Jesus, right there.*

Low air-conditioning notwithstanding, she'd brought sweat. Years of being with the same woman was an asset, not a detriment, as he'd once foolishly believed when he was younger. If there was ever any question about how to spend what might be their last private moment together, she'd answered it. *Take this to his grave, oh yeah—no problem.* Her hands and mouth were working in unison to kill him sweetly, anyway.

All of her collided against his senses at once . . . memories danced with the feel of her mouth, her breasts bobbing in time with her hard pulls, skin against skin, her nipples grazing his thighs as she took him in almost to the hilt without gagging and then wrapped her arms around his hips, not allowing him to fully pump until she was ready. He had to get inside of her, that was all there was to it. Time had been a patient lover, but he could no longer be.

"Together," he managed to gasp.

Making it to the bed was impossible, even though it was right there beside them. Already weak in the knees, he just let them buckle as she sheared away the last of his will. He punished her mouth for the exquisite offense, covered her, and entered her hard. Old times, their first time, he remembered it all as she clung to him and arched to his mount, riding the wave with him, knowing their dance by heart. Her intense shudder released his in due time, sending him to a place of near seizure that ended in twitching muscles that were only a reflexive response from spent cells.

Soft hands tracing his back lulled him into semiconsciousness. A tender kiss against the side of his face made him know that he was still alive. A hot whisper against his ear caused him to smile with deep satisfaction. Her wicked chuckle gently shook him and made his belly shiver.

"I guess that qualifies as great sex," she murmured into his ear. He just nodded with his eyes still closed and gasped more air. "Now I can think better," she whispered. "How about you?" "I'm brain dead," he muttered, not moving. She just laughed.

Chapter
7

"I've been thinking," Laura said, leisurely toweling her body dry.

James just peered up at her from the side of the bed, wondering how women did that. He was still liquefied after two hard hours with her and a hot shower, yet she was energized and refreshed, like she'd just come in from the gym. Her sly smile made him simply shake his head.

"I've got a copy of the old Haines will stashed in safe deposit down on Seventh and Market. We know what was in the previous one. But what we don't know is what was in the very first one—the one before he changed all his allegiances."

"And? Where are you going with this, Laura?" James stood and pulled on his pants.

"Check it out," she said coolly, slipping on a pair of jeans and a light cardigan. "When people came after us before, there was a will involved. Not that I think they have any monies due them by way of the deceased's assets, but it will tell us who old Haines thought of as close allies, and then we work our way backward, like reverse engineering, to figure out who might be seriously pissed off."

"Yeah, but the person who was his attorney of record before all the other bull went down is not one of *our* allies. Remember, we put his only son away for a very long time."

"True," she said, smiling as she finger-combed her damp hair and slipped on her shoes. "But his son's old lover is. Donny Haines, Jr., used to be hooked up with Alan Moyer's son."

James let his breath out hard. "C'mon, Laura. Donny went so far underground after that, we'd need a S.W.A.T. team to pull him out of hiding. He's not gonna just help us on a friendship tip."

She placed her hands on her hips and looked at him hard. "We saved his freakin' life, as I recall. Not to mention, unraveled a lot of family mysteries for him. He owes us."

"Maybe," James said, sighing hard. "But he might not see it as cut-and-dried."

"He's a smart man, and no doubt has been watching bodies drop. Oh, yeah, he'll talk to us, especially if he's not sure what's started the ball rolling again."

Tracking down Donald Haines, Jr., was harder than she'd imagined. James had been right, the man had gone AWOL. Rumor had it that he'd moved out to Delaware County, but another lead by way of good ole Rick the reporter had sent them to the right bar in New Hope, Pennsylvania.

The main drag had changed a lot over the years. Bikes littered the street along with noise level warning signs and pedestrians. The quaint little artist town that looked like something out of a nineteenth-century fairy tale—reputed haunted houses included— now sported the jarring contrast of chrome motorcycles and leather-wearing hog riders.

"Rick said he usually eats dinner at that little bed-and-breakfast over at the corner," Laura noted, motioning with her head while they circled the block for non-existent parking. "Quiet as kept, he has a permanent room there on the third floor and stays pretty much to himself."

James glanced at the old Victorian with white shutters, a small white-picket fence bordering the corner property's wide lawn that wrapped around to the next block. White wrought-iron chairs sat in wait under a grand weeping willow tree, and heavily cushioned white wicker furniture tastefully dotted the broad porch. If ever there was a retirement home, this was it.

"I'm sure they'll protect their local VIP from any intruders like us," James said with a skeptical tone as he pulled their unmarked, black Buick sedan into a space several blocks away.

"That's why we aren't going in to ask questions. We're taking a room, with dinner, and we'll wait to see who comes into the dining room."

"Yeah and what if dude is so freaked out that he only eats in his room?"

She ruffled her hair in frustration and simply got out of the car.

They both kept their eyes on the small boutiques and antique shops, hoping to spot Donald Haines, Jr., as they silently walked hand in hand like accidental tourists on an early evening stroll. New-age crystal shops, candle makers, tiny galleries, all set against the suburban escape route from urban chaos, made Laura sad.

The theme *you can run but you can't hide* replayed itself in her mind over and over again as they made their way up the wide front-porch stairs. Donny had been traumatized by his parents and his lover. Maybe James had a point; this sensitive soul wouldn't want to revisit all of that ugliness to unearth more of his father's political past life. It was almost as though the poor man had taken up residence in a home filled with strangers that were probably nicer to him than his next of kin, yet had located himself in what he'd always dreamed of—a quiet home away from it all, a house with a white picket fence.

Pasting on her most convincing smile, Laura walked up to the front desk.

"This is beautiful, isn't it, honey?" she said, for the benefit of the manager. She turned to James, gave him the eye to play along, and waited until her husband begrudgingly half smiled.

"If you like it, I love it," James grumbled, his steely grit on the manager, who remained uncomfortable.

"Sir," she said, ignoring her husband, "I know we don't have a reservation, but a dear friend of ours mentioned that this place was fabulous, especially the home-cooked dinners, and we were wondering if you had a room available?"

"I'm so sorry," the manager said, his gaze flitting between Laura and James. "We're booked solid in the spring and fall seasons."

She pouted and let out a sigh of feigned disappointment. "Bummer, after we drove all the way down here from Philly, too," she murmured, seeming helpless as she touched James's arm. "And at the newspaper they said how great your spinach soufflés are, and beef pot pies . . . maybe we can just have dinner here, honey?"

The manager cleared his throat as she barreled into James's arms, peering up at him with her back to the desk. Laura waited, knowing full well the policy was that dinner was only to be served to guests who had a room—but she was also well aware that business was business, media was media, and no establishment in their right mind would blow off a well-dressed, urban professional couple, that also happened to be African-American with friends at a major Philadelphia press.

"Uhmmm, ma'am—"

"Laura," she cooed, leaving James's loose hold to shake the manager's hand. "Is it too late for us to have dinner here?"

The slightly rotund man smiled weakly, shook her hand, and then smoothed back the few strands of hair that covered his semi-balding scalp. "Well, normally we're not supposed to extend that service to people who are not guests of the B&B . . . but since you folks traveled all the way here to be disappointed, we might be able to slip you in at a table, if you promise not to tell anyone we did so?"

She let out a quiet little squeal and leaned into the desk, glancing around and whispering. "Oh, sir, thank you—you'd do that for us? I promise to let my friends know how accommodating you were when they do the food reviews. We won't tell a soul."

The manager beamed at her and stood up a little taller. "The chef, my wife," he said proudly, "makes the pot pie crusts from scratch, and also does a fabulous baked salmon in pastry."

Laura swooned and smiled brightly. "Oh, sir, you've just made our night."

"How do you do that shit, Laura?" James said under his breath once they'd been seated. He glanced around at the small antique tables with graying couples at them in a cozy, open-air dining room that had been extended for space by a glass enclosed porch.

"What?" she murmured, smiling too hard as she sipped her lemon spiked water.

He shook his head and chuckled. "You worked me the same way when we met."

"Was that a bad thing?"

"My life has never been the same since."

She set down her water and stifled a laugh. "I repeat—was that a bad thing? Because this afternoon you didn't seem to mind."

He nodded and clinked his glass against hers. "'Nuff said. But what if our boy isn't here?"

"Then we have beef pot pie and salmon wrapped in pastry, and go to plan B."

"Which is?"

She chuckled. "I'm working on it. Give a sister a break."

"Ten o'clock. Don't turn around," James said, the smile sliding from his face. "You got your lucky break."

Laura calmly placed the white linen napkin in her lap and watched James's eyes. As she casually picked up her glass of water, she allowed her peripheral vision to note the movement of a rail-thin blond male who wore a powder blue Oxford shirt that seemed as though it had swallowed him whole.

"I'm going to excuse myself to go to the ladies' room, then become surprised by the fortuitous, chance meeting. I suggest you put a less menacing expression on your face. This is a delicate entry into a convo with Donny," she warned, and then stood, pecked James on the forehead, and left the table.

Calmly walking through the dining area that was beginning to fill with patrons, she stopped, waved at Donny, and ignored his stricken expression as she approached him.

"Donny, how are you? Oh, don't get up," she said using the balmiest tone she could muster. "Are you eating alone or expecting guests? Sit with us, please."

He awkwardly stood, kept his voice low, his expression strained. "Laura, you don't have to play games with me. I'm not exactly on the center city circuit anymore, so if you found me here, you had to be looking for me for a distinct reason."

She let out a weary sigh and nodded. "Your right, but we didn't want to invade your privacy."

Donny set aside his napkin in annoyance. "You already have."

Refusing to give up, she held his gaze. "And whenever I have, it's been for a good reason, hasn't it? I've been underground for a long time myself, so if I showed up with James—"

"All right," he said, moving toward Laura and James's table. "You've made your point."

Slowly following behind him, she hung back as James stood and kept his demeanor easy, and was grateful that her husband had taken her advice. The two men shook hands and suffered the overly eager waiter who eventually moved Donny's place setting to their table.

"So," Donny said on a weary exhale, "now that you know where I've relocated, where have you two been?"

"Out of the country," James said flatly.

Donny didn't react, just nodded and hailed the waiter for a glass of wine. "But I take it you've seen the news."

"Yes," Laura said in a quiet voice. "We're worried."

"Then, once again, you and my mother have something in common to share as unlikely allies."

Laura and James glanced at each other and let their worried gazes fall on Donny. His matter-of-fact response was chilling.

"Do you have any idea who might be severely agitated by the distribution of funds?" she finally said once wine had been poured.

Donny smiled. "How about half of the Pennsylvania legislators?"

"Anybody in particular with an axe to grind?" James said, his face stoic.

"About half of the Pennsylvania legislators," Donny repeated, his expression smug. "And, oh yes, two thirds of the city."

"But who's wrapped in tight with the old boys in D.C.?"

Laura's question wiped the smug expression off Donny's face. He took a deep sip of wine to poorly cover his new mental strain.

"That, I don't know," Donny finally admitted, glancing quickly between Laura and James. "How do you know it's gone that far?"

"A little birdie told us," James muttered.

Laura leaned forward; this was getting them nowhere. She dropped her voice to a low, conspiratorial tone. "A hit man with ties to the old federal Black Ops crew just blew up in his rental car in Washington, D.C. You did see the Consumer Report piece about refrigerant safety, didn't you?" She sat back and allowed that information to sink in. One thing she knew for sure, Donald Haines, Jr., abhorred violence, and anything that smacked of it gave the man the hives.

"How do you know he was a hit man with that sort of association?" Donny said, his bewildered blue eyes searching theirs as he breathed the statement out on a quiet gasp.

"He tried to kill my uncle," Laura whispered, leaning in even closer, making the waiter pause before bringing bread. "They ran his dental records, since that's the only way he could be identified once it was done," she added, weaving in theater and gruesome details to the half-truth fabrication, but leaving out the ruse Akhan had pulled to escape. "He was connected."

"Oh, my God . . ." Donny whispered. "It's really happening all over again, isn't it?"

James and Laura nodded together on cue.

"Then how do we stop it? What if there's some deranged individual trying to wipe us all out?" Donny's eyes went from bewildered to feral.

Laura placed a hand gently on his arm. "That's why we're here," she assured him. "If they'd wanted you, they could have gotten to you. There's more to it than that, and we can't figure out what it is."

"Yeah," James said calmly, sipping his wine. "Whoever did this isn't just some deranged fool looking to whack people. It ain't the mob, either—but don't ask how we know. We have sources. Period. This was planned and done with purpose. If we figure out the purpose, we can get ahead of the curve, feel me?"

"Well, what's this got to do with me? How am I involved?" Donny's gaze shot from Laura to James in sheer panic.

"We know what was in your father's adjusted will. We know who he had originally slated to receive assets before that . . . but what we don't have is insight into who he originally did business with before he started moving pieces around on the game board well before I came onto the scene."

Donny fervently shook his head no. "I can't go prying into all of that. I wouldn't even know where to begin, and frankly, if they're not looking for me, then—"

"You have access," Laura said, sitting back and picking up her glass of chardonnay.

"To what?" Donny said in a tight whisper, leaning forward.

"To whatever Alan Moyer's son—"

"No," Donny said, snatching his napkin off his lap and flinging it onto the table, ready to stand. "He's in prison for life for trying to kill me for my inheritance, being involved in my father's death, and then going after a material witness . . . for . . . I'm done with him, with that entire travesty, and—"

"You owe us," James said, his tone menacing. "We saved your ass a while back, and now—"

"You want money, I'll give you money. You want—"

"To live," Laura said quietly, coming between both men, who'd reached a dangerous stalemate. Her tone was urgent and for once contained the brutal truth. "*That's all.*" She set her gaze on him hard, but her expression was gentle in an attempt to break through to him. "Donny, I have sisters, family, nieces and nephews, an elderly uncle . . . I don't want to die; I don't want them to die— not over money, not for any reason. I want to find out who's been wronged so I can rearrange the money just as it was before, so we can all sleep at night. Can you seriously tell me that by just getting up from this table and leaving us with a target on our foreheads, when you could have done something about it—a very small thing—that you'll be able to sleep at night? If so, then let's just order, eat, and call it a night."

She glared at James, sending him a warning not to move or speak during this extremely fragile negotiation. If he pressed Donny, their ace in the hole would bolt and run.

"I don't even speak to Alan anymore," Donny murmured, slumping in his chair, hedging. "I don't visit that place. After the trial was over, I stopped any form of communication. I rarely even say his name."

Laura could feel a rush of hope beginning to make her palms moist. She practically bit her tongue to keep from speaking, and forced her gaze to remain serene.

"After all that ugliness came out at my father's funeral . . . and he was taken into custody, once the media onslaught was over, I packed all his belongings into a public storage unit and delivered the key to his father by courier. I never want to have anything to do with him again in this life."

Laura and James briefly stared at each other.

"You wouldn't happen to remember where you got a storage container, would you—or the number to the bin?" James glanced at Laura again. "Could be a long shot, but worth a try."

"It's engraved in my mind," Donny said, tears rising in his eyes, causing them to glisten. "How does one pack up a lifetime with one's lover? . . . each piece that the movers shoved in there had a memory."

Laura slowly reached across the table and squeezed Donny's hand in support. "I cannot imagine having to do that, but it's important that we know."

He sniffed and looked out the glass enclosure. "There's a large storage warehouse down on Delaware Avenue, near the Home Depot."

"I know where that's at," James said, sitting back in his chair.

"Bin twelve-seventy," Donny said softly. "But that was over a year ago. I doubt anything of his is still there."

James rubbed his face down his palms. "Fifty-fifty chance that old man Moyer was so upset by his son's behavior that he could have either left it there to rot, and not paid the bill—in which case, it's been sold by now—or cleaned out the unit and sent whatever was allowable to his son in the pen, keeping the rest as a—"

"He wouldn't have set up a shrine for him in his old bedroom at home, if that's what you're implying. His father was like mine, and would have burned it all first," Donny said bitterly, grasping the bottle of chardonnay by its neck and pouring a sloppy glass of wine to quickly down. "Besides," he pressed on, his hurt gaining momentum as he spoke through a gulp of wine, "what would seeing those old documents prove? I didn't even bother to open his lock box when I found the key hidden during the move. I'd already seen enough and didn't want to be devastated any more." Donny abruptly leaned forward, and spoke between his teeth. "I'd been through *hell*. I taped the key on the top of it with duct tape. I was through with all of it, and him."

Donny sat back, seeming spent. Laura poured a glass of wine for her and James, and waited patiently as the waiter came over to merrily take their orders.

"I've lost my appetite," Donny told the server, and turned away.

"A beef pot pie and the salmon," James said, eyeing the now confused and nervous server. "We're still hungry, even if our friend isn't. Maybe bring him the potato soup so his ulcer doesn't act up."

The server nodded, hurriedly took the order, and departed from the table. Glad that the small diversion had given her a chance to think, Laura picked up the threads of the conversation, coming in at a different angle.

"In each set of documents, there have to be social security numbers for the distribution of assets," she said as calmly and quietly as possible. "Through those, and with names, partnerships, etcetera, one might be able to track investment partners, and whomever else they're tied to."

Oddly, Donny blinked and leaned forward, but his gaze no longer just held pain and fear. A strange level of angry determination seemed to complement those roiling emotions as his brilliant legal mind briefly rose out of its traumatized state.

"Yes, you would be able to do that," he said carefully, appraising Laura. "I hadn't thought of that, because I never cared who my father used to do business with . . . but from the current will that held up, compared with the two before it, those documents should show his very mercurial dealings."

"We can track who got cut out, and then backward trend who suffered the greatest losses without repayment from that," she said, never taking her eyes off him.

Raking his fingers through his hair, Donny uncomfortably shifted in his seat. "That's all I have to do? Tell you where Dad's very old and outdated will drawn up by Moyer Senior is? All you want is the location of Alan's lock box?" Donny let out a hard exhale and rubbed his palms down his ashen face.

"That's all we want. You and I both know Alan had gotten old, confidential papers from his father when he'd clerked for him years back. You told me that out of your own mouth," Laura said, no judgment in her tone. "We had the most recent wills, but never had the one your father had Alan's dad prepare originally when they were still friends. Someone has to be mentioned in there that has federal ties, with enough juice and connections to call in the types of hits that they did. Someone with serious immunity. Icing a state senator isn't a trivial thing."

James smoothed his palm across his chin. "I'd put money on it that Alan's father never knew he had those docs, given their close relationship," he said sarcastically. "So, if the stuff in the unit where you stashed his belongings is still there, chances are, so are all the important papers."

Laura raked her hair with her fingers. Fatigue clawed at her. "Now all we need is a good hacker—once we get those social security numbers."

"A hacker?" Donny sat back. "Shit. That's illegal."

"So is breaking into a public storage unit," James said without emotion.

"So is putting a hit on innocent people to service a vendetta, but we're trying to keep the police and media out of it," she said, her gaze locked with Donny's. "This needs to be handled quietly, efficiently, and be permanently put to rest. Isn't that what we all want?"

After a long pause, Donny nodded but remained silent for what seemed like an eternity. "I have a friend at Penn," he eventually admitted as the server brought their meal. He looked down at his soup with disinterest. "Assuming you can get the papers, and assuming they show you anything worthwhile, making this just disappear as quietly as possible gets my vote. She's a pro on databases, and can hack. I trust her, and if I explain that it's something very personal for me, she might do it. She wouldn't breathe whatever you discover to a soul."

Laura and James shared a skeptical glance.

"I take it you've used her services before as an attorney," James said, ignoring the way Laura blanched when he accused Donny with his tone.

"I won't dignify that," Donny said icily. "My ex did things off the record and not always by the book to gain the advantage— even used my friends from time to time. His ambition knew no bounds, and Megan thought she was helping me. Alan called in markers he didn't own, but that's how I learned what she could do. Don't judge me." He glanced down, focusing on his cooling soup as he began to bring the spoon to his lips.

Then he suddenly looked up at both Laura and James, holding his spoon just before his mouth. "I don't want the police or media in this to start the whole scandal all over again. The next time will literally kill me."

James closed Laura's passenger-side door and strolled around the parked vehicle to the driver's side and got in. They both secretly held their breaths as he started the engine, and let out silent exhales when the motor turned over without incident.

He put the gears in reverse without looking at her, keeping his focus over his shoulder.

"Laura, I'm only going to ask you this one last time," he said, maneuvering the car into oncoming traffic. "Baby, how do you do that amazing shit?"

Chapter
8

His nerves pulled wire-taut, Akhan walked around the rooms of his daughter's home, thinking. No. Sitting and waiting for fate was not an option. He knew of places to go to hide that even his shrewd niece, Laura, couldn't fathom. The only problem would be getting Steve to blend in.

Akhan rubbed the newly appearing stubble on his chin as he gazed out of the sliding glass doors. If a black senator was killed, then it had to be because the man knew too much, and was therefore being cut out of deals he could no longer deliver on. The weak link in the food chain was always the first to go. *It's a shame bourgeois Negroes hadn't learned that lesson by now,* he thought, becoming irate.

Laura and James were going about this all wrong, the hard way, as young people often did. Getting a peek at Haines's original will would prove a dangerous proposition . . . whereas digging into a dead black man's effects by merely appearing to be his distant and vicious family, wouldn't raise any particular red flags. The key was to find out who the silent investors might have been in whatever supposedly minority contracts were apportioned to the dead senator and his also-deceased son.

Moving methodically through the house, Akhan stopped at the

doorway of the small office. Steve, Najira, and Jamal glanced up from the security system plans.

"Dad?" Najira said, her eyes searching his face with concern.

"Leave everything as though we're just going out for the day," her father said calmly.

"What's up, Pop?" Jamal said, standing, causing Steve to slowly set the blueprints down on the desk.

"Call it age, but I have a bad feeling. I want the three of us to drive to the airport."

"Hold it, Daddy," Najira said, standing and going to his side. "Laura and James said to—"

"Have I ever been wrong?" he asked in a tender but firm tone.

The threesome glanced at each other nervously.

"No," Najira said in a quiet voice. "I know we're all jumpy, but—"

"Get your purse and some money," Akhan ordered. "I'll be in the car."

He left the room without further argument. Within moments, Steve was behind the wheel with Jamal and Najira in the backseat.

"Where are we going?" Steve asked, nonplussed but curious.

"To Jamaica," Akhan said flatly. "I know some underground brothers there from the old days."

Mrs. Melville hoisted her purse up on her shoulder and turned to leave her home. Her husband gave her a quizzical glance.

"Where ya going, love?"

She smiled. "I know Mrs. Carter said she didn't need a ting, but . . ."

He stood, but didn't smile. "Don't."

Her smile faded. "Why not? I don't understand your mood."

"It's more than young people needing space to be intimate. Somethin' is wrong over dere."

She set her purse down with care. "Those nice people? You tink dey are into somethin' illegal?"

He nodded. "Cousin Bruce down at the airport said they got on a flight the next day after an elderly family member came.

Now, if they had company arriving, wouldn't you tink dey would need our services?"

His wife leaned against the wall for support. He simply nodded again and stood up from the sofa to go to her.

"Whole family in town, then she and her new husband go out of town. Doesn't jive. But I tink dat gurl is good of heart, because she got us out of the way."

"What should we do?" Mrs. Melville began wringing her hands. "If there's somethin' untoward happening in dat house, we cannot go back."

"I called cousin Hayward about it," her husband said, drawing her into a comforting embrace. "He deals with all sorts of tings like this in his bureau. Let the authorities quietly investigate, and if all is well, we can go back. If not, then we are out of harm's way."

Mrs. Melville tearfully nodded and rested her head on her husband's shoulder.

"I hope we're wrong," she whispered. "I liked them so much."

He cruised by the lavish villa twice. The house seemed vacant, save the landscaper who was out front busily pruning shrubs. Excellent. Why Vladimir couldn't have found the targets and dispensed with them was stupid and very sloppy. The dumb bastard deserved to die.

Gaining access to the back entrance would be a cakewalk. Planting a cell-phone activated explosive near the stove gas line, no problem. Then ditching his suit in exchange for touristwear and sunning himself on the beach until the occupants returned home was just another easy job. In fact, the gardener looked so numb that he could probably just walk right up to the man and ask him when James and Laura Carter would be coming home. He'd play it off as an insurance salesman, whatever. The help always responded to authority figures.

Picking up his briefcase filled with paraphernalia, he sauntered up to the man working on the front lawn.

"Excuse me," he said, in his most courteous, salesman voice. "I had an insurance appointment today with Mr. and Mrs. Carter. Would you happen to know what time they will return?"

The gardener surveyed the man with caution and deflected his gaze, playing dumb. "Why, no suh. They didn't tell me. But you could leave your information, and if I'm here when they come back, I'll be sure to tell them."

"No, never mind. I wouldn't want the papers to blow away. Mind if I step around to the back of the house to leave them some literature under their deck chairs?"

The gardener shrugged. "Suit yourself."

He smiled. It didn't get any easier than this.

The gardener watched the man in the sweat-creased khaki suit as he rounded the house and went toward the back. He took his time going to his truck, carefully hiding his hands behind it as he pulled out a walkie-talkie unit from his baggy trousers.

"Hayward, here. Got a very suspicious character here snoopin' around the Carters' property. Tall, athletic, six feet two. Brunette. Caucasian male. Car is an airport rental. He's carrying a metal briefcase. I'll call in the tags, run a check, and send me some backup in marked cars, immediately. I want him to open the case for you. Keep your two-ways on while you go behind the house so I can hear the conversation."

He had been able to easily find the lines to the security system, mimic a power dip so common in the Caribbean, and use his little black box and clamps to restore it before the alarm even sounded. Perfect . . . just like the very swift installation of the explosives had been. He slid the glass doors shut, dropped some brochures he'd picked up at the airport on the deck table beneath a Citronella candle, and smiled.

Footsteps made him quickly look up and remain still. He could see through the house that the gardener was still out front. Two Cayman Islands police officers walked down the side path. He remained cool. Perhaps he'd underestimated the paranoia of the Carters and they had installed a double system that he'd missed. He sighed. Maybe the silent secondary alarm did go off on a silent sensor. No problem. He had the gardener as a witness. His alibi would be simple: He tried the back door to attempt to slide his information onto the kitchen floor, rather than allow it to blow away on the deck. He'd shake the incompetent assholes in no time, and then be on his way without incident. Two dead officers would flush his targets and make them flee. That would be sloppy.

"Good afternoon, officers," he said brightly.

"Sir, may we see some identification?" the bolder of the two said, eyeing the man with outright suspicion.

"What brings you to this house today?"

"Oh," the man said, slapping his forehead and chuckling. "I had an insurance appointment with the Carters, they weren't in, and like a dummy, I tried to push the brochures through the door to the kitchen floor. Should have known that people this well off would have had alarms. The gardener said it would be all right." He motioned toward the fluttering brochures with a humble shrug. "ID, sure. My apologies for getting you worried for nothing."

As he reached into his suit breast pocket, the officers took a stance that now concerned him. They had guns, not a normal occurrence in the islands, and their holsters were at the ready.

"Gentlemen?" he said, feigning surprise, and halting his movements. "Aren't you taking things a bit far for an insurance guy just trying to make a sale?"

"Open the briefcase," the second officer said, no nonsense in his tone.

He watched beads of perspiration rise on shiny black faces. This was getting very complicated.

"OK," he said coolly. "Here's my identification."

He continued to reach into his jacket slowly, and then squeezed hard twice. Two silenced shots ripped through his suit. Two grunts and nearly simultaneous thuds sounded softly. Messy. He'd ruined a good suit. He was just glad that their brains had blown out onto the furniture behind them, and hadn't splattered his good shirt and tie. He glanced down at the two bodies with disdain.

The lawnmower in the front yard was music to his ears. But a small, very distinct popping sound, followed by a burning sensation in his back jolted him to a stop, spinning him around to look at the gardener's menacing face.

"Who are these people?"

Two men sat in the drawing room of a Chevy Chase home and sipped their brandy with concern.

"I don't know," the other murmured. "They have nine fucking lives."

"Maybe we should call this off for a little while. Let things cool off, before we go at it again?"

The other shook his head. "It's too late for that. We have to clean all of this up quickly. Need I remind you how much we've lost in real estate investments in the Gulf? Goddamned storms, natural disasters . . . if we lose key development opportunities in a major city like Philadelphia, too, we'll all be in the poor house."

The other man simply threw back his drink, wincing as the alcohol slid down his throat, and nodded.

"You are Detective Sullivan," James said, as he reached over Laura's lap to open the glove compartment.

She sat back in the passenger's seat and simply stared at her husband when he dropped a shield in her lap.

"You asked *me* how *I* did that shit?" she murmured, ogling the leather billfold that contained false ID that would put her on Philadelphia's finest team as a veteran detective.

"Don't ask, don't tell." James smiled and flashed his old shield. "Helps to have friends that have keys to certain rooms."

She shook her head as they exited the car in the abandoned lot. Her line of vision immediately went to the security guard booth, where a young man was sleeping and the blue flicker of a mini-television was visible.

"I've got this," James said. "Lemme speak the jargon, you look mean."

"Mean?"

He chuckled as they approached the booth. "Just give him that sister girl-don't-play grit you gave me when we first met and I'd crossed you wrong."

Laura cut him a glance from the corner of her eyes.

"Yeah. Just like that," James said, smiling. "Mean as a rattlesnake, and about as deadly, too."

There was no time to respond as James knocked on the booth hard. The sound startled the sleeping guard, and she wondered if they trained cops to knock in that bone-jarring way.

"Yo, what's up, man?" the guard said, glowering at James. "We closed."

"And we're Five-oh. Got a tip down at the department someone was stashing drugs in a unit. Need you to walk us around to bin twelve-seventy, and open it up."

The young man held both hands up before his chest. "Hey, man, I don't have the authority to—"

"Haul his ass in as a possible accessory, Sullivan," James said to Laura, using his voice as a weapon. "Print this bastard, run a microscope up his ass for making my night longer, and let's see how much authority—"

"Yo, yo, yo, I ain't in it, brother. I just work here, man!"

"Then make my night, and open the fucking bin." James sighed, flashed his badge, silently beckoning Laura to do the same. "I'm tired, need a cup of coffee, and don't feel like a lotta hassle. You make my job harder, trust me, I'll make yours unbearable."

"This shit is harassment, man," the guard said, opening the door and walking ahead of Laura and James with the keys. "Can make me lose my damned job, when all a brother got is this piece'a ass job. Shit!"

Laura just glimpsed her husband from the corner of her eye as they followed the young guard. The kid couldn't have been more than twenty-five, and the back of his bushy hair had a dent in it from where he'd been leaning against the wall. In that moment, she made up her mind. It wasn't about giving back a goddamned thing to those in power. They'd stolen enough. Had condemned too many people to life in the margins. New plan. Find the rat bastards, expose them, and send them fleeing to get caught on a sticky trap.

Keys turning in a huge padlock brought her out of her darkening thoughts. But she wondered if James would go for a smooth set up, or if he'd want to play it by the book.

The guard yanked away the lock and stared at James with defiance. "It's open."

"Stop playing with me, man," James said. "Lift the grate."

"That ain't my job," the guard challenged.

"See," James said, glancing at Laura. "A tough guy who keeps making me wanna haul his ass in just on GP."

The young man let out a frustrated breath and tugged on the steel grate until it rose, steadily glaring at James.

"Mind if I borrow your flashlight, or is there electric in the joint?"

The guard slapped the fixture on the wall, lighting the medium-size bin, and then flung the lock down on the ground and stalked away. "Close it up when you're done. I ain't responsible for the contents if you don't!" he hollered over his shoulder.

"My, you have such a way with the community," Laura said, smirking. "You ever think of running for public office?"

James ignored her as they shimmied their way into the tightly packed unit. Dust covered everything, and before long, they were both smudged and dirty. Lifting the edges of plastic, she watched James peer between picture frames that had been meticulously wrapped with brown paper.

"I feel sorry for Donny," she said, touching a lamp that had been carefully concealed beneath bubble wrap. "You could tell he loved this man to the end, even after knowing."

"How you figure?" James said absently. "He put all his shit in a bin and walked."

"Look at how he packed . . . as though he wanted his lover to know that, even to the bitter end, he cared . . . had enough class to not destroy his belongings and obviously wanted none of them."

James briefly stopped his search and stared at her for a moment. She watched the epiphany dawn in his eyes.

"Yeah, James. Loved him the old-fashioned way, because I can tell you—most sisters would have thrown his mess out in the street in green garbage bags, or sold anything of value."

James nodded. "Truth. Seen it done. You sending me a message, or speaking from experience?"

She chuckled. "Both. I helped my sisters part from men, and I can tell you, it wasn't this neat and lovely at all." She began picking through the contents with a sly smile on her face. "But I've never had a man to put out before—never let any of them get close enough to share my living quarters."

"Okaaay. Duly noted. So, then, where would a lover stash a box of important papers?" He waited and watched her every move.

"In an orderly fashion," she said calmly. "In an office desk, where it belongs, or in a bedroom bureau—somewhere private."

James walked over to the huge, polished oak desk that had been carefully wrapped in plastic. "Five dollars says the desk. Dude is too organized."

"I'll raise you ten dollars, and a Starbucks coffee when we get out of here, that it's in the bedroom bureau . . . sent as a message that all of this ruined what they once had. Underwear drawer, to be exact."

James waved his arm toward the bedroom furniture in the back. "Ladies first."

Frowning at the dust that marred her pants, Laura inched along the narrow walkway toward where James had motioned.

"Did you notice I was using my badge to touch things?" he said in a dry tone.

She drew her hand back and stared at him.

"I'm gonna wipe off anything you touched, and use your elbow to kill the lights on the way out. We'll let the guard worry about going back to lock up, feel me?"

"Shit," she murmured. "You could've warned me."

"Great criminal mind, and raggedy on the details—gets 'em

busted every time. Use the edge of your blouse to put your hands under it, and break that plastic seal."

"You do it," she argued, scrunching up her nose.

"Nope. You're the rookie cop on this detail. I'm already dirty enough."

She sighed, stuck out her tongue at him, and then worked quickly to make a big enough hole in the seal to allow the top dresser drawer to be opened. She shot James a smug look of satisfaction. "You know how I like my coffee, right?"

Chapter
9

She sipped her coffee in triumph as they pored over papers while sitting in the parking lot of the 38th Street 7-Eleven. "This isn't Starbucks, so you still owe me."

"Yeah, yeah, as long as I owe you, you'll never go broke," James muttered, leaning in to look at the papers, but not fully comprehending what they contained. "So do we need to pay a visit to this hacker chick, or what?"

"Uhmmm, hmmm, hmmm," Laura said, biting her bottom lip as she studied the papers. "Lookie here, lookie here," she whispered. "Micholi Foundation was to receive certain real estate assets."

James raked his fingers across his close-cropped hair. "And?"

She peered up at him. "You know who sits on that board?"

"No," he said flatly.

She let out an impatient breath. "A lot of Main Line real estate developers, several prominent attorneys—of which, Alan Moyer, Senior, Haines's old attorney, was one, along with James Devereaux from the Redevelopment Authority, Mike Polanski and George Townsend from the Micholi board, which I'd also bet, if we do a document search, has some cross-pollination with the old Scots-Edwards Foundation, chaired by the good senator's wife not so long ago."

"Damn, Laura," James said in a weary tone, rubbing his hands down his face. "The financial incest in Philly is worse than *The Sopranos.*"

"Ya think?" She shook her head and folded away the documents. "Now, the thing is gonna be how to find out which one has the biggest axe to grind, or the most to lose."

He started the ignition, peering over his shoulder to back out of the tiny lot onto Chestnut Street traffic. "Micholi sounds Russian to me, is all I know."

She placed her hand on his arm. "James . . . did I ever tell you that you were brilliant? Staring us right in the face!"

He kept his eyes forward, but her assessment of his skill quietly pleased him. "It was a basic, connect-the-dots, cop hunch. You've got one dead Russian hit man, a Russian-sounding foundation, highfalutin individuals with strong political ties to D.C. and the state, what's to figure?"

"Still brilliant," she murmured with appreciation as he pulled the car into a rare parking space on Hamilton Street in Powellton Village. She glanced up at the narrow brownstone guarded by a turn-of-the-century wrought-iron fence. "Think we should call, or just ring the bell?"

James opened his car door. "Chances are Donny gave her the heads-up. The fact that we'll be on her steps at this hour without warning is enough to let her know it's serious, even if he hadn't."

"OK," Laura said, "but let me handle this. She's a friend of Donny's and an innocent woman with a job to protect at Penn. We need something from her, and she doesn't need jack from us. So don't go banging on her door to scare the bejeebers out of her with a cops-at-the-door routine. All right?"

James saluted her as they strolled up the cobblestone walk and then ascended the few cement steps that gave way to a wide, wooden porch without furniture. Laura eyed the gingerbread-studded overhang that shielded the porch from the glare of street lights. Properties in this immaculate condition, especially in this part of town, were worth a mint. She wondered if the home had been purchased by sheer discipline and good investment with mortgage help offered to university employees, or if the sister had a little game with her?

Stepping in front of James, Laura rang the bell and then moved back from the leaded, beveled glass French doors. They could see a shadow moving inside the semi-dim house, and within moments, a slim, female figure entered the foyer, but didn't turn on the porch light. The lace sheers moved and a strained voice called out, "Who is it?"

"Donny sent us," was all Laura said.

The locks immediately turned, and a woman with long, rust-hued dreadlocks swept up in a ponytail cracked the door open, assessed them quickly, and then waved them inside. Laura hesitated, suddenly feeling a pang of guilt for possibly bringing disaster into this bystander's life. Megan Montgomery put her hands on her hips for a moment and pursed her lips as though about to say something before she'd changed her mind. Then she moved around Laura and James, locked the door, and toyed with her gray sweatpants string.

"C'mon in," she said in a begrudging tone, now twisting the edge of her U. of P. T-shirt.

"Thank you," Laura said, extending her hand, and trying to get the young woman to calm down. "I know it's late, and you have to get up early in the morning."

Megan's gaze hardened. "What did the bastard do to him now?"

Taken aback, Laura opened her mouth and then closed it.

"Can we step inside?" James finally said, feeling crowded in the foyer.

"Is it that bad that you brought a cop?" Megan shook her head and strode into the living room. "Got herbal tea. You want some?"

"No, but thank you," Laura said, still standing and glancing at James. "We're not cops, just friends of his. We think the people his old lover was connected to might be angling to find a way to physically hurt him and anyone close to him or his situation."

"Same ole bullshit!" Megan exclaimed and flopped down into a huge, electric blue butterfly chair. "Why won't they just leave him alone?"

"I take it you two are tight," James said in a matter-of-fact tone, sitting down heavily on the adjacent, lumpy sofa covered by a mud cloth throw.

"That's my boyie, okaaaay," Megan said. "Hell, yeah, me and Donny are tight." Sudden tears of fury filled her eyes. "I had his back in school. Loved him like a brother—we were tight. He'd do the world for anybody. He was in pre-law; I was dabbling in poli-sci courses, even though my butt was supposed to be in the school of engineering down at David Rittenhouse Labs. The bond was we were both artists having to do something we hated because of parental suggestion."

"So . . . from time to time, to help an old friend, you, uh, helped his lover out?" Laura asked, testing the waters.

"Hell no. I didn't do anything for Alan because of Donny." Megan stood. "I hated that bastard from day one. He was cheating on Donny with this brother . . . what was his name . . . tall, fine, treacherous."

"That would have to be Michael Paxton, Jr." Laura looked at James.

"Yeah. Him. The asshole that got shot by a cop and died. Good riddance."

James kept his gaze steady on Laura, willing her with his eyes not to go any further on the subject.

"So, why'd you do stuff for Alan, then?" Laura ruffled her hair as she watched Megan sit down again slowly.

"Because Alan had Donny's mind . . . would have broken up our friendship." Megan closed her eyes and leaned back. "I was going through changes, experimenting with different lifestyles, then . . . and my parents heard I had a girlfriend, freaked out, and stopped sending checks from Jamaica. Dad worked in the State Department, and my mother's people aren't evolved—old Jamaican bourgeoisie. Need I say more?" Megan opened her eyes and kept her line of vision on Laura. "Donny wrote out a personal check that covered my tuition for my senior year, just like that, no questions asked. When we both got into grad school, he went on to law school with Alan, and I stayed here." She chuckled sadly and sniffed. "He gave me the down payment here, and said it would always be between just us. Then Alan found out about it, and started some shit."

Laura nodded. James remained stone-faced.

"That's fucked up," James said, reclining against the cushions to help Megan relax.

"It was," Megan said. "So I did him a few quick and easy jobs, just so I'd have something on him, should he try to go there. But God is good; Alan got his in the end. His slimy ass is in prison." She let her head fall forward as she folded her hands between her knees. "I thought that after that Donny would be free and clear of stress, once it was all over and his old man was buried, too." She just shook her head, causing her long, thick ponytail to sway. "Then I get this panicked call from him that there's still some bullshit with his father's will, and that people could be after him to right some past deals that were still not entirely repaid." She looked up at Laura and James with remorse-filled eyes. "If all it will take is a little digging to find out who needs their itch scratched, I'm down."

"These people are dangerous," Laura warned. "If you can get into the system to find out some links off of social security numbers, maybe hunt for the docs filed that declare lobbyist activities, who sits as silent investors, maybe we can figure it out . . . but only if you know how to go in as a ghost so they can't come back to you."

"Shit," Megan said, standing, "if it gets real crazy, I can always go back to Jamaica."

"What my wife is saying indirectly," James said, standing to make his words sink in, "you have to be alive to get on a plane, unless you want to ride in cargo in a casket."

The room went still. Megan froze. Laura nodded and opened her barrel Coach purse to retrieve the documents.

"This thing goes real long and real deep."

Megan shook her head. "That's waaay too deep for me," she said quietly. "I love Donny, and all, but . . ."

Laura closed her purse and stared at the conflict that etched its way across Megan's stricken expression.

"I felt we owed you that much information," Laura said.

"I appreciate it." Megan began to tensely twirl the string on her sweatpants again. "Listen, I know old man Haines had a lot going on, at the Skull and Cross Bones Secret Society level, understand what I'm saying? Donny and I used to sit up nights sharing father horror stories. My Pop is how I have certain codes—I broke into his system years ago, and know how to navigate my way into any database that's out there, pretty much. But they have technology now that can track even the best hacker, and it's been years since I tried my hand at cyber-stealth. Like . . . I might get in, but there's a chance—"

"It's cool," James said, cutting her off. "We can do this the old-fashioned way, and just have to hope it won't be too late."

Both women stared at him for a moment.

"I've got this friend in Baltimore. Dude is scary on cyber shit. He works for a law firm . . . can go in to mask anybody from the firm, given he runs their local area network. He hates all his bosses, is always looking into their dirty laundry just for kicks, and likes to play games, send viruses, is basically out of his mind . . . but genius. Stays in the office all night, halfway sleeps there. If I make a call . . ."

Laura handed Megan her cell phone. "Why don't we keep you out of it, even as far as calling this friend tonight? If he's open, we're game." She glanced at James. "Baltimore is only a couple of hours on the road."

Megan slowly accepted Laura's cell phone. "He works in a plush mansion converted to a firm over on West Mount Vernon Place, a straight shot out of the Fort McHenry Tunnel, right off I-395 into downtown B-More." She punched in the numbers, but hesitated on pushing the send button. "This is really serious, isn't it . . . ? I mean, if you're asking me to make the call from your phone, and not mine?"

"Yeah," Laura said quietly. "But this is our crap, and I don't see any reason for an innocent bystander to get hurt."

"That's real cool of you," Megan murmured, glancing from Laura to James. "Wasn't sure what to think when I saw the big brother who seems like a cop." She laughed nervously. "Was hoping I'd paid my taxes and shit."

"He's cool," Laura said, motioning to James with a tilt of her head.

"How do I know?" Megan said, suddenly lowering the cell phone. "Like, if there's that much going on, I don't wanna get Sean screwed, either . . . even though he's probably done enough stuff to get himself into hot water." She narrowed her gaze on James. "I know I've seen you somewhere before."

"Probably in the paper," James said, nonplussed. "I was the cop that shot Paxton's ass dead. Is that enough of a pass for being on your side, or what?"

"Oh, shit," Megan whispered, her finger depressing the send key as a slow smile dawned on her face. "We're family, then. You should have introduced yourself like that from the door."

Akhan stepped off the Air Jamaica flight and glanced around. Insufferable heat immediately made his African print shirt stick to him. The trade winds didn't blow balmy in Kingston the way they did in Montego Bay or even in the smaller Caymans. Instead it felt like Manhattan on a hot, humid, summer day—but he felt free.

"This guy sounds like a nutcase," James muttered as they drove down I-95 South, and then pulled into The Maryland House rest stop to refuel. "Everybody's a nutcase," he added, becoming angrier as he gassed up the vehicle. "At three-fifty a gallon and climbing, I ask you, Laura, has the world gone insane, or what?"

She just nodded and watched her husband from a remote place in her mind, knowing full well that what had started his tirade had everything to do with his spent nervous system. It was their way; he processed information and discharged stress differently than she did. However, she was in lockstep with his thinking; this was some dangerous shit.

They rode the rest of the way in deep silence, without even the normal, complementary smooth jazz that they were accustomed to. On a mission, they kept their focus to the fast-moving white lines on the highway, each mentally absorbed in the hundreds of ways the scenario with an unknown variable, Sean, could play out.

James pulled the car into the Franklin Street garage, his eyes keened on the desolate environment. This late, downtown Baltimore was a ghost town. He casually pulled his leather shoulder holster out from under the seat and put it on, and then grabbed his bomber jacket before exiting the vehicle. Laura cut him a glance, but said nothing. He liked that about her. She was practical when it came to things like this.

His gaze sweeping, they walked a short half block to Cathedral Street, and then proceeded past massive four-story brownstones with elaborate architecture. From the street, the structures sported ten-foot windows that he knew contained ceilings twice as high. Marble steps sprawled past brick and ornate wrought iron. At the edge of the park, they turned down West Mount Vernon Place and visually scanned the mansions that lined the tree-ensconced promenade. This was definitely the high-rent district, if ever there was one. Laura took a deep breath, preparing herself for whatever come what may.

James motioned with a nod. "This is it."

They read the small, tasteful brass nameplate of the firm they were seeking and alighted the steps in unison, rang the bell twice, and waited. Before long, a slight, willowy built man seeming to be in his early thirties appeared at the door. He had on the requisite, conservative, Ivy-League navy Polo shirt and a pair of khakis, but his dark brown hair seemed a cross between urban chic mousse-spiked and punk. There was a subtle feral quality of repressed excitement in his eyes, shielded by thick, rimless glasses, and he gave James and Laura a quizzical look and then smiled. They gave each other a concerned sideline glance and then stepped over the threshold, trying not to gape at the sheer enormity of the elegance that surrounded them.

Highly polished woods met hand-plastered crown molding in twenty-two foot, expansive ceilings. Victorian sitting room furniture draped in ivory watermarked silk fabrics faced a huge fireplace. The fact that someone once lived here in such opulence had not escaped them.

"C'mon upstairs," Sean urged, dashing for the wide staircase. "The elevator is too slow, and we need to get down to business."

Staring up nearly produced vertigo as Laura glanced at the endless banister that terminated four long flights up with a stained glass skylight. Using only the dim illumination of security lights as a guide, they followed their eager host. At the top of the landing, the hallway was so large that there was another seating area, replete with two sofas, a Queen Anne chair and Chippendale coffee table that flanked another fireplace. By the time they'd made their way down the corridor behind Sean, and had been carefully sequestered in the back of the block-long building behind double-paned glass French doors, neither Laura nor James could hide their awe.

"Damn . . . so this is how the other half lived," James muttered, looking around.

"Live," Laura corrected. "And this was just an in-town property for most. The country houses put this to shame."

"Right you are, that's why I don't mind doing a little Robin Hood action, for the cause," Sean said merrily, firing up a computer and plopping down behind a cherry mahogany desk. "If it was earned from so-called honest money, I wouldn't have a problem with it," he added, and then looked at James and Laura hard. "But you and I both know that's not how it went."

Laura arched an eyebrow, but James's expression was impassive.

"Reparations now, sis," Sean said with a droll chuckle, and then extended his fist for James to pound.

James just looked at the younger man for a moment, and begrudgingly complied.

"Don't let looks fool you. We have the same roots."

Sean smiled when neither Laura nor James said a word.

"Oh, c'mon, guys," Sean prodded. "Don'tcha wanna know how I got here, or how me and Megan know each other?"

"Well . . ." Laura hedged.

"Cousins. My mother's side gives me my radical component," he said, chuckling and working on a computer system. "My father gave me a white boy passport. Most people can't tell. So you add that to the Ivy background, and the passable last name, and you'd be surprised at the places I can get into, and the things that get said about us when nobody thinks there's one of us is around."

"Deep," James said, moving closer to Sean to peer over his shoulder.

"Very," Sean said, triumphant. "You want to see the old boys' network, and nepotism taken to a whole new level, give me the digits and watch and learn. I see this shit all the time. Deals made on the yachts, at the country clubs, over golf, you name it."

Laura offered a tense smile as she approached Sean. "I have a few numbers for you," she said, not addressing the charge he'd made, but agreeing in principle without words. "Got a few names, too. Polanski, Devereaux, Townsend."

Sean nodded, his intense brown eyes glued to the bright screen. "Devereaux and Townsend are old families—Mayflower types. D.C. connections." His fingers flew across the keyboard in a blur. "Polanski is a newcomer. Watch for those, always, as they're usually more aggressive, have the higher-risk deals. The old-world boys are so thoroughly entrenched in the system that, they can work a deal clean without incident."

"Makes sense," Laura said, taking a perch on the corner of Sean's desk.

Sean's gaze traveled up her body with appreciation. "You're a new player, too. You obviously take a lotta risks, lady."

"That's why she rolls with security," James said, giving Sean a hard glare.

"My bad," Sean chuckled, and returned his gaze to the screen. After a while, he expelled a breath. "I see a Senator Scott in his filings, a Haines . . . several real estate holdings that got transferred . . . there were supposed to be land leases going to these guys from the Micholi Foundation, but they then transferred holdings to American Education First . . ."

"Bulls eye," Laura whispered. "What can you tell us about Micholi Foundation?"

"Might take me a while," Sean said, taking off his glasses and rubbing his eyes, "but it can be done. What types of relationships are you looking for?" He slumped in the high-back leather wing chair, suddenly seeming mentally exhausted as he waited for direction.

"How about something that would put dude in proximity of the kinds of connections that would be able to pull an old Black Ops favour— Russian variety, post-cold war era?" James had made the statement coolly without blinking, gaining a glance of concern from Laura.

"Oh . . . shit," Sean whispered. He stood and began pacing. "Not from here. You're talking a hack into State Department or CIA databases. If I go into Langley, they'd satellite track my ass down to the license plate and be able to have The-Men-In-Black-type roll up on me . . . with this new Patriot Act crap, I could really disappear."

"OK, OK," Laura said, slipping off the edge of Sean's desk. "Let's be judicious and work it with less dramatic flair. Polanski is a name from the old Eastern bloc region, just like Micholi is. Maybe we research just the foundation, any ties to that, through traditional paper-trail, sped up by cyber peeks . . . no heroics that could get somebody killed?"

James nodded; Sean ran his fingers through his hair and sat down.

"I want a common denominator. Someone who shows up wedded to everyone, in every new entity filing, transaction, or any contracts. Then, we research that individual . . . their resume, where they worked, how they climbed the ranks from college onward. We find out their approximate age, what college they went to, when, and who might have been there with them. Cool?"

Sean blew out his breath hard. "The CSI stuff I can do, lady. Easy. All I need to do is build a little program that makes relational associations, and I'll run it against the searches . . . of course, using my bosses' names for different searches on each would be client of the firm, that way, I cover my tracks." He smiled. "I don't care if they have any forthcoming issues—they're all as dirty as sin. So, hey," he said, shrugging, "all's fair in love and war."

"How long will it take?" James asked, growing restless.

"I'm an artist, OK?" Sean snapped. "Gimme a cell number and I'll get back to you. This isn't something I can just do on a dime. I need to think about it, figure out—"

"All right, all right, I hear you," James said, walking toward the door. "Let us know."

"What's in it for you, though?" Laura said cautiously.

"Artistic expression. Creative inspiration?" Sean smiled at James's glare. "OK," he finally said when he received no response. "Let's just say I have an old axe to grind, which I'd prefer not to mention."

"Like?" James said, steadfast.

Sean sighed and met James's gaze with a hard glare of his own. "Like Donny and I were very good friends, first—before Alan. All right?"

James nodded. "I'm sorry things worked out like they did. You would have been better for him."

Laura watched in sheer awe as the defensive tension left Sean's body. It was the last thing she'd expected James to have said, and the respectful tone he'd employed had no game within it at all.

Sean sat up a little taller in his chair. "Thank you," he murmured, and then looked at the computer screen. "I'll get what you need. Count on it."

For a moment, no one in the room spoke. It was as though they were all going to mental neutral corners and regrouping. But Laura's mind was still working the puzzle in a whir of fast-moving pieces. She needed to do something, anything, to flush the target out of hiding, so that extreme measures, like breaking into serious databases, weren't necessary.

"Before we go," she said as gently as possible, "are there any events, any fund-raisers, anything we might be able to attend to sweat these guys a little?"

"I like how you're thinking," James said, setting his jaw hard as he looked at Laura.

Sean's fingers went to the keyboard. "That's the easiest thing you've asked me all night. As system administrator, I can see the bosses' calendars, as well as anything their secretaries put on Outlook." Seeming satisfied, he pushed away from the desk with flourish. "The Smithsonian. Black tie. Gulf Rebuilding Relief Gala. Everyone who is anyone will be there." He glanced over his shoulder. "Micholi bought a table."

Chapter 10

She watched tension thread itself through James as they left the ornate office building and walked the few blocks to the garage. Her husband methodically paid at the auto-attendant station, and he again kept his eyes roving for the slightest movement. If he was worried, she was worried. It was not like James to unnecessarily panic. When he stopped at the vehicle, checked under it, and then warily opened the door, she knew they were on the same page—but she didn't speak on it.

His circuitous route out of the city was just as unnerving. Rather than heading directly for the highway, he went down Franklin Street until the houses became small row homes in disrepair. Dilapidated streets marred by blowing trash and abandoned structures took over from the posh, downtown environs they'd just left. Unable to contain herself, she turned in her seat and studied James hard. The muscle in his jawline was pulsing. That was not a good sign.

"All right," she finally said. "Tell me what's eating you."

"Everything and nothing," he replied, glancing up at the rearview mirror.

"Like?" she said, pressing him for an answer.

"A drive through the 'hood always puts things into perspective," he said too calmly.

She glimpsed the car behind them and then sat back, her eyes straight ahead. "Are we being followed?"

"Call Sean, tell him to get out of the building, and to maybe spend the night at a friend's."

Laura quickly dug into her purse, found her cell phone, and retrieved the number that Megan had punched into it. Sean picked up on the first ring. Her voice was brittle as she spoke and James blew through a red light. The car behind them sailed through the light behind them. "Get out of there. We may have been followed. Don't go home, go to a friend's and don't do anything else until we contact you again."

"OK," Sean said in a shaky voice. "But I'm scared. Where are you guys?"

"Drawing fire," Laura said, and then clicked off the call.

"Put your seat belt on," James ordered. "Tight."

She complied without argument, and glanced over her shoulder again. James turned down a side street, and the sedan behind them did, too.

"What are we gonna do?" she whispered.

"There may be a drive-by shootout in the 'hood, which will go down as a suspected drug thing," James muttered, pulling his gun from the holster and maneuvering the vehicle with one hand.

As soon as he'd sped through another light, the driver behind them became more aggressive. James went down a one-way street in the wrong direction, and the black sedan behind them followed suit, gunning the engine. Swerving to miss a light pole, James took their vehicle around the corner nearly on two wheels. She could see the panic in his eyes. They didn't know Baltimore well enough to know the street map by heart. In an all or nothing move, James hit the pavement and went down the sidewalk, spilling them out into oncoming traffic on 40-W again.

A hard thud made her almost chip a tooth as their vehicle landed, scraping metal to asphalt. Every conceivable fear raced through her as James topped speeds of eighty, headed for ninety miles an hour in a residential zone. Where were the cops? A collision with something was imminent, and she wondered which was worse, death by gunshot or gasoline fireball. Her cell phone rang.

"Answer it!" James shouted, driving like a maniac, sweat now evident on his brow.

She grappled with her bag, hands shaking, eyes darting at the blurred images of row homes. "Who is it?" she hollered into the phone.

"Megan!" a frightened voice yelled back into the receiver. "Slow down. I'm behind you!"

"Pull over," Laura shouted. "It's Megan—she's behind us."

James yanked the wheel hard, screeching brakes as the vehicle slid to a stop in the CVS lot. Breathing hard, he glanced at Laura and then the car that pulled up beside them. A pair of puffy, panic-stricken eyes greeted theirs.

"I needed some air to clear my head after you guys left. I walked down the block to go pick up some clove cigarettes, and I left the porch light on. It was out when I came back. . . . I was a block away and could see it wasn't on. I was only gone fifteen minutes. It was a new bulb." Megan had gasped out her statement, and then leaned her head on the steering wheel. "I always walk with my cell phone on me. I backed down the street, ran all the way to 30th Street train station, hopped on the airport line, and went to the only place I knew I could rent a car all night long!" Tears filled her eyes as she spoke between gulps, thick mucous making her words slur. "I knew you were coming here and didn't know what else to do. Maybe I'm crazy. Maybe I should have gone into Sean's. I'm worried about him. I . . ."

Megan's words trailed off with a sob. James and Laura were out of their car in seconds, going to Megan's side to extract the distraught woman from her vehicle.

"You did right," Laura said, pulling her into a hug.

"Roll with us to BWI," James said. "You got folks in the islands?"

Megan nodded. "My cousins and rest of Mom's folks are down there."

"You got a passport you can get your hands on?"

Megan looked up at James. "I only had my wallet with regular ID, some credit cards, and a few bucks cash."

"Give her one of yours," James ordered. "Tie your hair up, we'll give you one of Laura's suits—"

"James, her driver's license won't match any passports I have in the trunk."

Megan's stricken gaze shot between Laura and James.

"You know anybody in D.C. 'round the way that does this sort of work?" James ushered Megan to the back passenger's door and opened it for her to climb in.

"I don't know . . . maybe. I might be able to get a new driver's license, or something, down in Southeast? But I don't have enough—"

"We've got the cash part covered," Laura said, cutting her off as she climbed into the car. "You call your cousin, tell him to get his behind on the next thing smoking out of the states until this blows over. If you've got any old bogus ID vendors on tap in The District, that's where we're headed. From there, you sleep in the airport in a very populated area and wait on the next flight to Jamaica."

Megan wiped her face with both hands and sniffed. "What about the rental?" she murmured, motioning to it as James began to pull off.

He glanced at Laura, put the gears in reverse, and backed into the side panel hard.

Stunned, Megan's mouth dropped open.

"Call it in as an accident. Tell them you were in a very unsavory area of the city, and got a cab to the train station, and will file a report later—but as a female, you're not trying to stay in this desolated area."

"I like your style, Mr. Carter," Laura said, her gaze fixed to the road ahead.

Megan just dialed, continuing to stare at them both.

*   *   *

It had been a long time since she'd cruised The District. Everything had changed, and yet, it was all still the same. Pockets of opulence and grandeur in the power seat of the nation were still framed by poverty. Re-gentrification was in full effect. Georgetown still had its exclusive charm, albeit she saw more yuppies and students than ever before. The community, as it was in Chocolate City, was on veritable lockdown. Skyrocketing prices, a police force that kept the have-nots at bay from the haves, was the order of the night.

"I've never directly dealt with these people," Megan finally admitted, as they pulled up to a vacant-looking brownstone that had been sectioned into apartments. "I just heard from friends a long time ago that they used to come here to get phony ID so they could drink while in high school."

"Bad plan," James said, wiping fatigue from his face. "Got any good ideas?" He looked at Laura and she shut her eyes.

"No," Laura said. "Not at the moment." She sighed hard and glanced up at the building that had people slowly filing in and out. "If you ask me, this has crack house written all over it."

"Like I said," James grumbled. "Bad plan."

"Think, think, think," Laura muttered, dropping her forehead into her hands in exasperation. Then she suddenly sat up straight. "Take my driver's license and a matching passport." She turned to Megan and leaned over the backseat. "You put on one of my suits; we get you out of here with light, carry-on luggage. I've got a couple of days before I have to jump a jet, and can get a matching license later."

"Bad plan," James said shaking his head and pulling away from the curb. "You're a target, she isn't. If someone is looking for you, they'll come for her."

Megan had begun to hyperventilate in the backseat.

"Then, just give her a secondary one that doesn't have my name on it," Laura said calmly. "One that doesn't show U.S. citizenship—that way, she wouldn't need a license to confirm it."

Again, she glanced at Megan and petted her arm over the back-seat. "You're Lillian Braithwaite, citizen of Grand Cayman."

They'd waited in the short-term airport parking lot until just after sunrise, half dozing. Megan's brief call confirmed she'd made her flight. Sean was right behind her. Again, their world was spinning out of control. But they had a gala to attend. James needed a tux; she needed a gown. They both needed VIP tickets. That wasn't a problem, they'd be on the list as guests of one of the Micholi Foundation's significant donors—courtesy of Sean's old firm.

"Good brother, B," Akhan murmured, accepting an embrace from his old friend. He held Edgar Braithwaite away from him to stare into a pair of eyes that knew him well.

"Brother Akhan, long time, mon." Braithwaite smiled and jauntily tilted his head to the side, which caused his large red, black, and green crocheted cap filled with silver locks to lean. "Dis your family?"

Akhan smiled, as Brother B surveyed Steve with suspicion. "It is a very complex arrangement," he said quietly. "But, yes, this is my family. Two are still overseas."

Brother B rubbed his scraggly, gray-streaked goatee, pinching his dark, gaunt features into a soft scowl. "I guess it's all good."

Unable to operate on fumes any longer, James pulled their car up to the Florida Avenue Grille. "A brother's gotta eat," he said through a yawn. "Then at least three hours to crash and burn, before we do this thing tonight."

Laura was so bone-weary that she practically staggered out of the car, and once inside the small diner, she half feared she'd pass out if she ate a full plate of fried fish and grits. Coffee was calling her name, but soon the aroma of bacon, pancakes, sausages, and eggs, along with tender fried whiting made her stomach gurgle. James sat in a sleep depravation daze staring at the table, seeming to only be holding himself up on his elbows.

"This has gotta stop," he finally said, once the waitress had taken their orders.

"I know," she said quietly, sipping her coffee. "The circle of people caught up in the madness is getting too big."

"Then there's only one option," he muttered, slurping his coffee. He stared at Laura for a moment. "Bring 'em down, and bring 'em down hard—or go out in a blaze. I don't want anybody's death on our conscience."

"You been following the news?" Brother B asked as he pulled his rusted-out, old Ford station wagon up to the small shanty in Kingston.

"Not since we left," Akhan said, his eyes roving the streets he remembered from thirty years ago. He'd forgotten about the heat and congestion of Kingston and the economic decline. The three passengers in the back sat silently, as though holding their breaths.

"Was all over BBC News. They don't have crimes like that in Grand Cayman," Brother B said, glancing at everyone in his car. He paused as his eyes met Akhan's. "Two officers shot dead by an unidentified white man, claimin' to be an insurance salesman . . . but they said he was a terrorist, because he had bomb equipment in his briefcase. The policeman that shot him dead away couldn't make a statement until their investigation is over." He stroked his beard, winced, and then looked at his house, seeming unsure. "You gwan need to go up in de hills, mon. In de bush country wit da Rastas."

"Where, exactly, on Grand Cayman did this happen?" Akhan asked, glancing at Najira, Steve, and Jamal quickly, and then returning his gaze to his friend.

Braithwaite let out a long, weary breath. "House owned by Caldwell-Carter family. You know 'em?"

What had started out as crazy had become next to insane. Laura sat in the hotel room of the Watergate with her eyes glued to her laptop screen while James lay prone and snoring across the bed. Too wired to sleep, she worked. The CNN television crawl at the bottom of the screen caught her peripheral vision, and made her stand. Two officers murdered in Grand Cayman?

She sat down again quickly and pulled up each news service as fast as she could, then simply froze. Instinct sent a panic rush through Laura as she speed dialed Steve's cell, and waited. Why hadn't they called? She was about to wake James on the second ring, but Steve picked up.

"Where are you?" she breathed out in a rush.

"An island. A big one, with shaky cell phone reception—that's why we hadn't called before. Getting an outbound signal's been a bitch. But we're safe."

"Good, anybody hurt? You heard?"

"No. We're cool and, yes, we heard. Where's James?"

"Asleep. But I'll wake him." She quickly walked over to James, shook him once, and he sat up fast. "Steve. They had to move. I'll explain later, not on the phone."

James nodded and took the phone from her. "Talk to me, man."

"Up at Braithwaite's. We're good. Must be living right, because it was close. The old man had a vibe and moved us out."

"Cool," James said. "Stay in touch."

"No problem," Steve muttered, and then disconnected the call.

James instantly turned his attention to Laura. "What happened?"

"They found our house in Grand Cayman and sent a clean-up man. It's all over the BBC." Laura wrapped her arms around her waist, hugging herself. "They might not have made it. He'd rigged the house to blow from a cell-phone unit. What if they'd been there?"

"They're with some guy named Braithwaite," James said carefully, his line of vision following Laura around the room as she paced.

She stopped walking. "That's the last name on the ID I gave Megan," she said quietly. "From Akhan's contacts—his man in Jamaica."

"I know," James said, flopping back on the bed with his arm across his eyes. "But there's nothing we can do about that now. Get some rest, and save the fight for tonight."

"I can't cover for you any longer," Polanski said into the telephone, his gaze darting around the room. "This is so thoroughly out of control that we all stand to lose more than money." His voice became a strained whisper as only silence responded to his entreaties on the line. "Maybe we should just hold off for a little while, give them some time to react with a reasonable counteroffer and divest, or try to open lines of communication—now that they see things are serious?"

Receiving no response, Polanski mopped his brow, his voice pleading. "We can sway the contracts on the New Orleans clean-up jobs . . . we can make up the difference once they rebuild there—you know the feds will get eminent domain on the most lucrative areas and we'll get a piece of that as developers. We can probably also cut a deal to build resorts near the gaming districts in Mississippi, once the original residents get bled out by insurance companies that won't cover total losses. There's no reason to go after the old Philadelphia land sites that we lost, given how sloppy this whole operation is becoming." His voice dropped to a strained whisper. "Just think about it. I know this is personal, but it's getting too much visibility."

Again, only silence filled the line. Then an abrupt click ended the call, making Polanski close his eyes with a slight shiver.

Chapter
11

James stared in the mirror as he worked his black bow tie into a knot. Everything was set. Their extra clothes and sets of false ID had been sent to Jamaica via FedEx, guaranteed arrival the next day. The limo had been called, sent from Steve's contact, Caluzo's Philly people, to be sure there'd be ample security and a driver packing heat. The rental had been ditched and traded in for a new one under a different name, also parked only a couple blocks away from the Smithsonian, with two untraceable nine-millimeters taped under the dashboard—just in case.

He spied Laura through the mirror as she passed by the bathroom, readying herself for the event. Even under these circumstances, the woman was a knockout. She was wearing a backless white sheath with iridescent crystal beads that seemed like raindrops had splattered on her breasts. But the spiked, beaded satin heels were killer every time her legs swept through the slit in her gown. He stopped fumbling with his bow tie to give her an appreciative glance. "You look absolutely beautiful," he murmured. "Remind me to show you proper, once we do this thing."

She gave him a strained smile. "Not bad yourself, in a tux, Mr. Carter." She came to him, brushed his mouth gently, as not to disturb her flawless makeup, and then tied his bow tie knot for him.

As fantastic as her husband looked and smelled, they didn't have time to lose focus. Sean had blown her Blackberry up with new data that James needed to be aware of.

"Got a transmission from Sean," she said, smoothing James's black tuxedo lapels.

He just stared at her as she walked away to find her beaded clutch and sheer white wrap.

"The kid is brilliant," she said, offhandedly. "The old man who founded Micholi also had the same attorney as Haines before he died. Seems a then-very-young Alan Moyer Senior became the general counsel for that foundation. Polanski, Moyer, Haines, and Sutherland were all in school together. Harvard."

"Hold it," James said, leaning against the doorframe of the bathroom. "Sutherland, the doctor who slept with Haines's wife and killed Haines, was in their crew?" He smoothed his hand over his clean-shaven jaw and shook his head.

"Isn't it always the way?" She kissed James's cheek and then brushed the faint lipstick mark away from it with her fingertips. "That's why the old Mafia adage holds true: Keep your friends close and your enemies closer. The old boys on the Main Line invented nepotism and inner-circle deceit. I'm not surprised. I just needed to know."

James pushed away from the door and collected his wallet with phony ID. "If Sutherland is serving hard time, along with Alan Moyer, Jr., then we find old man Moyer and Polanski at this bull tonight, and lean on them a little."

"Just enough to let them know that we know," Laura said with a dangerous smile. "The only problem is, Sean's info didn't show any common assets that they might have held together. But where there's smoke, there's fire." She nervously fingered the beads on her purse as she hoisted the long strap over her shoulder. "One guess who also had Moyer as his attorney?"

"Senator Scott, for five hundred," James muttered with disgust.

"Five hundred goes to the man with the right answer," Laura said, no amusement in her tone.

"Suggestion," James said, looking up from the table and stashing his wallet in his breast pocket. "We go in with the media rush, have a glass of wine, walk the room before dinner, say what we've gotta say, and then be out—while the full media is still around to make it too visible to do a hit."

She nodded and draped her wrap around her shoulders. "I'm right there with you, brother. Shall we dance?"

She kept her gaze steady as their limousine pulled up to the grand entrance of the Smithsonian museum. Paparazzi were everywhere for the gala. Oddly, that helped her relax and she just hoped that those who were after her and James would employ enough patience and decorum to wait for a less visible moment. True, there was a debt to settle, but she doubted that they would be so foolish as to make a hard public statement; it wasn't like they were JFK or anything. Then again, one could never be sure.

When the limo stopped and the driver got out to round the vehicle and open the door, she took a deep breath. James squeezed her hand, and they exited the vehicle in high style as though they had actual invitations.

She gently threaded her hand through James's extended elbow and kept a media smile on her face. As they approached the small guest admittance podium just inside the huge glass doors, a small rush of butterflies escaped within her belly. What if Sean's little guest-list-addition trick hadn't worked? Then she remembered the oldest ruse in the book: Dress the part, speak the part, confidently appear like you belong, and that was half the battle—act like you know. Laura tipped her chin up and feigned the bourgeois attitude of entitlement.

"Mr. and Mrs. Johnson, from the American Education First Foundation—guests of the Micholi Foundation."

She felt James's bicep tense, but her man was cool ice on the outside.

"Oh, yes," the greeter said, after peering at the register a moment. "A late add-in, and we are so glad your schedule permitted you to attend. Welcome."

Laura gave the young White House intern a pleasant but dismissive smile and walked forward with James. They were in. She immediately felt his bicep relax as they scanned the room.

"This is your thing, baby. Work it. I don't even know what these guys look like," James muttered quietly in her ear.

"First off, smile," she said, ribbing him lightly. "Then when a butler comes by with wine or champagne, select a glass and sip it slowly."

He cut her a sidelong glare. "That part I've got."

She chuckled and swiped two glasses from a passing tray. "Then why aren't you smiling?" she asked, and handed him a chardonnay.

She watched him take the glass and try his best to smile. The man seemed pained. They had to go deeper into the soiree. The old boys always arrived early to give the best media sound bites and then shake the refuse of reporters so they could get down to business. The real VIPs and keynote speaker would make the final grand entrance. If her hunch proved correct, Polanski would already be here, and hopefully Moyer would, too.

Casually glancing around the room, she scanned the environment with purpose, soon spotting James Devereaux.

"Husband, let's take a walk," she said, moving in the opposite direction of Devereaux. It was all about timing, patience, allowing the targets to see her and to think that she hadn't seen them yet. "The Redevelopment Authority contact is here, which means so is his inner circle."

"Where?" James said under his breath.

"Six o'clock, but don't turn around. I see some folks from Harrisburg that we'll briefly chat with—state level, and then I'll give my condolences about the loss of a solid senatorial seat . . . and *then* we'll go see the people whose ticket we slid in here on."

The tension within James's body and within his strides was palpable as she made the rounds, exchanged phony air kisses, and engaged in small talk. But it was a necessary evil. Soon she'd glimpsed George Townsend, another member of the Micholi team, and had watched him slowly go over to Devereaux, confer, and then glance in her direction. That was her cue. She looked up, smiled, and raised her wineglass ever so slightly to let them know she'd be over to greet them in a moment.

"You don't mind if I scoot over to chat with some old friends from Philadelphia, do you?" she asked the small group of state officials standing near her and James.

"Of course not, Laura," the head of the Department of Community Economic Development said with a pleasant smile. "We hope to see you back in the game soon."

"Thank you, John," she said, gracefully slipping away as James nodded, shook hands, and followed her across the wide, marble floor.

They had to do this fast, she noted. There were too many people gathered within this Who's Who affair that knew her real name, and all she and James needed was to be summarily kicked out for crashing the event. Beyond the mere humiliation of that consequence, it would definitely create a credibility problem. Those being researched needed to be surprised by her presence, as though it were a mere coincidence. The goal was singular: to catch them off guard. So far, that had worked. Once they were sufficiently flustered, she could move in to possibly negotiate a deal.

"George," she cooed, coming up close to George Townsend and then turning to Devereaux. She touched his arm and smiled warmly. "And James Devereaux, you are a sight for sore eyes. What's it been? A year . . . maybe more, since Donald's funeral?" She shook her head as they blanched at the mention. "We should all do better at staying in touch, and that was such an unhappy circumstance to have had our last sighting." Before they could answer, she threaded her hand through James's elbow. "Let me introduce my husband, James Carter."

"Gentlemen," James said stiffly, extracting himself from Laura's hold to shift his wineglass to his left hand, and to then shake their hands. "Laura's told me a lot about you," he added, receiving a smile of approval from her.

The two men before him guffawed and stepped back with strained smiles.

"Wow, well . . . this is new," Devereaux said tensely. "Congratulations."

"Yes, welcome, uh, congratulations," Townsend said. "Really, Laura, you are always full of surprises."

She chuckled and sipped her wine, peering over the glass at them. "Always, gentlemen. A little sun in the Grand Caymans can change a woman's perspective."

They raised their glasses toward her and James, but their eyes belied the smiles on their faces.

"So, are you back home now, in Philadelphia?" Devereaux asked. "The landscape has dramatically changed since last year."

"Yes, we just got back, and are consolidating households now. We're looking at property up in Radnor, maybe Chestnut Hill," she lied, glimpsing James from the corner of her eye as he simply sipped his wine without emotion.

"Are you thinking about restarting Rainmaker's, Inc.?" Townsend asked coolly, polishing off his glass and setting it on a passing tray to claim another.

"I don't know," Laura breathed out with a sad sigh. "I've lost my passion for it." She turned to James and gave him a brilliant smile. "We're both semi-retired and looking into real estate investments as a quiet option."

Both Devereaux and Townsend fixed their gaze on James.

"Ah, it's coming back to me," Devereaux said, his smile containing a warning. "You were the officer in that big, nasty case with Paxton."

James chuckled, and the sound of it startled Laura into taking another sip of her wine.

"Yes, I'm the one," James said coolly. "But like Laura said, I'm semi-retired. Figured if I can't beat 'em, might as well join 'em. She has a way of developing the sweetest compromises."

Both Townsend and Devereaux laughed, but the sound was brittle.

"Please tell me Mike Polanski is here?" she crooned, giving James's arm a little shove, like a love pat for theatrical effect.

Again the two men before her and James exchanged nervous glances.

"Yes, uh, I believe I saw him a bit ago," Devereaux hedged.

Laura glanced around the room and spotted him in deep conversation with some men she didn't know. "Well, before the night is over, I must say *hello* to him."

"We'll let him know you're here and asked for him," Townsend said after a healthy swig of his wine.

She kissed Townsend's cheek and gave Devereaux a brief hug. "Thank you, gentlemen. You know I wouldn't miss giving my best to Mike for the world."

"OK, break it down," James said under his breath as they melted back into the milling throng of dignitaries. "What's with the real estate and whole Cayman thing?"

"I needed to let them know I was back, or make them think I was, and that I was fishing for an in . . . which meant that I was oblivious to the attacks—or didn't associate myself with them, but that I was also holding real estate aces. Second point was, I blithely told them about the Caymans so they wouldn't know whether my comment alluded to the fact that I'd not yet heard about the attempted bombing of our home, or that I had. Keeping the bastards off balance. They'll kiss and tell Polanski, who, if they're still connected, will inform Moyer. Just some cheap insurance that word will make the rounds, if we can't tonight."

"I love how your mind works," he said, pecking her cheek.

"Not bad yourself. You didn't blink or stutter when they made you as the cop that shot Paxton. Very cool, Mr. Carter. It let them think you came in here on the guest list as yourself, and don't have a clue that anyone's been after us."

For the first time that evening, James offered her a genuine, sly smile. "I've been known to play a good game of poker in my day."

"Touché. I stand corrected," she murmured as they slipped into a group of men standing near Polanski.

"Forgive me," she said to the unknown men around Polanski.

"But I just had to say hello to an old friend." Using the feminine prerogative, she stepped around them, inserted herself into their midst, and extended her hand while James hung back and watched her work.

"Mike, we'll leave you to this lovely friend," one of the men said, and moved away to another group of guests with the others.

The floor had cleared around Polanski, which let her know that those men previously standing close had been ready to bolt from the conversation that they'd been having. An instant distancing meant only one thing—whatever Polanski was lobbying them for wasn't being heard, and there was resistance to whatever he'd proposed. Good. That left him isolated with thinning allegiances.

"Laura," Mike said, trying to sound upbeat as his eyes flitted between her and the men who'd vacated his presence. "Long time." He looked at James as he walked up. "I don't believe I've formally met your escort." By rote, Polanski extended his hand and shook James's. "Mike Polanski."

"James Carter," James shot back, shaking the man's hand in a vice grip.

Laura smiled. "My husband." She watched the color drain from Polanski's face.

"Congratulations, and, uh, forgive me if I'm too bold . . . but haven't I seen you somewhere before?" Polanski's eyes studied James for a moment.

"I guess I just have one of those memorable faces," James said evenly, and then took a sip of wine. He let the comment hang, and enjoyed how Polanski twisted in the brief, uncomfortable silence, knowing how he'd process the unspoken reference to all black men looking alike.

Laura glanced between both men without elaborating and also allowed the comment to dangle a bit for theatrical effect. He was pleased that she'd followed his lead on this one. They were on the same page in throwing a key target off balance.

"No, I'm sure of it," Mike Polanski said, pressing the issue and raking his fingers through his thinning hair. "In Philadelphia . . . but I just can't . . ."

"Maybe in the newspapers?" Laura said, mischief tugging at her mouth.

Polanski tilted his head for a moment, and then his eyes widened. "The Paxton case."

James smiled. "I don't like to talk about it. Not every day you have to take a man's life."

Polanski's and James's eyes locked, until Polanski glanced away and sipped his wine.

"I don't suppose so, Detective," Polanski said, giving James a respectful nod. With that, he turned his attention to Laura. "Well, married, back home from the Caymans, what's next for you, Laura?"

She and James shared a glimpse at each other from the corners of their eyes. She hadn't told Polanski they were in the Caymans or that she was back in Philadelphia, plus Devereaux and Townsend hadn't crossed the room yet. OK. Time to play. He was in it.

"Real estate," Laura said with a threat in her smile. She didn't bother to inform Polanski of the fact that James had retired, either.

"Really?" Polanski said, nervously twirling the stem of his wineglass.

"Really," Laura said in a flat tone. "I have access to old program properties via very trusted friends in the grassroots community, but . . . it is becoming somewhat of an overhead burden for them, given the recent change in funding priorities. We may consider just purchasing it from the state outright, or whoever was ultimately granted that property—since the nonprofits are beginning to fall behind on their lease payments."

She watched Polanski's mannerly smile fade to a tight line of concern. They both knew the state no longer owned that property, and that Akhan, her uncle, did. But it was a delicate game of unmentionable knowledge.

"In fact," she added, throwing gasoline on the fire that quietly raged within Polanski's eyes, "James and I may manage those leases and buildings ourselves to take the tax incentives, or recommend that they donate a good portion of it away to a larger, worthy foundation, if I can be assured that the paperwork will be handled properly." Laura allowed the tender offer to dangle as a negotiating ploy.

Polanski nodded fervently. "I'm sure Micholi Foundation can help you with that. Our general counsel is excellent."

"Alan Moyer is renowned for his meticulous handling of such affairs," Laura said to let him know she was well aware of his foundation's power structure, and then took a cool sip of wine.

"Moyer will work with you," Polanski said in an unnaturally quiet voice.

"Can you set up a meeting between us?" she asked, now toying with her wineglass. She waited and glanced at James as Polanski took his time responding.

"I'm sure I can," Polanski finally said, but there was uncertainty in his voice. "I just need to let Alan know a general framework . . . what we're talking about."

Polanski had to be out of his mind if he thought she'd give back lands deeded to Akhan's personal neighborhood nonprofit—the one he'd founded and ran practically alone as executive director, and that now held several newly renovated buildings, courtesy of Haines and also housed several huge, new economic development nonprofits. The revenues off the leases alone were worth a mint, and the land itself represented ridiculous, primo, urban real estate that they'd definitely have to kill her and Akhan to acquire.

Laura smiled and pushed a wisp of hair behind her ear. Yeah, she heard him and fully understood why she and Akhan had been a target. If her uncle died, the lands were then under her control as cofounder, and the board and bylaws were stacked to elect her as the next executive director to run everything. With the two of them gone, the board would have no focus and could be persuaded into anything, and the little caveat in the bylaws about original founders controlling land would be moot.

"I think, given the current executive director's age and health issues, and my new marriage," she finally said beaming at James, "most, if not all, of it could be transferred to a larger institution that has the resources and wherewithal to deal with the constant problems of building maintenance, upkeep, late lease payments, security . . . all of that is so daunting."

Polanski rubbed his palm along the edge of his jaw. Cool, repressed excitement glittered in his beady, gray eyes. "Well, then, Laura, I'm sure Alan would love to meet with you as soon as humanly possible."

Something indefinable tugged at her gut. Polanski was obviously just a middleman. She and James needed to know who had called for the hits and sanctioned them, and then she had to be sure to keep an ace up her sleeve that would guarantee their lives if any so-called transfer was made.

"Isn't Alan here tonight?" she asked in her most innocent tone.

Polanski shifted nervously where he stood. "Uh, I'm sure he'll be here shortly, but I haven't seen him yet."

Interesting. Moyer was arriving with the senior VIPs and keynote, time-wise? *Very* interesting. She glanced at James, who hadn't said a word since the conversation began. She monitored her husband's tension as James carefully set his empty glass down on a passing server's tray and kept a steely grit on Polanski.

"Is there a number where he can reach you, Laura?" Polanski said quickly, noticing the way she and James had fallen silent. There was urgency in his voice, as though he were trying to keep the deal on the table and from unraveling before Moyer had a chance to weigh in.

"How about if I call him, to save him the long distance call to the Caymans," she said, offering the thinly veiled excuse. They both knew a call there was nothing for Moyer to pay for, but it also indirectly said that she wasn't giving him a definitive stateside location or a cell number, which added pressure to Polanski's hope of holding on to the deal.

Reading her signal, James took her by the elbow. "You know, Laura, maybe we should have this conversation with several of the other major foundations and nonprofits. The Red Cross, for example, and The Salvation Army, both could use the properties as semipermanent housing and facilities for all those good people displaced in the Gulf . . . and I bet there will be new nonprofits, or even older, more established ones, getting into the post-hurricane relief and family settlement business. That land and the subsequent buildings on it could be leased to a variety of worthy causes, to take the burden off of Akhan's smaller organization. So, honey, why don't we think about this some more?"

She kissed James's cheek, but spoke to Polanski without glancing at him. "Do you see why I married this man? He helps me to sleep at night."

"In all due respect, Laura," Polanski said, clearing his throat in agitation. "You and the Micholi Foundation go a long way back, and have very positive history—based upon your relationship with Donald Haines. I think first right of refusal is in order, don't you? So let's not be hasty. I'll find Alan, and we'll set up a meeting quickly."

"In Philadelphia? Say tomorrow?" she cooed.

"For you, Laura," Polanski said, dabbing his brow with a nervous smile, "I'm sure Alan will clear his calendar."

Chapter
12

He didn't like it. They were supposed to get out of there before the serious VIPs arrived, and while the waiting media rush to mob them was in full effect. The way Laura was lingering was messing with his mind. But he knew she had to do it, had to see who came in with Moyer. He also knew his wife well enough to know that she was creating a strategy on the fly. So he waited, chilled, and kept his gaze scanning the guest-filled room.

She hated this shit. Once playing the political wine-and-cheese circuit had been her forte, but more than a solid year away from it had her wondering how she'd ever hung in there with it so long. As she looked at her husband's nervous system drawn wire-taut, and at the feigned smiles and coy glances, the position-jockeying that was going on amid the exhibits, she knew. Never again. No more Rainmaker's, Inc. No more galas for whatever reason or cause. She was out—just as soon as this was over. If anything, she'd become a radical philanthropist. Maybe she'd fund kids like Megan and Sean to become cyber-pirates and help watchdog agencies . . . but these people . . . never!

"I can't stand it," she said to James through her teeth, brandishing a tight smile that bordered on a snarl.

"I hear you," he said after a moment, but held her gaze as though worried she might snap.

"Just look at them," she whispered in a hiss, turning away from the crowd to compose herself by only staring at him. "People died like dogs in the streets, were denied food and water and shelter and human decency while these fat cats sat around with their thumbs up their privileged tight asses, and now they have the gall and audacity to host a fund-raiser as a media photo op to show their concern!"

Laura drew a shaky breath and smoothed her hair as James stepped in closer to her to shield her expression and her words from others.

"You've got insurance lobbyists in here, James, pleading their cases for why they shouldn't be financially impacted by all those tax-paying homeowners down in the Gulf who paid them hard-earned wages, believing that . . ."

"I know, baby. But you have to keep focused—"

"You've got other nonprofits in here trying to ensure their taps don't get turned off while funds get diverted to New Orleans, Mississippi, and Alabama, because donor fatigue has set in, and the little people, the American public, just gave up a cool billion from hardworking households to help." She could feel hot tears rising in her eyes. "All this happened while we were away. Did you hear the conversations as we passed by the chic huddles? Private corporations are in here lobbying to get a chunk of the rebuilding, the cleanup, waste removal, you name it, while you've got politicians in here using this tragedy as election platform fodder. People died because they were poor. Any trust I had in any aspect of the so-called system has been shattered, James. Shattered fucking trust, is what I have now." She briefly covered her face with her hands and took a deep breath and then summarily straightened.

"Laura—"

"I'm all right," she said quickly. "But this is why I used to do what I did."

"That's why I used to do what I did, too," he said quietly, his steady gaze holding hers. His eyes only left hers to scan the filling room. "Justice always meant just us po' folk going to the pen while larger, more serious crimes that impacted masses of people went unchecked . . . so I was trying to make a difference at the street level. You were real good at it, Laura, like me." He smiled at her sadly. "We did this thing before as straight-up vigilantes."

She nodded and caught a glimpse of Elizabeth Haines entering by the door. "Well, I'll just be damned," Laura whispered. "Two o'clock. Mommy dearest Haines."

"Your take?" James casually glanced over his shoulder and then back to Laura.

"One of two things," Laura said, her gaze on Elizabeth becoming lethal. "Either she's a part of this, which I wouldn't put past her, or she's trying to keep her son out of it, given they might take him as a proverbial hostage."

James shook his head. "No, baby. You're allowing rage to cloud your judgment. You've gotta detach and think about this like a cop. Donny isn't on any papers, and wields no power. There's no way for her to get to anything Haines left to Akhan; I'm too sure the old boy had a legal electric fence around his estranged wife to keep her from getting her claws into any assets he didn't want her to have. Think." He stared at Laura, took the glass from her, and set it down before it cracked in her hand from her too-tight grip.

"She's being groomed for succession. Perfect fit. The wife of their dead colleague, Donald Haines, Sr. That would be politically correct as well as media salable. On the surface, honorable. Old Liz would be easy to manage, because then they could take Donny Jr. as a hostage; if she doesn't play the game as their pawn, something tragic could happen to her boy . . . whether violence, or a media rape."

James nodded and blew out a slow, controlled breath. Laura let hers out in an exasperated rush.

"That's my baby. Dead on target," he said. "Now tell me, who did she walk in with and is her expression media-friendly, or tight?"

Laura reached for another glass of wine, just to position her body and James for a full frontal view of the door. "I'm not sure who she walked in with," Laura admitted, "but Moyer just graced the door right after the ex-director of Homeland Security, who used to be the governor of Pennsylvania." Her voice trailed off in an awed whisper. "Check out who's in the little party by the door . . . the ex–FEMA Director, two big Philly real estate developers, and a coupla guys in suits I don't know."

She took a quick sip of wine. "Now we study the crowd to see which way the big fish move. They may have come together, or not—that I'm not sure of, and neither is anyone else in the room. Moyer could have timed his and Elizabeth's entrance with theirs as a power ploy, something the pros do all the time to give the illusion of connections that don't really exist, and those guys could be uninvolved. That's just the thing, James. Ya never know."

James moved her slowly through the room toward the gala entrance. "Polanski just went over to Moyer."

"Alan," Mike Polanski said calmly, fawning as he moved to where Alan Moyer stood with Elizabeth Haines. "May I steal him for a moment, dear?" Polanski's eyes begged for her understanding and a private audience.

"No problem," Elizabeth said with a weak smile, and slipped away to talk to his colleagues, James Devereaux and George Townsend.

Once she had removed herself from their conversation, Polanski launched right in on his urgent point. "Laura Caldwell is here with that cop, Carter. She married him."

Alan Moyer declined a passing tray of wine, his small, intense hazel eyes set deep in his puffed face. He stared up at the gaunt man before him with disdain. "I saw. So she married him. Why am I not surprised?"

"She wants a meeting. Tomorrow, in Philadelphia," Polanski said, his eyes nervously darting around the crowd as he spoke. "She's ready for a truce. She said she'd confer all the land back to Micholi, the way it was before Haines—"

Moyer held up his hand to stop Polanski's excited flurry of words. Polanski watched a slow red tinge of fury overtake Moyer's face and creep along the gleaming bald surface of his scalp between the perfectly barbered wisps of his silvery white hair, although his expression remained impassive.

"It has already gone too far," Moyer said calmly. "A meeting at this juncture is unnecessary. It's out of my hands."

Polanski leaned in closer, against his better judgment, and pressed the issue, panicked. "He's *a cop*. A detective. If anything happens to his wife, the guy will be relentless, and if anything happens to him, they'll investigate this until they can nail someone to the cross. That's how *the equipment* left in North Central near Akhan's landed at Philadelphia Police Headquarters," he added in a choked whisper. "Who knows who they know? Haines always had his finger on the black pulse, so did Scott, but we don't have anyone with such insight anymore. We need to back off, consider her offer. The Devereaux family is well-connected in New Orleans, and we could just cut our losses in Phila—"

"I see some people I need to speak with," Moyer said, dismissing him. "You worry too much, Polanski, and that can be bad for your health. I suggest you let it go and meditate on serene subjects."

Laura watched the two power brokers from the Micholi Foundation confer, and also saw Devereaux and Townsend hang back. When Polanski left Moyer's side, his expression seemed haunted. Moyer looked in her direction briefly, his old jowls set tight and his eyes burning with hatred. It was the same expression on his face when he'd appeared in court for his son's trial. . . . Oh, shit.

"We need to leave, now," she said in a tense whisper.

"I thought you wanted to pick Elizabeth's brain and find out if Moyer's gonna agree to a meeting."

"There won't be a meeting," she said quickly, threading her arm through James's to move him to the door. "The decision has been made. Liz got the lucky pick. Me and Akhan are in the way—"

"But that's so sloppy. It doesn't make sense, if they can get what they want through a clean transfer."

"It makes all the sense in the world, because it's personal."

She didn't have to say another word to James, and she was glad that there was enough trust between them for him to take what she'd told him at face value. James murmured to the door attendant that his wife had a brewing migraine, and then grabbed his cell phone to hail the limo. Her phone was out in seconds as they went to the front steps and waited. She deftly punching Megan's number on speed dial.

"Tell Sean to dig up anything he can on Moyer, asap. I wanna know how and when he got into bed with the Micholi foundation people, if his people are Old Russian extraction, anything you got on the man." She closed her phone without a good-bye, and almost ran down the wide, cement front steps with James to greet the limo when it pulled around the corner.

The driver got out and opened the door. He seemed confused, but asked no questions. Laura almost ducked into the vehicle, but hesitated.

"I don't feel so good, James," she said loud enough for the driver to hear. She stared at the driver and then her husband. "Give me a moment," she told the driver. "I'm pregnant, and don't want to upchuck in the vehicle. "Can you wait here while my husband walks me inside to the ladies' room?"

The driver nodded. James's grip tightened on her arm as he hustled her back into the gala.

"The driver's a blond, and we had an Italian jobber drop us off," Laura said quickly, almost not stopping at the door greeter.

"Is everything all right, ma'am?" the greeter asked, seeming concerned.

"I'm just a little nauseous from the headache. Can you tell me where the ladies' room is?"

The greeter pointed them in the right direction, and James was practically welded to her hip.

"You got good eyes, Laura," he muttered, hustling her along.

"I'm sure security is gonna be a nightmare, getting out of the back door impossible," she said, panting as she hurried down a long corridor to the restroom.

"Plan?"

They stared at each other.

"I'll go in, slap my face, spill water down my front, and come out with a towel, blotting my front. I'll claim VIP humiliation, and refuse to walk out the front—and you beg mercy not to have your wife's dignity assailed by having her go through a gala with vomit on her dress. Cool?"

"Done. Meanwhile, I could use a little assist from the boys. Lemme make two calls. Hurry."

Without delay, she dipped into the ladies' room, slapped her face hard twice to make it look flushed, ruffled her hair, and splashed water down the front of her gown. She was out of the restroom by the time James had closed his cellular.

"I told Steve that Caluzo might need to have someone check on his boy, who no doubt ain't breathing any more. Got a squad car on the way to detain our problem out front by giving the limo driver a hassle. Let's go find a brother working security. Now would be a good time for tears."

They slipped behind velvet stand turns that had been placed to keep guests from straying to sections of the museum beyond the gala. Within moments they were hailed by two security guards.

"Hey, hey, hey, sir, ma'am, this is a restricted—"

Laura heaved and covered her mouth with her hands. "Oh, my God. I never thought pregnancy could be so vile, or I would have never let them do the fertility process on me, James. Get me out of here!"

"Ma'am, the front exit is—"

"I can't go that way," she shrieked, looking truly crazy, and lowering the paper towel away from her breasts.

The young security guard looked at his older partner.

"Man, listen . . ." James said in a calm tone. "My wife is about to die a thousand deaths because she just upchucked in the ladies' room and can't walk through that crowd smelling like that, and her gown all messed up." He pulled Laura to him and rubbed her shoulders as she turned her face away. "They don't let a lot of us in events like this, feel me? So, she's . . ."

Laura timed fake sobs perfectly, and both guards glanced at each other in full accord.

"Look, brother," the older guard said. "We could lose our jobs. You know they've got events like this on lock. All doors except the front one are supposed to be off limits. But, damn, that's a shame to have her walk through all those folks like that."

"Man, I hear you, and would really appreciate the favor," James said as humbly as possible. "You've got the power brother—to make her die going out the front, or let this sister save some face, going out the back."

"Aw-ight, look, if we let you out that way, you ain't get there 'cause we was involved. Cool?"

"Thank you," Laura breathed into James's lapels.

James extended his fist for the two guards to pound. "Thank you. I owe you."

"Cool. Well, then, hurry up," the older guard urged, and began walking quickly in front of Laura and James, while the younger guard kept his post, glancing around nervously.

Half running, half jogging down the corridor behind the older guard, they kept alert, and within moments he'd ushered them through the control room past several other guards, made some sort of eye signal not to ask questions, and allowed Laura and James to slip out the back, closing the door behind them with a thud.

Fresh air allowed them to take a deep breath, and then begin a flat-out dash to the waiting rental several blocks away. She stopped once, took off her heels, and resumed the pace on cold concrete, but the moment they hit lot gravel and glass, he scooped her up and kept moving.

It was only for a few seconds, but the action of being picked up so that her feet wouldn't be injured by debris was surreal. It was also spring, she noted. Here she was a woman of her age, and again she was running barefoot, after an altercation, in a gown . . . just like on her damned prom, and fighting for her life, her dignity. And strangely, this time like before, she had a real man from around the way to step up and help her . . . just like that kid who'd given her an unmolested lift home did. She'd never gotten that kid's name . . . but the man who'd shoved her into a rental after checking it thoroughly had a name she'd taken—James Carter.

He pulled out of the self-park lot like a man possessed, and barreled down the street, yanking a firearm out from under the dash. "Change of clothes, under the seat. Do it now."

She complied, knowing that Dulles airport was out of the question. They'd expect that. BWI was the closest option, and they'd have to change tickets in transit.

"James, I don't think your boys stopped the limo," she said glancing over the backseat.

Gunshot report was the answer that shattered the back window as she screamed. James swerved away from oncoming traffic and headed up Fourteenth. Before she could remove her hands from over her head, James had hollered at her to take the wheel, never slowing down. She gripped the wheel, eyes wide, her ability to control the car, fragile. He leaned out the window and sent three shots into the limousine's grille, then quickly leaned back into the car, grabbed the wheel from her, and spun out to go in the opposite direction.

"He can't maneuver in that big rig like we can, so hold on!"

Sirens were everywhere in the distance and gaining. Cars and pedestrians screeched to a halt and jumped out of the way.

"Grab my cell, hit Cap, and tell him we're taking fire in the streets of D.C. proper! Then get a damned gun and hold the bastard off, but try not to hit any folks in the street!"

She was motion itself, grabbing the cell from James's waistband at the same time she dipped low and snatched the second gun from beneath the dashboard. She hit the unit and pressed the phone to her ear. "They're shooting at us in the District!" she hollered to whomever answered the line. She didn't know if it was even Captain Bennett, nor did she care, because another shot whirred by them and put a neat hole in the front windshield.

She dropped the phone on the seat and rolled down her window, pointed the gun behind her, and closed her eyes as she squeezed off several rounds. The limo swerved behind them. Police lights entered the drag race from two side streets and cut the limo off. James floored the accelerator, turned into a side alley, screeched to a stop, and jumped out of the car. He grabbed his phone and the small bag of clothes. Laura was still barefoot and he threw a pair of sneakers at her. "Change as we run—gotta ditch the ride and get to a subway. The corner. We jump the rails, come out walking slow and easy. Seen it done by perps trying to get away from us every day. Let Cap straighten it out on the back end."

By the time he'd finished his statement, he had on a hooded sweatshirt, had lost the cummerbund and jacket, but kept his tux pants, and his feet had been jammed into sneakers. She ran behind him, yanking a sweatshirt over her head, and only stopped for two seconds to rip down the gown and pull on a pair of sweatpants. When they exited the other side of the alley, she'd been transformed, like James, and they were on their way down a flight of Metro steps. She ditched her beaded purse, taking only her cell, ID, and Blackberry out of it to shove into her pockets. James had the bag over his shoulder, which contained money, his wallet with a different ID, and her laptop.

Pacing, they waited in the white-tiled space for the train to come, not even caring if they were on the right line or not. They just had to flee the scene, as the main priority. Later, once above ground and away from the sirens, they could navigate the city by cab and get to Amtrak. From there, the airport was within reach.

Laura bent over, gulping in air as the wait ground her nerves down to a thin filament. In a subway, there was nowhere to run, nowhere to hide, if a gunman came for them—or if the police did. Every time she opened and closed her eyes, dots of light danced like floaters within her vision.

She'd fired shots in an open street. A limo driver had tried to kill them, had tried to actually blow the gas tank of their rental car! They'd created a serious security breach in Washington fucking D.C., and had hacked a computer to get on an A-list using bogus names, when everyone there knew their real names. Canada no longer gave exile to American fugitives. Mexico was out. She'd take her chances in prison before going underground there. Multiple felony charges swirled in her head until she thought she'd pass out. Instead she dry heaved, and then felt James's hand on her back.

"I want you to stand up, lean on me, and breathe slowly, until the train comes," he said in a firm, quiet tone. "All right?"

"But James," she gasped, wheezing out the words. "The many legal implications—"

"Breathe in and out, and lean on me before anyone walks down here and gets suspicious. You look like you've been running, and that's not good."

She nodded, went to him, and leaned on him, forcing herself not to cry. Panic was eating a hole in her brain. Claustrophobia was setting in. She wanted to be free, away, moving. Standing still was making her crazy. The train came, and she almost tore away from him to jump through the doors, but he held her firm, and walked slowly to get on and sit down coolly. Only when the doors closed and they'd passed several stations did she feel and hear him audibly exhale.

He'd been prepared for the worst, and the worst had come. But had it not been for his skill and planning, she knew she might well have a bullet in her skull right now.

They hailed a cab once they surfaced. She glanced around, but couldn't tell what section of the city they were in for a few moments. Then it hit her, Georgetown—the only place, other than by the station and tourist areas, where a cab would be available at this time of night. D.C. was not like Manhattan, in that regard, and she thanked God in heaven that they'd ended up on the right train.

Union Station looked like a sanctuary, and they booked the last thing smoking out of there to Newark.

"Newark," she whispered, as they walked away with tickets from the automated machines.

"You see all these cops in here?" he whispered, keeping his

back to the milling patrols that scoured the echoing, marble ter-
rain. "We dip into a bar in here, go buy a drink, and quietly fade
into the backdrop of weary travelers. By now, they've got a drag-
net at Dulles and BWI with our pics probably posted, plus probably at Philly International as well, knowing that's where we'd
most likely catch a flight from. So get on that BlackBerry of yours
and get us tix out of Newark or even JFK for Jamaica."

Chapter 13

Caribbean sunshine never looked so good. She didn't care that she appeared to be a vagrant, or that what she was wearing was ridiculously hot under the outrageous sun. Sleep on the flight and a chance to breathe and think had done wonders for her mind, not to mention her spirit. They'd agreed not to contact Akhan and the rest of the family until they'd gotten a hotel, checked in, and were sure they weren't being followed.

Enduring the slow customs process was their greatest challenge at the moment, but they'd survived. James kept a protective arm over her shoulder the whole time, even once they'd entered the cab that dropped them off in the center of Kingston. He'd been on her hip while she quickly selected a few sundresses, T-shirts, and pants for them, and gathered toiletries that he could stuff in the small knapsack. Eerily quiet, she monitored his mood, but understood it. He was now freaked out after the near brush with disaster, like she had been during the heat of everything.

"Baby, breathe," she said quietly as they crossed the street. "We'll get inside a nondescript hotel or rooming house, no majors . . . get you something to eat, a cool shower, and a change of clothes. Then we call Akhan."

James just nodded and watched her buy some fruit and bottled waters and juices to take to the room in a small, cement walk up that simply had a painted sign that said HOTEL.

American cash being the universal language, they had no difficulty getting an out-of-the-way room for the night in Kingston. The fact that there was spotty hot water was not an issue, given that it was already hot as the blazes outside. She let James hit the shower first, and set out mango slices and oranges, cheese and crackers, and water and juice while he freshened up. Knowing that he'd feel calmer once out of his getaway clothes, she didn't tell him about the plan that had formed and taken shape in her mind while on the plane. She simply got in the shower behind him and allowed the tepid spray to wash away her worries for the moment. That was the key to remaining sane: Take each moment by moment.

He was already dressed when she reentered the bedroom, and had pulled on the pair of khaki slacks, white Polo knockoff collared shirt, and generic brown leather men's sandals she'd laid out for him. He'd eaten half the spread of goodies she'd left on the dresser, which was also a good sign. His color looked better and he appeared to be more relaxed.

"How'd everything fit?" she asked, stripping her towel off and finding a bright orange sundress to slip on.

"It worked, but you forgot drawers," he said with a smirk.

"No, I didn't," she said chuckling, and finger combing her hair.

"I put on the swim trunks, instead."

She poked out her bottom lip. "Bummer."

He laughed. She had him.

Ever so casually, she sat down on the side of the bed, swiping a mango slice and a bottled water. "I've been thinking."

He stood. "Oh, shit, here we go."

They both laughed.

"OK, what, Laura? My nerves are shot."

She peered up at him, munching on mango. "We need backup."

"Tell me something new."

"We have backup we're not using."

He sat down on the bed and gave her a sidelong glance.

"They messed up this time, and hit an Italian jobber. I have a direct number to the head guy down at the casinos in Jersey, who might be interested to know that Russians did it."

James ran his palms down his face and stood again. "Oh, shit, Laura . . . have the Italians go after the Russians? Woman, are you crazy? After we narrowly got out of that casino-inspired jam before, you wanna call Joey Scapolini?"

"Yeah. Why not?" she said, smiling. "Caluzo got us a security car, on Steve's call, right? Now, how do we know if it was casino family or not that got whacked in the limo? The guy who tried to hit us definitely didn't know that we, of all people, might have had an Italian jobber as a driver, and just eliminated what he thought was some Joe-regular guy."

James fought a smile, but didn't commit.

"These Main Line assholes wanna play hardball, so let's play—street variety," she said, pressing her point. "Last I saw, Scapolini had Tony Rapuzzio as his driver, so who knows who this kid that was our driver was related to?" She stood and wagged her finger. "Never make assumptions, and you know the Italians already have an axe to grind with the Russians moving into Philly and Jersey. Now add on the indignity of the same folks that almost snatched the casino-charter-building contracts out from under them having a hand in trying to mess with *friends* of theirs—which resulted in a wrongful death of kin . . . heeeey. Who knows what might happen?"

"Well we damned sure don't want 'em to think we had a direct involvement in them losing one of their own—that's for sure."

"My plan has merit, James." Laura put her hands on her hips. "Besides, it's a poor rat that has one hole."

"You know this will get construed into us owing the Mafia. You ready to deal with that?"

She let her hands fall away from her hips and blew out a breath. "If I have to give them some of the land, so be it. I'd rather burn it to the ground than see any of that Micholi rat pack have it."

"Six in one hand, half a dozen on the other, if you ask me." James stared at her.

"Both sides are deadly, James. So why not deal with the friend-liest element we can negotiate with for now?"

"All right," James said grudgingly, and smiled. "You call Scapolini, but make sure you let that bastard know you're married."

"I will . . . if it comes up." She gave him a sly smile, which he returned.

"You're not a part of the bargaining process. Ever." He gave her a look with a smile, but in a way that told her not to play with him.

She nodded respectfully and got some crackers and cheese and didn't say another word for a moment.

"We're gonna have to clean up that D.C. incident, though," he said, lost in thought, swiping another orange section from the dresser top.

"Been thinking about that, too," she said, guzzling water. "Got more untapped resources," she added, dabbing her mouth dry with the back of her wrist.

"Like?"

"Like Megan's father works for the State Department, and I'd bet Sean's people are tapped into some high-level governmental post as well, given they're cousins, went to the schools they did, and are living in the U.S. If those families thought their kids were at risk because some greedy, Philadelphia Main Line bastards had lost some land to inner-city black folks—through a legal will and legal deed transfer . . . hmmm . . . I wonder what they might be able to dig up on the old boys, if provoked?"

"Damn, Laura," James said quietly, leaning over to stroke her cheek. "You have an evil mind."

"I have a practical mind," she whispered, kissing him more deeply.

"I'm glad you're feeling better," he said in a low, sexy tone. "Last night you looked beautiful, even running in bare feet."

She laughed and flopped back on the bed. "I didn't thank you, though—did I?"

He covered her and chuckled. "Nope."

Joey Scapolini put the phone down slowly. "Tony . . . we've gotta call a meeting. It's your nephew. He didn't come home last night."

Anthony Rapuzzio set his drink down slowly and swallowed hard. "What happened to little Eddie? It was just a limo job for Caluzo. That kid is only twenty-three, twenty-four. What the fuck coulda happened, Joey? What am I gonna tell my sister? Oh, Christ. How bad?"

"Russians. Vladimir Chertoff blew a hit on Laura and her cop. They got another one to stand in, and he fucked up the job in the Caymans—house job on 'em. Then they sent an enforcer, real pro, he took lil' Eddie's limo. Kid never saw it coming. Silencer. Ordered by Main Line developer boys. Now it's personal."

Scapolini balled his hand into a fist as he stood and went over to his hulking bodyguard cousin and hugged him. Bitter sobs wet his suit shoulder and made him look up to the ceiling.

"We have to fix this, Joey. It ain't right!"

"First we send the Main Line a message, then go have a conversation with those Russian muthafuckas."

Prison COs stood around the body scratching their heads.

"He was in solitary confinement, yo. How in the hell did another prisoner get to him to slit his throat? This one was only in here because he was a doctor and couldn't go into general population till he got moved to a country club facility. There wasn't enough time for him to have made any enemies. Damn!"

The other guard scratched the hair on his neck. "This is gonna be some fucked-up paperwork and long reports," he said with a weary sigh. "Get Sutherland's body out of here, before he draws flies."

* * *

Megan clicked her cell phone off and walked through her parents' British-styled home like a slow-moving shade. Her entire life had changed through one visit, one attempt to help a friend, and she wanted her world to go back to the way it had been. Shunning privilege as an option of rebellion was one thing, but truly living impoverished and on the run was unacceptable. She'd spent so much time lambasting her father for selling out, working for the man, big government, but today, after what she'd heard, she hoped that he had connections, strings, favors, markers, anything out there in the universe that he could call upon to protect her and Sean.

She found her father in the study, where he normally took his afternoon tea and pored over dense portfolios while on the phone, before going back to his office downtown or catching a flight to Washington.

"Daddy," she said in a quiet voice. "Can we talk?"

Her father looked up from the stack of folders on his wide mahogany desk and peered at her over half, Ben Franklin glasses.

"You haven't called me daddy in years, baby," he whispered.

Tears rose to her eyes and she swallowed hard, then glanced around his impressive sanctuary filled with leather bound law books. "I'm in trouble," she whispered.

He was immediately on his feet to rush to her and embrace her. "Megan, tell Daddy what's wrong. Your mother and I can fix this."

She buried her face against his shoulder, wetting his blue Oxford button-down shirt with quiet tears. "People in the government are chasing me and Sean because we found out some things we shouldn't have."

He held her away from him, wiped her face, and stared at her hard. "What people?" he demanded. "If they are not as high as the President, then I know for a fact they don't want me on their ass over my daughter."

* * *

"What happened to your cousin's nephew is as upsetting as what happened to our Vladimir," a thick Russian accent said into the phone. "Our client double-crossed us and went to freelancers when they became unsatisfied with Vladimir's work."

"Then you got our message, that we're unsatisfied by the way you guys don't have checks and balances on your fucked-up Russian freelancers," Scapolini said. "Shame about that fire that burned out several stores in K. and A., and, oh yeah, my condolences on one of your old, Main Line clients . . . a doctor, I think? Prison's a bad place for an educated man to be."

"He wasn't our client," the voice snapped through the receiver. "How many times do I have to tell you that? He was cut off from his associates, a nobody now! Who cared if he died in prison—he wasn't one of our paying customers."

"Oh, no? Then a colleague maybe? A vodka-drinking buddy from a long time ago, huh, maybe?" Scapolini was on his feet walking with the phone. "All I'ma say is this—you guys fucked up. You need to become more organized. You made a grave error. An apology is in order. Some show of good faith that it was really an accident. Accidents happen, true, but you still gotta repay the family for the inconvenience—Capice? So you tell your client that I took a head for my cousin's nephew's, but I still ain't really feeling a complete sense of total satisfaction!"

"What?" Akhan whispered, as they all sat on the back porch of Braithwaite's hidden house in the bush.

Laura and James calmly took turns relaying the chronology of events as small insects dove at them, despite the smoking pots of Citronella candles. Steve, Jamal, Najira, Akhan and Brother B sat with plates laden with jerk chicken, fried plantains, callaloo greens and cabbage, pigeon peas and rice, with tall glasses of sorrel punch gathering gnats, but nary a fork moved as the couple spoke in hushed tones.

Fully sated from making the critical phone calls, taking a nap, and making love to release tension, James spoke between bites of home-cooked food, while Laura also dug into her plate with abandon. It was what it was; wheels had been set in motion. The Main Line had pressed their backs up against a corner, and they came out fighting like any good street rat would—no holds barred. That was the one thing that the boys at Micholi had discounted; yes Laura and James were educated, had reached a significant level of affluence, but they had roots from 'round the way.

"But you called the casino boys?" Steve said, still incredulous.

"Eat your food, man, while it's still hot," James said, stuffing a Johnny cake into his mouth. "We figured, why not, after all was said and done."

Laura shrugged as she picked the meat off a chicken wing. "Screw waiting around for them to find us," she said, monitoring her language for the sake of Akhan and Brother B. "We got the State Department in a bit of a lather, too." She took a swig of sorrel and watched her cousin Jamal slowly begin to eat.

Akhan looked at Braithwaite and slowly smiled. "I told you she was a Scorpio."

Braithwaite nodded and blew out a long breath. "Shame she wasn't around during the sixties."

"Ashé," Akhan said with pride. "Risky, but brilliant. I suspect that a chain of events will begin to unfold. Those who were only involved on the tertiary level, will run for cover and begin distancing themselves. But those intimately involved will have to make a move now. That's what we must watch."

Braithwaite nodded and took a deep swig of sorrel. "Indeed, just like dominoes. They'll drop."

"What are we looking for, though?" Najira asked, beginning to eat slowly, as her nerves calmed.

"The clean up and recovery," James said. "First the cover up. The whole thing at the Smithsonian won't be marred, if I were a betting man. It will be just a random event—played off as a drug dealer's limo and turf fights between drug boys in The District. Cars will find their way mysteriously back to rental car lots, repaired . . . shit like that. Any abandoned weapons will be associated with dead men and drug boys. The media spin will be that everything that went down was just more local crime, and the need to keep up the war on crime, but it will never be linked to us, because then it would necessarily have to be linked to the high-level people after us."

"What about my gown and your tux, not to mention our ditched fake IDs?" Laura asked as she stopped chewing for a moment to look at James in the waning sunset.

"If D.C.'s finest got to it, with the calls to Cap, it will get lost, permanently, just like a lot of evidence does all the time."

"Damn," Jamal murmured. "And here I thought I was just Conspiracy Brother."

Steve shook his head. "A lot of dirty shit goes down behind all closed doors, even in precincts."

"Elizabeth, just be careful," Polanski said in a harsh whisper through the phone. "You were always a good egg, and no matter what you and Donald were going through, some things are just . . . I don't care what you and Sutherland had going on before Donald died. That was between you two. The man was a doctor, was in our circle, and even your husband didn't turn the dogs against him, affair or not. But they slit his throat in a jail cell. It's gone too far, Elizabeth, and I want out of it all. You should stay out of it all, too."

"They killed him in prison," she whispered, disbelieving. "I had come to loathe him, but I would never . . ."

"I know. That's why I'm getting out now, before anyone else gets hurt."

"You be safe," she said quietly, looking around her condo with fear.

"You, too, Liz. I have to go before Marian gets worried. We're going to play bridge tonight with friends."

"Bye, Mike, and thank you."

He hung up the telephone without responding, and called out to his wife as he heard her move through their Radnor home. "Marian! All right! I'll be down in a moment, stop eavesdropping for heaven's sake!"

Angered by the silly games she always played in hoping to catch him in an affair, he crossed the room in a huff, and yanked open the door. A pair of male eyes greeted him, barely visible through the ski-mask. Before he could yell out, a soft whooshing sound, followed by a bullet, pierced his forehead.

Chapter
14

Night sounds of the bush, voices, and laughter blended in with the low, steady timbre of Bob Marley filtering from deep within the house. Pops and cracks laced the old album's croon, just as the lights sizzled and popped from unwary bugs that ventured too near them. The weary group sat rapt, listening to Brother B and Akhan tell stories about the glory days of civil rights protests, Panthers, and power to the people.

It was their way of chasing away the harsh realities of the present, by going back to the past and recounting the wins and losses, analyzing "the struggle," which by any other terms would have been called a civil war. Their little party became a tribal council of sorts; all that was missing was a center fire to give ablutions to the ancestors. By any means necessary, they were still standing, after the first round of volleys.

Laura smiled, oddly content to be here, versus many of the other places she'd been. Rum punch at one-hundred-and-fifty-one proof was taking a toll on them all, except the elders, who seemed accustomed to the strength of the brew. Jamal had slid down in a porch chair with his eyes closed, and finally Steve relaxed enough to gather Najira against his shoulder to doze. His acceptance had been delivered through a singular statement by

Braithwaite; "You cool—had you been your age back then, you would have marched with us." Acceptance conferred. Akhan yawned and set off a chain reaction in the group.

James had his head back against the stucco wall, looking so mellow that he could have been poured into a tall glass. Laura cast a lazy glance toward the house, which was more like a barrack than home, but comfortable.

It seemed as though Braithwaite had set up a camp without soldiers. His home in the bush was one long, rectangular structure that had a bend in it to form an *L.* In the short section was a small kitchen off a tiny bedroom and bathroom beside a place where a long picnic table with benches served as a dining room. The living room was a tight, cozy space chock full with an overstuffed sofa and floral-print, lumpy, overstuffed chairs, an antique breakfront with mismatched china, an ancient TV and record player, and colorful throw rugs. Local art and family photos covered the walls, along with a mural of Haile Selassie. Windows had screens, some with shutters, some without, but there was enough dense foliage around the house in a profusion of hibiscus to serve as natural curtains.

Down the long corridor were three bedrooms on either side, each sporting a large double bed made by hand, and handmade dressers, a wicker chair, washing bowl, and mirror. Behind the house were the chicken coops, a small vegetable garden, an outdoor wood-burning stove that could handle huge pots and cauldrons, a free-standing shower, water pump, and an outhouse that had undoubtedly been left over from yesteryear.

Everything was neat and clean and Spartan, just like the elderly warrior who proclaimed the revolution was still ongoing—and was right. Even through the rum haze and fatigue, Braithwaite's eyes held subtle, barely repressed excitement, as though he'd been waiting all of his life for it to begin again . . . for a group to visit and commune at his oasis once more, like old times, now that his many children were grown, educated, and gone, and his wife dearly departed. Laura knew this place was no less a shrine or institution within the fabric of this community environment than Akhan's North Philadelphia hostel had been. She wondered if she'd ever put down roots long enough, or live to see the day when, wherever she and James set up permanent housekeeping, they'd grow old and gray with many stories to tell the next generation.

"You all must be bone weary," Braithwaite finally said, refusing to admit that he was also exhausted. "Pick a bedroom. All linen is fresh and towels are in the dressers. My room is near the kitchen, since I really don't use the long part of the house unless company comes." He stood, stretched, smiled, and then yawned, and finally went into the house, leaving the screen door to clatter shut behind him.

"Good night old friend," Akhan called out sleepily. He rubbed his bald head with a sigh and stood slowly. "We should all live like this," he murmured. "Off the land and free."

They watched him go into the house, and Jamal stood, stumbled a bit, and headed toward the door.

"Whew," Jamal said, rubbing his eyes. "All that was missing is a blunt, and a brother would have been righteous." He glanced out into the darkness as Najira scowled. "They probably got it growing ten feet away out here in the wild." He waved off his sister's brewing complaint and went into the house.

James and Steve looked at each other, and Laura watched the male dynamic from a remote place in her mind. Steve's eyes held a question; James's offered support. No words were exchanged for a moment, and only the thick, humid night cloaked the foursome on the porch.

"It's cool," James finally told Steve. "I don't think you have to sleep in separate rooms. That's why the old dudes went inside to crash first."

Najira's eyes sought Laura's, and Laura simply nodded. As the younger couple stood and slipped into the house, Laura snuggled down closer to James on the cushioned wicker porch furniture.

"Guess it's just us old-timers left to fight the bugs, turn off the lights, and lock up," James said with a sleepy chuckle, and nuzzled her hair.

"You think we're gonna grow old together, and have one of these big old homesteads for everybody to come back to?" she asked in a distant whisper, her thoughts leaping through time and space.

"Yeah . . . when it's all over, we'll have that big old raggedy house that everyone comes back to for holidays, making us crazy, and we'll be fussing about when they're going to leave."

He kissed her gently, making her chuckle in contentment and attempting to chase away the fears that neither wanted to name. The one thing that they'd never discussed, but loomed large nevertheless, was the fact that a majority of their assets were down in the Caymans—a place that didn't play and would seize all until they returned to help sort out the investigation there. Unlike the States, the Cayman Islands had virtually no crime, and the murder of two innocent police officers had sent a shock wave through the region. State Department officials couldn't clean that up or make that evidence disappear, like slightly damaged rental cars or an ill-placed gown and tux. The Mafia couldn't blast that away, either. Nor could all the fancy maneuvering in the world address what had happened there. And if they explained what was going down, it would indeed become a huge, international incident with implications neither of them could fathom at the moment.

Rather than go down that very slippery mental slope destined to renew panic and despair, she felt her husband try to solve the problem with touch, his gentle ministrations to her skin a balm to her weary spirit. She returned his kiss in the thick night air in kind, a gentle homage to what this man meant to her.

Soon the probability of being left destitute or confined fled with each quiet sigh. James Carter was a wise man, his hands a tender conference of patience. The heat of his long, gentle strokes down her arms as his kiss consumed worry, made the air around her seem cooler and caused sudden shivers. Annoying gnats and mosquitoes were soon forgotten, and the song of the night replaced the thousands of nagging questions dancing through her head.

"You ready to go to bed?" he whispered, sending a warm, moist current against her lips.

"Yeah . . . I think so," she replied quietly, brushing his mouth. "Tomorrow is another day."

She'd slept like the dead, and now a foreign, bleating noise was tugging at her senses. It was a half screech, half wail, and she opened her eyes to James's lopsided smile. He hadn't opened his eyes, but she knew he was awake.

"What the hell is that?" she grumbled and pulled in closer to him.

He laughed softly. "A rooster."

"Oh, my God," she said, dropping her head against his chest.

"We're in da bush, mon," he said, teasing her and pulling her against him. "Cock-a-doodle-doo."

"Man, stop," she said, struggling against his hold and not wanting to address his morning erection.

"The rum kinda made my best-laid plans go awry last night. Fell asleep before my head hit the pillow. But this morning . . . I'm much improved."

"James, we've got a lot to do today," she argued to no avail, giving in to his body as he pulled her on top of him.

"I know," he whispered. "But first things first."

She laughed and kissed him, warming to his hold. There was something about his relaxed countenance, the fresh mountain air, the stillness of the house, and the heat of his hands as they washed over her backside, pushing up the oversize T-shirt she'd slept in. He'd lodged against her so subtly without entering her that it made her gasp, his movements beneath her a slow stroke down her slit until it plumped and swelled, spilling her slick essence to bathe him.

"You sure you wanna get up with the chickens, or stay in bed for just a little while longer?" he murmured against her neck, finding her breasts beneath the too-big T-shirt and crisp white cotton sheets.

"No," she murmured back, swiveling her hips to capture more of the sensation until she could actually hear the sound of her wetness each time he slid over her engorged bud.

His smile had faded to a grimace, and she bent to suckle his nipples till he arched, but she still denied him entry, prolonging the dance between them. She didn't understand what had ignited her body beyond the obvious. Perhaps it was the sense of freedom, the pending threat they faced, and him all combined. But the playful mood had turned frenetic—him trying to enter her, her denying him access, his hands now roughly kneading her fleshy bottom, pulling it open wide as he sought her haven. She'd tugged off the T-shirt and flung it God knew where, needing his tongue to lap at the overly sensitive tips of her breasts, and almost crying out when his mouth captured one, his tongue a spiral of pleasure around the heated, hardened surfaces.

His intermittent suckles were making her as crazy as the quick jabs at attempted entry that repeatedly ended in an accidental sliding between passion-slicked lips, now so swollen with need they hurt. Unable to stand the torture she'd imposed on both of them, she ground her pelvis against his, her bud lathing his base, nearly swooning from the slow building orgasm. Too overwhelmed to lift her head, she pressed her flushed face against his cheek.

"Two seconds before I cum, put it in," she rasped in a harsh whisper.

He felt her shudder, and obliged the request with a stifled groan, not caring that she'd bit into his shoulder to keep her pleasure from echoing throughout the quiet house. The immediate sensation of being inside her the moment her body contracted around him in orgasmic pulses made him half sit up, grasp her around her waist hard, and thrust in offbeat jags. His voice buried between her breasts was the only sound he could muffle. The bed springs be damned, he couldn't worry about all of that, no more than he could stop moving or stop the convulsion that swept through his sac, clenched his stomach, overran his base, and released up his shaft forming tears in his eyes.

He was twitching when he'd landed on his back with a thud, Laura a heap of spent flesh against him. Now he felt the heat, the humidity of the island morning. Now he heard the movement in the rest of the house and smelled coffee. For a long while, all he could do was pet Laura's velvety curls. Reality made him slowly open his eyes. What if by some fluke they did federal time, twenty-five years to life without this? He'd been a cop, too . . . and there would be hell to pay from all those he'd sent up the river. No, today it was time to get a realistic plan and stop running.

"You OK?" she murmured, pushing herself up to kiss the bridge of his nose.

"Yeah, but I think we woke up the whole house."

"They didn't hear us," she whispered, smiling wide.

"Like hell," he said, smiling despite his sobered mood. "The springs gave us away. There's always something even the best criminal forgets to address."

She cocked her head to the side and then covered her mouth with her hand, eyes merry.

"See, the problem with you, Laura, is you like living on the edge."

"Moi?" she said, placing a palm against her chest. "You started it this morning."

He was annoyed but had to laugh. "No, I was gonna be discreet . . . a quickie. Not—"

"Let it get all messy, and hot, and wet, and juicy, and good," she said in a low, deliciously wicked murmur.

He swallowed hard. "Yeah."

"But isn't it more fun this way?"

He closed his eyes, somehow knowing she was talking about more than their lovemaking. "Yeah."

James had made up his mind; he wasn't going to address the sly smile Steve gave him, or even glance in Jamal's direction. Nope. He was a very private man, and his business had been exposed.

He was just glad that Najira hadn't started, but kept her gaze on the stove, and Akhan seemed to be old and wise enough to keep his own council. Thankfully, their host, Brother B, was in a separate wing of the house. He'd get his shower after Laura, eat, and then develop a plan.

He listened to the water go on in the bathroom and affixed his gaze to the mug of java Najira had been kind enough to slide under his nose. They had to go back to Grand Cayman, simple as that. If they reentered the island, spoke to the detective, cop to cop, maybe, just maybe, they could use the chaos of Carnival Batabano as a cover to come up with a joint sting operation.

Laura allowed the weak shower spray and chilly water to cover her body and help her think. James had been right. All of this, even their interlude this morning, had been too open, too exposed, and too unplanned, and as a result a lot of people were involved that shouldn't have been. She thought hard about it all as she washed off and got out of the shower. They had to go back to Grand Cayman alone, draw whomever was chasing them there, and put an end to the nightmare for multiple families.

When she passed James in the kitchen, their eyes met and a common understanding bound them. Later in the bedroom, alone, after breakfast, they'd talk. She just hoped he'd understand.

James Devereaux sat numbly watching the morning news. Polanski, shot in his own home? He reached for the telephone and called George Townsend. George picked up on the first ring.

"I want out," he said quietly, not even bothering with a formal hello.

"Me, too," George said in a shaky whisper. "But how?"

"We have to let them stand on their own. I'm diverting what I had to family connections."

"They won't let you just do that without a fight."

"I know." Devereaux paused.

"What are you going to do?"

"I'm not sure. I just wanted you to know that I'm getting out."

Devereaux hung up the telephone without saying good-bye. His next call was to a few friends very high up at the federal level. He knew people that had always wanted in on prime lands he owned, and he stared at his wife and children's pictures on his desk.

"I have a family," he said quietly into the telephone receiver. "I want to make a statement, and I want amnesty. I'm stepping down from my board position at Micholi, and whatever I owned down in the Gulf is negotiable, if you can provide me and my family protection."

"Not on the telephone," the voice said. "I'll come to you."

"No," Devereaux said quickly. "I just saw what happened to Polanski while he waited for someone to come to him. They did. The wrong person. I'm sure my phones are tapped." He hung up and dashed through the house, finding his wife in the garden. "Get in the car," he ordered. "We'll pick up the children from school on the way."

Disoriented, her blue eyes shone with fear, but she stood and looked at her husband. "James, what's wrong? What's happened?"

"I'll tell you on the way. Mike's dead."

"What?!" she shrieked, but followed him as he hurried her into the driveway, and pushed her into their silver Mercedes.

He turned to her. "I love you," he whispered. "No matter what, I did everything for you and the kids." He rubbed his palms down his face and inserted the key in the ignition.

"I love you, too," she said quietly, but never got to finish the thought.

The moment he turned the key, the car exploded.

"Polanski was a show of good faith; Devereaux and his wife were personal. We didn't like how he treated my nephew, any more than we liked how Sutherland did. Vladimir has been avenged. So, in that regard, my friend, I salute you for doing us a favor. Were you here, I'd raise a vodka to you."

"Yeah, salute. Just after you put a bullet in my head. So we're even. So squash the shit like men, and your stores and whatever else you peddle stays on your side of the line, untouched." Joey Scapolini pushed back in his leather chair and surveyed the casino floor below him, then hung up.

Tony Rapuzzio looked at his boss as he hung up the phone. "Did they do their part, Joey, or is it war with the Russians?"

"They did their part," Scapolini said carefully, studying his henchman's face. "The thing that's bothering me, though . . . I can't put my finger on it. There's an opportunity here; I can smell it. This all got wrapped up too fast, too neat, and there's gotta be someone higher up that has his hands dirty. If we know, then we can put a little pressure on the son of a bitch for a favor one day."

Tony nodded. "I hear you, boss. It would make it easier to take Eddie's death. At least there would have been a reason. The shit still gets under my skin just thinking about it."

Joey nodded and stood. "A lot of things get under my skin, Tony." He smiled suddenly and shook his head. "That Laura Caldwell broad is one of 'em. But she's always dead-on." He looked at Tony hard and polished off his drink. "An honorable thief. They don't make 'em like that anymore."

"Sounds like she's a little more to ya than just business, boss. Be careful. She may be dead-on, but she's also deadly—all barracuda."

"She's gonna make me divorce my wife one day, or get killed."

"Probably both, if your wife finds out." Tony chuckled and went to the bar to fix them another drink.

Chapter 15

Technology had once been her friend, but now it had become her mortal enemy out in the bush. Cell phones had died, batteries needed charging, and there were no chargers to be had. Wireless laptops couldn't get a Wi-Fi signal. None of the gadgets that would have connected her to the States and the news at large were working, and Brother B's television had a wire coat hanger stuck in a hole where the antenna once was. Out where they were, power dipped and swayed like it was doing a waltz, and the plugs in the wall matched nothing they would have had on them anyway.

Sitting on the side of the bed in defeat after stilted conversation at breakfast, Laura looked at James, who had obviously come to the same conclusion when he flung his cellular on the dresser. Then it dawned on her: the FedEx box. They'd missed a delivery!

"James, we have to go back into Kingston and go to Lillian Braithwaite's house."

He closed his eyes briefly and let his breath out in a rush. "Damn. The FedEx."

"Yeah. The FedEx."

"But if that house was safe, then Brother B would have taken the whole crew there from the getgo."

"I know," she said, standing and chewing her bottom lip. "Here's the thing, though. Megan came into the country using Brother B's dead wife's name and her old family property. That's the shell game, that's where the box is supposed to be delivered, and if anyone came calling there, we need to know to secure the rest of the people with us."

He nodded, hating that she was right, and that peace had just been a fleeting, twenty-four-hour experience. "All right," he said, giving into the inevitable. "Just make sure that Brother B drops us off to a cab, and is far enough away from the house when we enter that nobody can follow his station wagon back here."

George Townsend sat with his attorney at FBI headquarters in Philadelphia, quietly horrified as he slowly related his story. Sutherland had had his throat slashed in prison? Devereaux and his lovely wife had been murdered in a car bombing? Polanski had been shot in the head by an assailant that had entered his home? The executive director of Micholi, Polanski, and the foundation's treasurer, Devereaux, gone, and now, he, the secretary and CFO was the only one left from the old guard?

Hell no. He'd spill his guts, sing like a canary, give up whatever information he had for federal witness protection and having his name kept out of the press, so that he could quietly live abroad for a few years, returning once the storm had passed. Elizabeth Haines could take the helm of that sinking foundation. They could then hire whomever they wanted to fill the other two key vacancies—Devereaux's and his. He had friends at the State Department.

Rick stared at his boss in disbelief. "I'm laid off? Me? After all these years? Why, John?"

"Knight-Ridder is consolidating. You know that. All the newspapers in Philly are going through a trim down, and all us old-timers are on the chopping block. They can get two fresh-out-of-college journalists to replace you as part-time freelancers, with no bennies. You and I cost too much. I can't do anything about it. I'm sorry."

His boss looked away ashamed and raked his fingers through his profusion of white, scraggly hair. "This shit sucks."

Rick stood and folded up the lay-off notice into his pocket. Fuck that. He had a wife and kids in college to feed. It was time to negotiate and take any info he could find to the highest bidder. It was time to call in all markers and Laura for a favor.

They exited the cab and looked at the small, clapboard house that sat within the crush of close-together homes in the center of Kingston proper. A missed-package sticker was on the door. FedEx had obviously come, and no one was home.

James glanced at Laura, and as their eyes met, the silent message was clear. Let him go in first, packing heat. He calmly extracted the antiquated weapon that Brother B had given him and shoved it into his waistband, pulling his shirt over it to hide it from neighborly view. During the four-hour trek from the hills into town by way of narrow, slow-moving roads and then through thick urban traffic, they had their nerves on edge.

"Maybe I should try to find a cybercafé somewhere first, or see if I can buy a temporary cell phone to dial into my voice mail remotely?" she offered, glancing up at the house, her nerves raw.

"Six in one hand, half a dozen in the other," he muttered, beginning to round the house to see if there were any signs of forced entry.

"James, what if the door is rigged to blow?"

He hesitated, watching the few lean stray dogs snuffle at curbside garbage. "And what if we miss the second delivery attempt, and all our shit gets shipped back to the States?"

She sighed and nodded, but kept her eyes on the dogs in the street. His line of vision went to them as well.

"There's a food vendor not far down the block," he said in a faraway tone, glancing down the street.

"I can't believe you're hungry!"

"I'm not," he said calmly, motioning to the dogs with his chin. "But they are."

She wasn't sure what he meant, but she followed him down the street and watched him buy a grilled pork sandwich, and then hit another corner grocery store for some duct tape. It was amazing, just watching him work, as he tore off bits of food to ball in his hand as he loosely wrapped the sandwich, taped it to the back doorknob, inserted the key to turn the lock and then took cover by the adjacent house, tossing a handful of food toward the hungry dogs that scoured the streets for a meal.

Before long, several dogs had picked up the scent and snuffled their way toward the back door, snapping at each other through yelps and low whines, and then began to pull at the sandwich that had been affixed to the door. The dogs' aggressive efforts rewarded not only the street scavengers that finally got the meat away from the knob, but also Laura and James, as the back door eerily creaked open without incident. No bomb. They were in.

"Whoa . . ." Laura breathed out, once the dogs had run down the street battling over a ragged pork sandwich. "Where'd you learn that MacGyver shit, James?"

He didn't answer her as he cased the house, smelling for a possibly broken gas line, and searching for a hidden intruder. "Don't turn on the lights or open the front door," he said carefully as he continued to scout the tiny, neat home for any evidence of tampering. "They wouldn't expect us to come in through the back door. But I don't know what else has been rigged."

She nodded and wrapped her arms around her waist. "What do we do now?"

"We wait until four o'clock for FedEx to come. When they ring the bell, we go out the way we came in through the side alley, get the package, come back in, open it, get what we need, then we're out."

She looked at her watch, her gaze taking in all facets of the home for any clue. They had an hour. This house, like Brother B's, was neat, old-fashioned, with furniture too big and too formal for it, with all mantles laden with family photos, but not much more. Her line of vision briefly lingered on a yellowing photo in an oval, silver frame that contained her uncle, Lillian Braithwaite, and Brother B in a candid beach shot from years gone by. Both she and James simultaneously looked at the telephone, and she went to it first. James simply nodded.

There were three messages on her cellular that she had to access remotely. The first was from Megan. The second was from Rick. The third one almost made her heart stand still.

Megan's message was very short and very concise: "My father says that it's best that we end our association, and I agree. This last bit of information that my cousin sent you is our way of saying good-bye under good graces. Don't try to return my call or his. Our cell-phone numbers will be disconnected after this and our phone records to you purged. Be well. Take care of yourselves and Donny." The message ended without any signature or name, but she knew the frightened female voice well by now.

Rick's message was less cryptic and contained a level of urgency that gave her an idea. It simply said: "Laura, what the *hell* is going on? I just got fucking laid off from the paper! Where are you? Call me. I need a favor, some contacts to get me back in the game and positioned well. Don't leave me hanging. I love you, and you're still my favorite girl. Tell me you've got a marker you can call in and a story I can use to bargain my rusty ass back into a media job somewhere."

Yeah . . . she might be able to accommodate Rick, after all.

Then came the call she'd never thought she'd receive again in life, the one from Elizabeth Haines.

"This is Liz. I know it's been ages, but I don't know what's going on, Laura," a nervous female voice said in a heated whisper. "Someone murdered Sutherland in jail. Polanski got shot in his own home." There was a long, static-ridden pause. "James Devereaux and his wife were blown to bits in their family driveway. No one knows where George Townsend is . . . and *people* want me to become the new executive director of Micholi. I'm afraid. I don't want to be a part of this, and I want my son to be all right. Do you know what's happening? Please call me on my new cellular, and here's the number." A quick number was rattled off, and then the voice mail electronic message came on to denote that Elizabeth's urgent call was the last message in the queue.

"Talk to me," James said, his eyes holding a steady, intense beam of worry as he watched Laura's expression.

"Our friends are bailing," she said, and then relayed the three messages word for word for him.

"Lemme use the phone," he said, taking the antiquated receiver from her. "I might have something on voice mail that could prove interesting."

Sure enough, he had one message—from Captain Bennett. It told him all that he needed to know. The shit was getting rugged, and George Townsend was in with the feds, cutting a deal. While that took some of the spotlight off them as key players, and could help them bargain with the authorities in the Caymans, it also meant another long trial was in the offing that would ultimately drag them back to Philadelphia as material witnesses.

That was an unacceptable option, until they found out exactly who was after them, why they wouldn't just crawl back into the hole they'd slithered out of, and how to diffuse the bounty that was on their heads.

"What?" Laura said, her eyes glued to his as he slowly lowered the telephone.

James quietly relayed Cap's message as she remained mute and still, trying to formulate a plan in his head as he spoke.

"I need to get my laptop up and working," she said quickly, rummaging in the knapsack he'd brought along. "Once I see what Megan and Sean sent as a parting gift, from there I can feed enough of it to Rick to give him a media-in to bargain with—which will give our side of the story further credibility way before we try to negotiate with Cayman authorities."

"Yeah," he said calmly. "Let me get a call off to Cap, tell him we need some courtesy cover through his boys on the fed team as an entrée to the squad down in Grand Cayman. I'd rather be treated like VIPs who are coming down there to help them solve a case as freelance PIs, rather than be met at the airport and taken into custody in cuffs."

"Make the call," she said, nervous perspiration wetting her skin with sheen. She got out her laptop, waited until James had finished his call to Bennett, and then searched for a place to plug it in. "Shit!"

"What's wrong?" James folded his arms over his chest.

She held up the old phone cord and sighed. "It's not a plastic adapter. This is old, hardwired to a four-pronged wall jack!" She rubbed her palms down her face in total frustration. Being in a foreign country had its merits and distinct limitations. The dusty, thick air in the house was stifling. "I've gotta find a cybercafé. That's all to it."

"Then we wait for FedEx," he said, trying to remain calm.

"Why don't you do that thing on the front door with the dogs, so we can just open it and act normal when they get here?" she said, frustration making her tone brittle, and the request come out as a command.

"After FedEx comes and goes. Whatduya think will happen if the door possibly blows before then?"

He walked away from her in frustration, his nerves tight enough to pop.

"OK. I'm sorry," she said, stuffing her laptop back into the knapsack. "We're both edgy. I just hate sitting here in the house, waiting."

The sound of the doorbell almost made her squeal; she was ready to jump out of her skin. They both dashed to the back door, but James held up his hand, shoving his gun into his pants waistband under his T-shirt again.

"Let me slide out of the house, then go around the front, in case it isn't FedEx. You peep through the shades on the side and give me the nod if you see a real FedEx truck. Cool? But stay away from the window."

She nodded and watched him exit the house through the back, holding her breath, and gave him the thumbs-up the moment she spotted the familiar, marked truck.

He collected the package without fanfare, and rounded the house with a box. They tore into it like thieves, and quickly shoved the contents into his knapsack.

"Now, we leave," James said, a slight tinge of annoyance and triumph in his tone that irked her.

"We still need to test the front door like we did that back door," she said. "If Brother B comes back here for some reason, after we're gone, I can't have anything happen to—"

"I know, I know," James said, hurrying with her down the street back to the same food vendor. "You ask where you can hook up your laptop, but stay in the store. "I'll go do my thing, and will be back in a minute."

This time she listened, every muscle within her strained to the limit as the slow process of getting served took place. Nothing happened quickly in Jamaica. Everything was done at a leisurely, mind-wracking pace of no worries. Once James left the store, it was all she could do to keep up the pleasant, idle banter, and seem like a casual, American tourist on holiday while her heart slammed against her breastbone.

The sudden sound of a blast made the few milling patrons, the clerk, and Laura shriek, drop everything, and tear out of the small, sparsely stocked store. Billowing black smoke could be seen where she stood, but there was no James in sight. Instant terror made her feet move toward the blaze. Tears filled her eyes—where was her husband?!

Commotion ensued in the street. A jumble of patois-strained voices and shouts to call authorities rang out. Dead, mutilated dogs left in bloodied bits against the curb, parked cars, and in the street almost made her vomit at the sight. But no James.

"Oh, Jesus," she whispered, swallowing hard, and running in the opposite direction from the horror to find a way to get to the house from a back street. She had to find James's body before the house burned to the ground.

A man stepped out of the alley, yanked her arm, and she screamed—but her voice was drowned out by the sound of the shrieking neighbors and sirens.

"Let's go," he said, and pulled her nearly off her feet.

It took a few seconds for her brain to sync up with her vision. It was James, their knapsack over his shoulder, and pulling her into an adjacent street with a steel-force grip. He jogged them through several alleys, ditching the gun in one trash can and the bullets deep in a Dumpster a block away, lest neighborhood children accidentally discover the weapon. She knew what he was doing as he stripped the weapon clean, wiped his prints off of it with his shirt, and kept moving, eyes roving. If he'd died in the blast, her soul would have died right along within him. But she didn't have time to think about all of that as he pulled her out onto a main thoroughfare, then flagged down a cab before additional gridlock ensued.

Shaking, she gave the cabbie the location of the cybercafé as though they'd been oblivious to the blast like the cabbie was. They went in the opposite direction of the mayhem, paid their fare, and jumped out onto the sidewalk.

"Get on your laptop; I'll call the house to get our family out of there. You send whatever to Cap and Rick, and we head to the airport in ten minutes."

"Oh . . . baby . . ." Rick whispered as he stared at his Blackberry. "This is a Pulitzer in the making." He licked his lips quickly, closed his eyes, and forced himself to wait for the right moment, just like Laura had said. "You are still my favorite girl."

"Yeah, this is Joey," Scapolini said, walking through his expansive Cherry Hill, New Jersey, home sipping a beer. He stopped in the middle of his kitchen and waited as a rush of information filled his ear.

"But see, this is why friends should come to friends—and only friends, first," he said as a smile tugged at his cheek. "We wasn't even invited to the party. Is that how you treat friends, after all these years?"

Again, more urgent words filled the receiver, and he opened the fridge, nonplussed, to hunt for some lunch meat.

He stood, growing agitated. "Listen. I don't fuck with the feds—creates tax problems. Especially when there's no incentive." He waited and listened, still not happy with what he was being told.

"No. That wasn't us. We're not sloppy like that. See, you shoulda come to professionals. Friends who are professionals. Those guys are new to the game. Do shit half-cocked. Ain't our style."

Joey slammed the refrigerator door. "Now you want us to clean up after them? Look, you guys have a lotta nerve—"

The caller's urgent pleas cut off his argument, and Joey leaned against the center butcher-block island in his white-on-white kitchen, listening to bullshit that was beginning to make the beer in his stomach curdle. Something wasn't right.

"This much I did hear," Joey said, angling. "You know the network has ears. It didn't involve us, but we heard that some Russian guy's cousin bought it, and they took offense, on account of the fact that their client ordered the job on the jobber. Bad form, if I must say so myself—but you didn't hear that from me. . . . I'm just saying, word travels, rumors get spread. Anyway, from my take, that's when things got messy. Went ova the top. I'm glad I'm just in the casino business and building trades, ya know. But, a little waste management contract down in the Gulf might help me become more interested in your problems. Capice?"

Joey smiled. The Main Line fat cats were so stupid, for all their political clout. Blessed Mary knew he wasn't about to admit to any involvement over some freaking phone. Pin it all on the Russians. Bastards.

"Laura Caldwell? What's that broad got to do with it?" Joey waited, becoming suspicious. "I ain't heard from that black chick in, what, more than a year . . . if memory serves me. Mighta been longer than that. Only time I saw her was when she came to play some blackjack. Your point being?"

Every instinct within him told him to play it cool. George Townsend never called him directly. OK, so they wanted to play games.

"That cop, Carter?" Joey pushed away from the center island slowly. "I'm a law-abiding citizen, George. I try not to mix with cops, unless it's a friendly game of cards down at my establishment. I don't think I can help you on this one. Like I said, neither the cop or the broad have been whispered in my ear as a problem. But shame what happened to Devereaux and Polanski, though. Sutherland, too—a man should be able to serve his time and get back into society, once his bid is done. My condolences to all of Micholi Foundation, on that. Seriously. It's a fucked-up sin that a man can't even enjoy his own home. What's the world coming to?"

He keened his ears, listening for any unusual clicks or hum on the line.

"Yeah, yeah, yeah," Joey finally said, growing more uneasy. "Tell you what. You ask your people to break Joey off a little waste-removal job, and I'll see what I can do. Does that sound fair, reasonable?" He waited, now more sure than ever before that Laura had told him the truth. "I can't make any promises, since, like I said, not to be redundant and repeat myself, but I just hear things—don't get involved and that kinda business. I'm strictly legit."

He passed on the bait, and ended the call with professional courtesies. Laura and James owed him, and in a way, he owed them for the heads-up on contracts that would have gone down without him. They could come to terms and settle up later, but not during what he was now sure was a federal wiretap. George Townsend was a dead man walking. Nobody set up Joey Scapolini and got away with it.

"He didn't take the bait," the federal officer said, looking at Townsend with an icy glare. "Got any other bright ideas, or people we should call? If your story doesn't check out, you've got hard time staring you in the face, buddy."

"Brother B, listen to me carefully and quickly," James said under his breath from the cybercafé. "Go to the U.S. Embassy." He cut off the elderly man's words, too hurried to argue politics with him.

"Put Steve on the phone." James paced as Steve got on the line. "Yo," he said in a rush. "Get everybody out of the house, they blew the one in town—you're sitting ducks in the bush. Go to the U.S. Embassy. Call in Milton Montgomery, Megan's dad, if you need a witness, and you probably will. Then give 'em Cap's number in the States. You guys go in unarmed, scared, as victims being hunted that need governmental protection. And, you spill the beans—it was Russians, by way of some Main Line boys. Whatever you do, don't mention Caluzo or Scapolini. You're just victims who are scared shitless and fully cooperating, and you don't know shit about where me and Laura are at the moment."

"Shit," Steve murmured. "That role won't be hard to play at all."

Laura's semi-charged cell phone vibrated on the side of her purse as their cab took its leisurely time to get to the airport. She opened it and stared at it, showing the text message to James: *Watch your back. The feds are in it. GT called from an FBI joint, gut hunch. You owe me. Will settle later. It's all good. Your pal, JS.*

"Oh, shit," James said, leaning his head back and closing his eyes.

"It costs to be the boss. Gotta break him off something, anyway," Laura said, her tone philosophical as she stared out the dingy back window, hoping they weren't being followed. "It's the way of the world."

Chapter
16

Full-blown paranoia strangled her as they waited for the next flight to Grand Cayman within the bustling airport. Each time a Jamaican officer passed, or anyone with a uniform on for that matter, her eyes felt like they would bug out of her head, even though James's contained the command to be cool. The extra sets of phony ID that she'd stashed in her brassiere and underwear were making her sweat bullets. If they didn't get on a flight soon, she was sure that she'd fall dead away from the stress. Now she owed the mob big-time, too?

Her hands were shaking as she used the last of her minimal battery to make a call. She wished that she'd had more time to get a solid charge on the unit, but that was the primary issue— they'd run out of time. She punched in Elizabeth Haines's new cell phone number. She'd only heard it once, but had memorized it instantly. James's eyes held a question, but he didn't say a word as she worked. Their communication had deepened to glances and pure trust.

"Liz," she said quickly, huddling down to make her muffled words private to the airport throng. "My battery is going. Listen to me carefully. The only way to get your ass out of this sling is to give Scapolini something he wants. Break him off a piece of the

Gulf cleanup, somehow, and tell him Laura sent you. That will make him your friend."

"But—"

"No buts!" Laura said in a tense whisper. "You do it. I have to go." She hung up and looked at James. "Debt paid in full, I hope. At least that will temporarily keep Scapolini off our asses, and make him know that I heard him. Might even save Liz's sorry ass."

"Good move," James said, impressed. "I just hope Cap worked some magic on his end, before we touch down."

The flight seemed interminable, even though it was a short hop by flight standards, island to island. Yet the fact that it was nearly dusk when they landed didn't improve her case of the jitters. This situation was so different than the smooth operations they'd pulled in Philly so many years ago. This job had death-trap written all over it, and she hated not being in full control with a stacked deck. All of it was high-risk, high-stakes poker with an unknown wild card in the mix. This evening, she wasn't inclined to be a betting woman.

The moment she saw what was clearly a plainclothes officer waiting by the Customs area, both she and James bristled. His line of vision went directly to them. Two more men in khaki suits were with him. His face was vaguely familiar. Tall, lean, handsome, dark brown complexion . . . where did she know him from? He had cop oozing from his pores; it was the no-nonsense grit. James had clearly seen it, too.

"Be cool," he told her under his breath, and handed off their forms to be stamped at the desk. "We walk by, nice and slowly. They're looking for someone, might not know who, exactly, and you just smile, lean on me, and chill. We're weary travelers. We do this like Union Station."

She nodded, but her instincts told her that the thin plan wasn't going to work. Her hunch was corroborated the moment they cleared Customs and three detectives advanced.

"A word, Mr. and Mrs. Carter," the man in the lead said, not waiting for them to respond. He flashed an official shield, causing a mild stir of interest from onlookers.

James nodded and complied, and they crossed the small airport to get into a police minivan parked outside without a struggle.

"I'm Detective Hayward," the man who'd accosted them said. He nodded to the driver. "That's Officer Dowell, and the man beside you is Officer McFadden."

Three sets of serious eyes greeted Laura and James within dark brown, deadpan faces.

"I've seen you before," Laura said, trying to wrap her brain around the authorities that held her, and gain insight into their position.

Hayward nodded. "It's always a surprise when you meet people out of context, isn't it, Mrs. Carter?" His glare held quiet fury. "You put my family at risk."

Instant memory soaked into her brain. "Mr. and Mrs. Melville . . ." She glimpsed James, whose jaw muscle was working overtime in his silence.

"My elderly cousins who would have been at that house—"

"Which is why we sent them away," Laura said, leaning forward. "Ask them."

Hayward sat back in his seat and looked ahead, carriage erect. "We'll discuss it all down at headquarters."

Three very skeptical officers sat on the edges of desks and took to folding chairs in a small interrogation room as a very ornery-looking captain remained unreadable. James kept a close eye on each man's body language. He knew cop unspoken language well, and was fluent in it.

Laura produced her laptop for them to inspect. "I have a missive from a person with State Department contacts. You have word from a police captain and the FBI in Philadelphia. See for yourself," she added, theatrically, turning her laptop toward them.

"All these men have been in business together for years. You have a copy of the original will, the more updated ones, and can see how me and my family were put at risk because of it."

Hayward finally nodded. "I can see that much with my plain eyes. But what I don't understand is this—why would they need to be so bold, create so much havoc, when they could have easily sent a messenger to threaten you into their position? This is the part that we cannot fathom."

"Nor can we," Laura said flatly.

"Listen, man," James said, speaking slowly, his eyes going to each man in the room, but finally settling on the one who had the most at risk, since his family had narrowly escaped tragic involvement. "I'm proposing a sting, Hayward. We need to do that to bring your case to a close and seek justice for those two officers that got killed. I used to be a cop, too—and we both know good and damned well that it ain't over till it's over, once they've killed one of our own. They got two of yours."

"You got dat right," their captain said. "Not on my island."

James eyed the man who'd finally spoken, and then sent his gaze back to Hayward, negotiating hard. "Me and Laura *have* to do it, to get the bounty off our necks." The two men's gazes locked in silent struggle. "Even if you just send us up the river to tidy up your paperwork, and to make it look good for the people on Grand Cayman, me and Laura will still be working to solve this crap from behind bars with a time bomb ticking over our heads."

"Send us up the river, make us have to await trial, if you want to . . . but how do you know whether or not they'll send a cleanup crew after anyone who's been in our house, might have seen anything, might have been in our employ—like your cousins?"

"All right!" Hayward shouted and stood. "What do you propose?"

Strained glances fell on Laura and James.

"We use the chaos of Carnival to see if they still have a gunman on our asses," James said in a flat tone. "You put us in a downtown hotel, near the action, with a wire, and several men walking point.

You take any bastard down that comes for us—with a tranquilizer gun—and then lean on his ass, if you get him. We're gonna need a trust factor between us, though."

"So, if we agree to your proposal, you're talking about a possible incident in a crowd of tourists," the captain said, shaking his head. "We depend on tourism as one of our primary industries, and it is already bad enough that there's even been a hint that terrorism has reached our beautiful island!"

"That's why you don't do any blind shooting into crowds and only use tranquilizers to numb any target you profile," Laura said, her voice straining with urgency. "Correct the bull in the media with a leak, stating that it was an unsavory Russian-inspired business deal gone down, linked to something in the U.S., not terrorism, so people can rest easy and think it's gone back from whence it came. Give them a shred of the truth to go on; two Cayman officers simply got in the way by accident. Meanwhile, if you do capture an aggressor, tell them he's being shipped back to the States so all can go back to normal here. But, ultimately, James and I are going to have to get back to Philadelphia to set up the ones behind this."

"We're not allowing you to leave here without assurances that you two aren't more directly involved. The deaths happened here, thus, justice will be served here."

James gave the men around him a disgusted scowl. "You want us to take lie-detector tests? Whatever."

Laura allowed her tone to become more civil. "Listen, gentlemen," she said coolly. "We'll take whatever tests you want, and you can work out the details of détente with our stateside authorities, even if that's a hand-off from you all to them, with a guarantee of our return here, should things not pan out." She glimpsed James. "We're heavily invested in the Caymans, as I'm sure you know by now. I'm also sure you can seize our assets as a good-faith gesture, to ensure our return, if you haven't already."

She held Hayward in a steady, serene gaze, and then turned it on his captain. "Besides, think of the feather it will be in your respective caps to have solved an international crime that involved a senator from the States, several VIPS, a gun battle in the streets of Washington, D.C., and a filthy U.S. foundation . . . as well as your unfortunate officers—who were simply victims that were in the wrong place at the wrong time, but due to Hayward's shrewd observance, didn't die in vain. That gunman was killed on the spot, justice served neat, from his revolver," she said dangling the career-enhancing options before all the detectives in the room. "Even our local police and FBI in the U.S. couldn't solve it alone, nor could Jamaican authorities, which experienced incidents on their island. You can send a clear message to the people of Grand Cayman that your expert involvement was the lynchpin that cracked the case here, and that will go out over the BBC. I have friends in the U.S. media, trust me."

Laura sat back, folded her arms over her chest, and waited for the tender offer to sink in. James didn't move a muscle.

"Fine," the captain said, finally standing with the others. "But if you die trying, it will not be on our heads."

"This is a loosely constructed, raggedy-assed plan, if ever I heard one, Laura," James grumbled, changing into a bright red Polo shirt as she slipped on a bright red dress. "We've got targets on our backs," he muttered, referring to the bright colors they wore so they could be easily spotted in the street crowd that was growing below the balcony of their hotel.

She didn't immediately answer him, but simply listened to the steady calypso beat that thrummed through her as the noise of revelry cascaded through the closed sliding glass doors and windows. "We go downstairs, blend into the crowd, buy a rum and coke, and sip it calmly at a very open, outdoor café," she said flatly, picking up her purse.

"And if the hit man puts a neat bullet in our skulls?" James folded his arms over his chest.

"Then we died fast and quietly," she said picking up her purse. "And nobody else we love gets hunted or hurt."

"That's bullshit," he said, following her out of the room.

"These guys down here ain't used to high drama, SWAT maneuvers, or anything else!"

"I know," she said coolly, walked down the exit staircase, undaunted. "That's why they probably won't catch anyone, if there's still anyone tracking us, and we'll get a free pass home to wrap this up old school."

James kept his eyes moving on the passing crowd of partying tourists and native revelers. Masks, giant floats, and colorful costumes moved like a sea of liquid human color. His wife was insane, so were the Cayman authorities. This plan had failure etched all over it, but as crazy as Laura was, she did have a point.

She was ice-cool. He observed the way she took a sip of rum and coke, glanced up at rooftops, windows, and then through the throng, her motions steady, unflinching, like a spider waiting to trap a fly. Suddenly, without warning, she leaned across the table to kiss him, and he lifted his drink between them to salute her.

Instantly, the glass shattered in his hand. Pandemonium broke out. They were on their feet, screams shattered the festival, and people ran like roaches scattering in the light. A blur of costumes and halted floats almost made the filled thoroughfare impassable. Café tables overturned, shouting officers and sirens blared. Chaos was in full effect.

Breathless, they took cover in a restaurant, rushed through past tables and shrieking patrons, hit the kitchen unsettling angry chefs, and ran out a back alley exit into the darkness. Unsure of which way to turn, they hesitated, and another shot hit a Dumpster and a trash can. James pulled her into a darkened doorway, and then they both made a flat-out dash to another building, hiding beneath the fire escape.

Police vehicles careened by both ends of the alley, flashing lights and making the crowds disperse and run like fleeing lemming in all directions. More shouts from authorities, and then several plainclothes men rushed past them. Within moments, the two-way that James wore squawked. "We got him!"

*   *   *

"He won't be fully conscious for several hours," the doctor said, his worried gaze going to Detective Hayward and then to Laura and James.

Hayward signaled to his men. "You both stay armed, in his room, and when the bastard comes to, you call me."

"I guess that's a pass for a flight to the States," Laura said, trying to keep victory out of her tone.

"I'll call the captain," Hayward snapped, looking at both Laura and James with fury. "You just make sure that your media friends get the story right. An incident like this during Carnival will have a bad effect on tourism for us."

"Too close for comfort," James said, rolling the tension away from his shoulders as they sat in the airport under heavy, plain-clothes authority guard. "Any bright ideas for the move when we get back to Philly?"

"No 'thank you, baby'? No 'that was brilliant, sweetheart'?" she said under her breath. "No 'not bad for thinking on your feet'?"

"No 'you were right, James'?" he muttered under his breath. "No 'glad a bullet missed the kiss, darling'?"

He didn't answer her. She didn't press her point. They had work to do.

"All right, gentlemen," Laura said quickly as several FBI agents met them at the gates. "You've been briefed, I take it."

They nodded without words.

"I'm gonna need a blue business suit, a wire. James is gonna need a car that can move." She glanced at them. "Can you guys get into my old house on Pennsylvania Avenue, and sweep my Jag to make sure it's not booby-trapped?"

"We'll send somebody over there," one of the suits said. "We'll put the wire on you both down at headquarters—we've got a coupla cots down there you both can sleep on. Better stay with us, have several conversations, then we can discuss the plan in depth."

*   *   *

"That's a crazy bold move," Captain Bennett said, adding his two cents into the discussion as FBI officials took weary seats around the war room. "Maybe we should just send in a team to arrest the bastard."

"On what charges?" James argued, fatigue making him irritable as he sipped his fifth cup of bad coffee from a Styrofoam cup and rubbed his eyes. He wondered how he'd ever been able to hang as long as he had on the force. The fluorescent beam was creating a throbbing tension headache. Laura looked washed out and exhausted, too.

"Cap, be serious," James said, pressing his point. "If this guy is involved, we still don't know exactly why someone as well-connected as him, with as much to lose, would start this level of bullshit. Besides, last I heard, being in a silent partnership wasn't exactly a felony. It might represent a significant conflict of interest, but if you go after this guy, you've gotta nail him with something that will stick. We're still not even sure if he's the big fish, or just a mid-level player, like Townsend. So, you've gotta let her go in with a wire to see if she can draw him out in conversation, then we wait to see if anything jumps off whack, after that."

Captain Bennett peered at the assembled group, his nerves on open display. "Listen, I just don't like sending her into a downtown highrise building all alone to waltz into his office and directly confront him."

"We'll have undercover men in the building, several, who will appear to just be office workers, cleaning staff, you name it," an FBI agent assured Bennett.

"I have to go in, cocky, like I have a bargaining ace up my sleeve and rattle his cage," Laura protested. "If I go in there with James, he'll immediately know I'm not just fishing, but have an army outside. He could panic, like Sutherland did . . . *then*, it could get ugly. But the man isn't crazy, just ruthless, and isn't about to have an incident go down at One Liberty Place near his place of employ." She glanced at James for support. "The one thing he seems to have been very good at is keeping on the periphery in a defense of total deniability."

"I'm not worried about One Liberty Place," James said flatly, turning his line of vision on Bennett, and then the others in the room. "My concern is after I pick Laura up, and we supposedly go back to her place to chill and wait for his phone call. *That's* where it could get intense, just like before."

"We've got agents in the house already sweeping it for any listening devices, explosives, with snipers concealed. No one will be able to get in or out without our guys spotting 'em," another FBI agent said in an authoritative tone.

Bennett looked at James and Laura hard. "Yeah, well, we all know that even in the best of circumstances, one slipup, one blink, and a pro can breach a line, do a hit, and slip out clean— no offense, gentlemen. Not to mention, there are so many quiet partners in bed with this guy, from other elected officials to people with serious financial juice that who knows if this guy is even our man, truthfully?"

"That's the problem, sir," Laura said raking her fingers through her hair. We don't know. But there's only one way to find out."

"Lean and lean hard, make him place a call, make a move, meet someone and get a quiet photo op," James said, standing to pace. "That's the only way, at this point."

Chapter 17

Laura took a deep breath, smoothed the front of her Ellen Tracy suit, lifted her chin, and glimpsed her reflection as she passed through the chrome and glass doors of One Liberty Place. Pearls, white blouse, low-heeled Prada pumps, Coach bag, light dusting of makeup, she looked like any attorney or businesswoman going to work on a Monday morning.

She signed in with the security desk without even looking at the guard, confident, like she belonged there, and rode up to the fifteenth floor, keeping her eyes on the ascending numbers in the crowded elevator. Without stopping to glance around, she walked right up to the wide, double-pane glass doors, pushed her way in, and impatiently waited at the receptionist's desk.

"May I help you?" a pleasant-looking, older woman with a tasteful silver chignon asked.

"Alan Moyer," Laura said, glancing at her watch as though she had somewhere else more important to be.

The woman buzzed the inner office, giving Laura the once-over. "May I have your name?"

"Laura Caldwell," she replied, not batting an eye. "If he's not in, do let him know I was here."

"One moment," the receptionist said, seeming confused. "Do you have an appointment?"

"Yes," Laura snapped. "A standing one."

The receptionist spoke in a low, confused tone to the executive assistant behind the rows and rows of partitions and walnut décor. "Uhmmm . . . he's not expecting you, and has a full calendar this morning," she replied after a moment. "Would you like to make an appointment?"

"Please tell his assistant that he can either make time for me this morning, or he can explain to his boss why I bypassed his office and went to speak to the FBI." Laura batted her eyes, smiled tensely, and leaned on the desk peering down at the woman to help her decide.

"I think you may want to come out here and have a conversation with Mr. Moyer's client, Joanne," the receptionist whispered in a tight voice. "Something about the FBI?"

Within moments, a very efficient-looking, middle-aged blonde rounded the corner. Her hazel eyes smoldered with indignation as she peered at Laura over her gold-rimmed glasses that draped pink and black crystal beads behind her ears.

"I'm Joanne McLaughlin, Mr. Moyer's executive assistant. May we help you?" Joanne said, clearly peeved. She swept her hand down the front of her pink knit cardigan set and fumbled with a message pad and pen, as though about to take Laura's information.

"Alan Moyer would want to have a conversation with me before I get nervous and go to the police about his various holdings and conflict of interest at Micholi Foundation," Laura said in a low, civil tone that contained a warning. "Or, he can blow me off until his schedule frees up later in the week, and by then, it will be a media travesty." She gave Joanne a wink. "Ask him that for me, would you? Then, check his calendar and see if something opened up. I'll wait."

If looks could kill, Laura would have been taken from the building in a body bag. Joanne hurried away from her to the inner offices, while the receptionist kept her eyes on Laura as though waiting for some signal to call security.

"Would you like a seat?" the receptionist finally asked.

"No, I'll stand," Laura said, her tone frosty.

She hated the whole charade. What she really wanted to do was go into Alan Moyer's office and bitch slap him. It didn't matter if he actually called for the hits or not. He was as guilty as sin and involved somehow; she could feel that through her skin. The problem was what it had always been, there were so many well-shielded players, who knew where to begin.

Micholi had been cross-pollinated with so many others, boards were overlaid with boards, good old boys from the same elite high schools, boarding schools, same country clubs and golf circuits, old alma maters, and shared past-present-future CEO or corporate merger tycoon status . . . how did one unravel the thread, pull one string and hang them all—or at least the ones who were directly fucking with her and James? In that moment she realized again just how much she missed her old sparring buddy, Donald Haines. Yes, he was a thief, like the rest of them, but at least he was genteel in the sport of being a robber baron.

Laura jerked her attention away from the large picture window that gave one an impressive view of City Hall when Joanne hastily reentered the lobby.

"Mr. Moyer said you can steal a few, *unscheduled* moments of his time. But he can only spare a few moments without wreaking havoc to his other appointments that had been scheduled well in advance."

Joanne McLaughlin could kiss her natural behind. "Yeah, whatever," Laura said, straightening her spine to stand even taller. "You can tell the boss I won't steal anything more from him than he's been trying to steal from me. Lead the way."

Entitled fury filled Joanne's eyes, but rather than respond to Laura, she pursed her lips, spun on her penny loafer flat heels, lifted her chin, and strode down a corridor. "Follow me."

Joanne turned abruptly as they came to a halt before a massive set of double walnut doors. She glared at Laura again, knocked gently, and turned the brass handle. "Ms. Laura Caldwell, sir," she announced. "Would you like me to stay and take notes?"

A man in his late sixties looked over his half-moon horn-rimmed glasses, and leaned his elbows on his highly polished mahogany desk. His eyes burned with a mixture of intensity and curiosity as he studied Laura for a moment. Bright sunlight gleamed off his scalp, making his silvery white tufts of hair sparkle. His thick jowls moved ever so slightly as he laced his fingers together and made a tent with his hands in front of his mouth. "That won't be necessary, Joanne. Our conversation will be brief, I'm sure."

Nodding, but keeping a lethal gaze on Laura, Joanne stepped back, allowed Laura entry, and then quietly shut the door behind her.

"Well, and so we finally meet again," Laura said, her gaze sweeping his office. "Impressive. I like the digs," she said calmly. "When did we see each other last? Was it Haines's funeral, or your son's trial? I can't remember."

"You have a lot of gall coming here, Ms. Caldwell," the senior attorney said, watching her move around his office and not take a seat.

"Or, a lot of balls," she said, pruning a plant for him by the window that was already in immaculate condition. "And, by the way, it's Caldwell-Carter, these days."

"Get to the point," he snapped.

"Fine," she said, turning to calmly face him. "My point is this. I hear through the grapevine that it's too late to try to rectify things the civil way . . . with a donation made to Micholi, one that would heal old wounds."

He smiled. "I'm afraid too many balls have been set in motion. I'm sorry you wasted your time returning to Philadelphia to discuss a moot point."

She smiled. "Then I guess I'll have to turn over the records that some friends at the State Department accidentally e-mailed me."

His smile faded and he just stared at her.

"Isn't it a conflict of interest to be the attorney of record for a large foundation that has millions in assets, but to own those assets . . . by way of power of attorney for a son that is now incarcerated on felony charges . . . and to also invest, quietly through silent partnerships, in the holdings of the foundation's larger clients? Hmmm, donors and clients, all in the same bed?" She pressed her hand to her chest and tilted her head. "I'm no attorney, and don't know the fine points of things like this, so I'm just seeking legal advice. Your expert opinion on said matters."

His gaze hardened. "Get out of my office," he said quietly.

"All right," she said with a sly smile. "I wouldn't want you to call security. The Russians are so messy . . . have been botching assignments from here to Grand Cayman and back. Shame they hit the wrong limo driver, though."

Moyer leaned forward, but didn't speak. Damn, she was counting on the fact that he'd say something, anything, to give her a clue. But the old man had blue-ice water in his veins, not blue blood.

"The one thing I see that you haven't invested in is the casinos, though. Shame. That's a tip I learned a looong time ago," she cooed, moving toward the door. "I've passed on the hot stock advice to some of my best friends down there that they might want to invest in the privately held prison corporations on the NASDAQ."

"Are you threatening my son," Moyer said in a low, dangerous tone, "after all you've done to him?"

"Would never dream of it," Laura said, absently studying her manicure. "I'm just saying that a man in your position might want to divest in ventures that could pose conflicts of interest, and you might want to spread your portfolio a little more . . . that way, you wouldn't have all your eggs in one basket." She looked up and smiled, but her eyes were hard. "I did a tour of duty on Wall Street years ago. I'm retired, but it's just some free advice."

"If anything happens to Alan in prison, like it did Dr. Sutherland, I'll have you and your Italian goons arrested on murder one," he said, standing slowly behind his desk and leaning forward.

His voice had escalated, and his face had become beet red, even though he'd said nothing incriminating that would help her case or make the wire she was wearing any more comfortable. In fact, what he did say only incriminated her and possibly Joey Scapolini. But, she had gotten a rise out of him.

"Nobody is going to attempt to go near Alan Jr.," she said, feeding Moyer more to enrage him and possibly make him sloppy. "*He's* our man. The one already shown capable of murder. The one already known to have a serious axe to grind, and already locked up with people who could get the word on the outside to people who could do a payback job . . . and he clearly has the financial wherewithal to pay."

Laura stopped, pursed her lips with her forefinger against them for a moment. She'd been yanking the old man's chain, but as she went down the slippery slope of logic, the more it made sense.

The epiphany hit her like a ton of bricks as she watched Moyer's eyes and his expression become pale. Oh shit, they'd been tracking a bunch of dirty old men on the outside that hovered around polite society and stood to gain, but never went behind bars to the young Turk who might actually be pulling the strings. Junior was already serving time and out of the way. His elders would benefit in the short term, and with power of attorney could move money in his behalf as directed, make payoffs, make high-level connections, and cover his tracks for him, and then find a way to get him an early parole and ankle bracelet to work from home, given all the judges and parole boards they owned.

If anything went down shaky, they could pin it on the man who was already serving time. If they slipped through undetected, then they could all get rich and party—they'd be dead from natural causes; Alan Moyer, Jr., would still be a fairly young man and set for life when he got out. It made so much sense, she shivered. Power never ceded to anything but power and old money didn't let itself get lent outside of the circles it had been born in. Deep.

"You are playing a very dangerous game with me, Laura," the

old man said, and rounded the desk. He'd spoken between his teeth. "Get out."

"Have a nice day, too," she said. "I'll be sure to send Alan a note of thanks to brighten his days in the joint."

Laura slipped out of the office, passed Joanne McLaughlin, and headed for the elevators, not even looking back at the receptionist. Her palms were moist; the wire taped to her body was itching. She could feel eyes watching her everywhere. No wonder Scapolini had stayed close to home with his message—a hit on Sutherland, Alan's old partner in another facility.

The mob boys had to have known the orders to engage the Russians came from inside. They just hit the wrong one, or maybe that was their intent all along, to hit the one inside that would cause them the least collateral damage to their contracts and relationships. Either way, they broke a loose link in the chain on the inside as a warning, and now she understood why. From there, the drama had escalated. *Now,* she *totally* understood why.

Pacing down Market Street to Sixteenth, she rounded the corner and headed toward Chestnut to the lot a few blocks away where James would be waiting in her Jag. Even though it was a spring day and still cool, by the time she power-walked, half dashing, half jogging to her destination, her silk blouse was drenched. She glanced at James and climbed into the white florists' van that sat double-parked at the mouth of the garage. Federal agents helped strip the wire as James's voice boomed through the two-way system they'd rigged.

"I'll be damned," James said.

"We got it," an agent said, glancing at Captain Bennett.

"The time bomb is ticking," James said, wishing his old partner Steve was there to ride shotgun with him.

"We know. She didn't get enough to fully incriminate the old bastard, but at least we have a warm trail to pick up on."

Laura looked at the agents and cops that had huddled into the van. "Alan is as slick as dishwater," she warned. "He won't have made a call. His father didn't even go collect his belongings from storage. It was all a ruse to make it seem like they were estranged. But I'll bet someone on the inside of the pen where either Junior or Sutherland were serving time will have made a call to Moyer. Cell phone records, office calls, his house. Or, it may have come in third party, like through Polanski, Devereaux, or Townsend as couriers." She stopped and looked at all the officers around her hard, unconcerned with modesty as they lifted her blouse, dug into her bra, manhandled the most private parts of her flesh, trying to quickly extract the listening devices from her body. "Or, Elizabeth Haines!"

Everyone in the tight confines of the van stopped moving for a second.

Captain Bennett rubbed his palms down his face. "Do we need to expand the warrants, or can we just snag her shit under the new Patriot Act?" He looked at the federal agents in the van.

"Go Patriot Act," the lead agent said. "There was a bombing, deaths, and shootings in The District near the White House, plus international bullshit. We use that these days to do whatever we have to without the DAs, judges, and paperwork hassles. Fuck all that personal civil rights crap. Do it."

Laura remained very still and just stared at them all.

"I know," she said quietly to James as they drove. She pressed her finger to her lips, looked around the vehicle, and reached in the glove compartment for a piece of paper and a pen. She scribbled furiously and showed him her note when he stopped for a light, careful to keep it low.

From now on, we're on the fed's radar.

James nodded, took the pen and jotted a quick response.

Since when do local Philly cops share jurisdiction with the feds? They're not colleagues. Are competitors.

She arched an eyebrow, nodded to let him know that hadn't escaped her, and quickly took the pen.

Since Homeland Security?

James shook his head no and wrote a fast response.

Not hardly. SSDD.

"Same shit, different day," she whispered.

"Yup."

She shrugged, giving him a wide-eyed expression to ask, *what gives?*

He shrugged. He didn't know any more than she did, but he felt a setup. True, a state senator had been shot. Two men killed in prison that were all linked to business deals . . . Senator Scott's son was the first to bite the dust. Then Sutherland got waxed—but that was courtesy of Scapolini. Still, something didn't completely fit. They'd killed their own hit man, Vladimir Chertoff. Lost another one in Grand Cayman. Sent one to track them down in Jamaica. Then iced their own from Micholi—Polanski, Devereaux, and spouse, and had Townsend on the run. Excessive. Multiple, local municipalities were involved . . . Philly, D.C., Baltimore. The State Department was in it, courtesy of Megan Montgomery, and her cousin, Sean. The feds were in it. Jamaican and Cayman authorities were in it. Russians, and Italians by proxy, were in it.

The question remained . . . what the hell was big enough to have stirred the pot this seriously? The only person who went back in history far enough, and who might be able to provide answers to that, was unreachable and was currently bargaining his way home out of Jamaica—Akhan.

Laura and James looked at each other at the same time.

"Your place or mine?" she said with a low chuckle for the sake of the probable bug that had been embedded in her Jag.

He motioned for the paper and pen at the next light along the Ben Franklin Parkway. "Yours," he said aloud, but quickly scribbled the alternate response.

Neither. Yours or mine is a death trap.

Where?—she asked with her eyes.

He wrote the reply swiftly and gunned the engine at the light.

Akhan's, then Liz's.

Laura kissed his cheek and calmly began making note paper confetti in her lap.

Chapter 18

They knew they were being followed, but they didn't care. The places they were going, a tail would stick out like a sore thumb. The neighborhood would be their shield. Checking on their uncle's abandoned property was their excuse. But the authorities knew that it was a delicate, fragile dance, if they were hunting them—and at the moment, no one was above suspicion. The only reason they believed that they weren't dead, yet, was because all the badges needed them to lead them to somewhere or something significant. They just wished they knew what it was.

Simpatico in thought, James bypassed her street turn off the Parkway and took the scenic route up Kelly Drive, heading for Hunting Park. Each time they spoke, they gave each other careful eye signals and glimpsed in the rearview for their unmarked escort. Spring had created a lush green canopy of foliage. University sculling crews were out on the water, making their drive seem like the most normal thing in the world as they passed Boat House Row. She motioned to her clothes and James nodded, both keenly aware that a chip could have been inserted in the fabric hem or sleeve of anything the feds extracted from their homes for them to wear.

"I just want to check on my uncle's house, since we're here in

Philly," Laura said, purposefully sighing. "He'd have a conniption if crack addicts or thieves razed his place . . . that's all that old man has in the world."

"I figured as much, honey," James said, giving her a purposeful glance. "My nerves are shot after you did that walk-through up at Moyer's. No sense in going directly to your place to just sit and wait around for some hit man to come knocking."

She mouthed the word *honey*, and then stuck out her tongue with a smile. He shrugged and smiled. Yeah, he never called her that. OK, then, that would be the code word for when they were kicking bullshit.

"Shot nerves?" she scoffed. "Oh, *sweetheart*, I could use a Valium right now."

He mouthed the words *sweetheart* and *Valium* and then rolled his eyes with a sly smile and then winked. She never did drugs, nor called him sweetheart. Theirs was an *oh, baby* type relationship. OK, he got it.

"Think maybe our boys in blue might open the door so you can do a walk-through?" James looked at her with a careful glance.

"Maybe we can ask them when we stop?" she said, aware that he'd rather have a bomb squad expert open the door than have to rely on stray dogs and a cheesesteak to be sure that place wasn't rigged.

"Yeah, when we pull over, I'll see if they can arrange it . . . but, uh, you sure you wanna go into your uncle's joint in that suit? I'd hate to have you get your good designer rags all filthy. Who knows what condition the property is in at the moment?"

"That's why I love you, sweetheart. You're always thinking and so considerate. Maybe I can just pop into a thrift store on North Broad before we go in?" She wrinkled her nose for theatrical effect to make him smile and made her voice sound as haughty as she could. "I love my uncle dearly, but he does live in a really old home in a borderline neighborhood. I'm sure if the place has been a crime scene, and doors and such left open for the authorities to walk in and out until it was sealed, there'll be vermin and all sorts of insects infesting the place by now."

"Baby . . . honey," James said, correcting himself. "I'll get some throwaway clothes, too, then. This way, I can do the really nasty stuff, and you just point to anything you want shifted or moved. All right?"

"Thank you, sweetheart," she murmured, and then nestled back into her seat for the balance of the ride.

The agents within the car looked at each other and radioed to their command post.

"Houston, we've got a problem. They're going into the house in North Central."

"That's where we want them to go."

"Yeah, but the lady is squeamish about the environment, and is gonna ditch her clothes while she's in there."

Silence crackled on the line for a moment. "What about Carter?"

"She's got him in honey-do melt down. He's gonna ditch his, too, so she can tell him what to move and clean up for her."

More silence entered the line. "All right. Then just try to keep a visual on them when they enter the house. Go in, sweep it for them by the numbers, then fall back so they don't feel crowded, get nervous, and clam up. Right now, they think we're solely on their side."

James pulled the Jaguar up to a large white building on North Broad Street just below Lehigh Avenue that looked like it had once belonged to a storefront church turned thrift shop, and got out of the vehicle. He glanced at Laura's purse.

"I think you should just tuck some cash in your pocket, and put that expensive designer bag in the trunk, honey."

"Good idea, sweetheart," she said, noting that it, too, could have been planted with a bug.

They worked quickly in unison, him opening the trunk and body-shielding her efforts from pedestrians as she got cash and then slammed the trunk shut. On a mission, they both quickly entered the large shop that was crammed with a combination of dilapidated furniture, worn velvet wall art depicting voluptuous black goddesses and tigers, half-working lamps, partial sets of china, knickknacks, plastic bins of shoes that ranged from animal print stilettos to sneakers, racks of clothing in odd sizes, and bargains, if one had all day to hunt and peck through the disarray.

"Good morning," a cheerful old man said with a smile as they entered the shop.

His merry brown eyes practically twinkled at the prospect of customers so early in the day, and he scratched the gray stubble on his narrow chin, clearly trying to figure out what had brought the likes of Laura and James to his establishment. He hoisted his gray cotton work pants up over his potbelly and pea green sweater, and then looped his thumbs under his suspenders. "What can I do you fer?"

"We have to clean up my uncle's house," Laura said with a warm smile, engaging the shopkeeper, "and we need some work clothes."

"You came to the right place, purty lady," he said, giving James a wink of appreciation. "We gots plenty of clothes—sweats, jeans, lots mo' bargains in the bin." Not waiting for them to respond, he hollered toward the back of the store. "Gots some VIPs in da house, Red. Bring dese people the good stuff from da back!"

"Got you, Pops!" a young man in his mid-twenties called out, and then wheeled a rack out from a storeroom. He gave Laura and James a curious look through light hazel eyes while scratching his wild profusion of reddish brown Afro. Freckles dotted his almond complexion, and he leaned his gaunt, muscular frame against the wall, studying them while chewing on a toothpick, as though watching a show.

"We save this for folks who seem like they want something nice and kin pay."

Laura swallowed away a smile as James nodded with a grin.

"Cool," James said, glancing at the rack of sequined and leather trimmed designer sweatsuits that looked five sizes too large for Laura. "How about just a pair of plain gray sweats and flats for my lady—since she'll be tying her head up in a rag and dropping Lysol everywhere, and some work pants already splattered with paint for me with a T-shirt, and a pair of work boots, brother?"

"Aw, c'mon, now," the older man protested. "She's too purty to be . . ." His voice trailed off as James raised an eyebrow, leaned on the counter, and produced a fifty-dollar bill. "But since you insist, who am I to judge how you dress yo' woman?"

The younger man's eyes became wide as James produced a twenty and held it between two fingers.

"Can she change in the back, and can you put her clean clothes in a plastic bag for me?" James smiled as the older man discreetly took the bills from James.

"Can a duck quack?" he said, glancing around and noticing the sedan that had pulled up behind their car through the window.

"Yep," James said coolly, accepting an armload of clothes from the younger man and tipping him well. "We'll be out of the storeroom in a minute."

"Aw'ight. Y'all take your time. I gots jackets and whatnot, too. Just holler."

James and Laura exchanged quick glances as they quickly went to the back of the store, slipped into the storeroom and changed silently. When she'd stripped down to her underwear, he signaled her to lose that, too. She nodded; a bra was a great place to hide a mic. She cringed at the thought of going bare back in a pair of sweats that had come from God knew who, but she dealt with it. He seemed to take the challenge in stride, ripping off his boxers and calmly tucking himself into a pair of previously worn work pants. She squinted. Men definitely had different sensibilities.

Hastily folding their clothes up into a neat pile, they exited the storeroom and went to the front desk. Both the older and younger clerks gave her unfettered breasts casual glances of appreciation, but kept their gazes sufficiently lowered out of silent respect for James.

"Well, that was fast," the older man said. "Y'all need a receipt?"

"No, just a bag," James said, and then fished in his pocket for more cash. He waited until their clothes were shoved into a bag and it was dropped on the floor. Then he picked up the pen on the counter and wrote a quick message on the edge of the C-note he held, then slid it across the table to the store owner. The message was simple: *Got a phone in the back?*

Laura kept her eyes on the man at the register and pressed a finger to her lips. He nodded.

"The little lady ain't happy with the gray sweats, is she?" he said, glancing down at the note. "Why don't she go in the back and see if there's something on the wall she might wanna use?"

James nodded. "Appreciate it. Laura, honey, go on back there and see if there's something you can work with. OK, honey?"

"Sure, sweetheart." Laura paced to the back of the store, prayed that one of the cell phones with her family was charged or hadn't lost power. She also hedged a bet; Jamaica's U.S. Embassy wouldn't be as technologically adept as one in the states. The building would be more open, cell-phone reception more possible. Security not as intense. If she could get a call in to Akhan, she had critical questions that needed answers.

Dialing quickly from the store's wall-mounted phone, Laura drummed her fingers against the plaster. Steve's phone immediately rang over to voice mail. That meant a couple of things, none of which made her relax. Either his battery was dead, reception where they were was dead, or they were. Growing frustrated, she tried Najira's phone. Same thing. Instant voice mail rollover. Akhan and Brother B didn't have units. "C'mon, Jamal." She tried her cousin next, and hoped that for all the whiz bang gadgetry he had on his phone, but with no one to really talk to, he'd be charged and able to receive. On the second ring, she hit pay dirt.

"Who dis?"

"Jamal—don't say my name, answer me in one word answers—it's Laura."

"Oh shit."

"That's two words, but I'll let it slide. You all okay?"

"Yeah."

"Where are you?"

"The Embassy."

"Is everyone all right?"

"Yeah."

"Can you talk?"

"No."

"Are you under arrest?"

"No. We cool. They fed us good, gave us blankets and a place to lie down. It was late when we got here and it normally would have been closed. But every American that was downtown is here," Jamal said in a low voice, breaking their code of offering only a few words. "There was a blast, everybody is trying to roll up outta here, worried it might be some—"

"I know, I know, don't use that word on the phone," she warned, cutting him off, but relieved that everyone was accounted for. "Put your father on the phone."

She heard the phone rustle like it was being passed. Their fake ID was holding, they might be able to get out of Jamaica without incident.

"Uncle?"

"Young queen sister."

Laura closed her eyes and leaned against the wall. "We're OK, you're OK. Jesus."

"The universe is beneficent."

"I'm on my way to your house, because I know I'm missing something . . . care to elaborate?" She *knew* there was something all these badges and shields were looking for, and if there was ever a time for her uncle to be forthcoming, now was it. Whatever it was, she didn't have it, nor did James.

"As I said, the universe is beneficent, but also efficient," Akhan replied in a maddening riddle. "X always marks the spot." He paused to allow the riddle to sink in. That had always been their way, and she now totally understood why he didn't trust phones, having been the very recent recipient of eavesdropping technology on her body.

"Yes, and things sometimes come full circle," she said, picking up on a hunch.

"They come home to roost . . . by any means necessary."

The huge framed poster of Malcolm X that graced Akhan's dining room immediately came into her mind. Yes . . . X marked the spot, and portions of his famous quotes.

"I understand," she said quickly.

"But we must also overstand to gain insight, above all else," he said, dropping his voice. "The efficiency of the universe is as neat as mathematics."

She rubbed her hands down her face. Math. OK. X could also be the Roman numeral ten. "Ten to one, everything always runs its course."

"Ten to one, indeed." Akhan said.

This was the essence of crazy-making! She wanted to scream. Ten to one could be numerically ten plus one, or eleven. One hundred and one. What?

Sensing her frustration as her hard sigh filled the line, Akhan pressed on. "One times out of a hundred, if you travel by *bus*, train, plane, whatever, you'll run into snags. But if you're patient, bring something along to read, then you'll be able to endure the tests of time. Just remember the *key* is going back to basics and *land*-ing on your feet by employing patience." He sighed. "You understand?"

"I think so. Thank you. I love you. Travel well, and be safe. See you guys soon."

"Ashé."

Laura hung up the telephone quietly and paused, and then changed into a different sweat top to go along with the ruse in case the feds were getting nervous outside. A key was in the house. Near or above the poster of Malcolm X—"overstand" meant above it, or over a stand near it. A bus terminal locker, one hundred and ten, had something for her to read. *Land*—ing . . . land was involved. Real estate. What was Akhan into with Haines?

"You ready, honey?" James asked when she'd rejoined him at the counter.

"Yeah, I liked this one better," she said, turning around to show off the pink and white baseball shirt and then striding out toward the fresh air and waiting feds.

The old shopkeeper slapped his helper five once James had cleared the door. "Lady's got good taste . . . bouncin' and behavin', have mercy!"

*   *   *

"You think you guys can get us into her uncle's house for a quick look around?" James bluntly asked, leaning into the agents' passenger's side window after he'd stashed the bag of clothing in the trunk.

"It's not on the detail," the driver said flatly.

Laura placed both hands on her hips and glared at the men who strangely resembled The Men In Black to her. "If we're not under arrest," she said in a quiet voice, leaning into their window. "If his house is no longer an active crime scene," she added. "If I'm risking my life to aid an investigation that you gentlemen desperately want to see wrapped up nice and neatly . . . I'd like to go to my uncle's home to check on that poor old man's property to be sure it's all right, and all his belongings are still there. After all we've been through, is that too much to ask?"

Sure that the house was sound-wired, Laura crossed the threshold once agents had gone through to clear it. But they didn't have to tell either of them twice to stay away from the windows.

Everything in Akhan's North Philadelphia row home had been riffled through, pored over, examined, and violated by external hands and eyes—the long arm of justice, seeking his assailant, but victimizing his privacy in the process.

All his papers, clothing, food boxes in the metal kitchen cabinets and pantry, items on the tiny linoleum kitchen table, his dining room breakfront . . . posters and pictures had been moved about, and she had to use her old memories of where he'd always placed things to find Malcolm, who was cast on the floor.

She didn't need to go upstairs, just seeing the upheaval on the first floor. Floral sofa cushions had been overturned, chairs pulled away from the wall. Her uncle's worst nightmare had come true; *the man* had come into his fortress with impunity. She could only imagine the sense of utter violation a proud and very private man like her uncle Akhan would feel, or the roiling emotions that would sweep through her once she opened her own front door. Homeland security, kiss her ass. This was a police state, a nation under siege. The Patriot Act was a fucking joke that wasn't funny—conspiracy theory manifest in a political manifesto.

The worst part of it all was egress had been taken by force within her Philadelphia and Cayman island oases. No home was left sacrosanct. That was unforgivable. But she focused on the task at hand, namely, finding the key so she could overstand it all.

James shadowed her as she made quick work of righting pillows for the observant eyes outside the house, calmly body-blocking her as though he were her human shield . . . but it served a dual purpose of blocking their view as she made her way to what had been Malcolm's wall.

Clearly, they'd been looking for a wall safe behind the tossed pictures. Laura glanced up. Overstand . . . She walked up the steps and looked at the badly cracked crown molding along the edge of the living room ceiling that was too thin to slide a key between. She walked back down the stairs in frustration, then glanced up at the central ceiling light, then to the floor. The small poster light that had been affixed to the edge of the ebony framed poster by double-back sticky squares had never worked, to her recall. It lay on the floor, yanked down from its sticky back placement. A small brass thing with batteries in it. She went to the poster, James blocking her from window view, and quickly opened the back of the light unit. A small silver key slid into her palm, which she immediately shoved into her pocket.

"There's nothing for me to do here," she said loudly with disgust, "but to call a cleaning and restoration service." Laura shook her head and strode out the front door. "Nice work, gentlemen," she said with attitude, and jumped into the passenger's side of her Jag.

James was in the driver's seat in a flash. "You wanna go home now, *honey?*"

She shook her head no. "Sure, *sweetheart*. But first I need to stop at one of those cell phone/beeper stores . . . I think there's one up on Cecil B. Moore Avenue. In all the drama, I lost my cell phone charger. I can at least plug it into the lighter and maybe see if I can call family to be sure everyone is all right."

"Sure, honey," James said, pulling off from the curb. "Anything you want."

Chapter 19

They entered the electronics store and watched the agents lean against their head rests in exasperation. There was nothing like a woman to drive a man insane, and if they wanted to play games, she could play all day, driving them in errant circles. She knew what she wanted, a way to get the key to Rick, and it was simple.

With James as her shield to the window, she picked up an inexpensive prepaid phone and charger.

"I want to buy this stuff," she said, calmly producing cold cash. "But I want to be sure it works before I give it to my friend."

"Do what you want, sis, but once you break the seal on the box, you bought it." The young clerk dismissed her with a glance.

"OK," she said, and passed him the payment, then hurriedly opened the box, entered the prepay code and dialed Rick, half shielded by James and a rack. Laura discreetly slid the key into the box and waited for Rick to pick up. "Listen to me," she said quickly under her breath. "There's a locker with papers in it downtown at the Greyhound Station. One-ten. This will put topspin on your Pulitzer. I'm going to give you the location of a phone store. Pick up a phone I just bought for you, and find the key in it. Get the papers, then call me once on my cell, one ring, hang up, and meet me at Kinko's on Spring Garden. Got it?"

"Yeah," Rick said, sounding out of breath. "What the hell—"

"When you go to Kinko's, you make me a good copy of whatever you find. Use self service and accidentally leave it on the copier. You don't know me or James when you see us. We'll pass each other like strangers. I'll pick the papers up. You keep going with the originals. Scan them, send them to a safe source in the media, put them in a vault, lock box, wherever. Do not screw this up, Rick. I'm not sure what's in them, but this probably goes all the way to Washington—Deep Throat action. OK? Ditch the phone after you call me once."

"Done," Rick unnecessarily whispered.

Laura hung up and called the bored, young male clerk over to assist her again. "It works. OK. Can I leave it here for my friend, though, in a bag that says paid? He's all slow, I can't take it to him right now, but he said he'll come get it in an hour."

"This ain't no layaway joint, and I can't be responsible if the phone walks," the young man protested.

She discreetly passed him a twenty. "He'll be here in an hour, okaaaay. Can't you just put it in a bag under the register with a note that says 'paid,' and when he comes, just hand it to him—if you ain't too busy?"

"Aw'ight, aw'ight," the clerk grumbled. "What's his name?"

"I'm hungry," Laura announced, once they got back into the Jag.

"What do you feel like?" James said, issuing her a lopsided grin.

"A deli sandwich. There's a great diner right down on Spring Garden, not far from my house. Around Eighteenth or Nineteenth, I think? You know . . . right next to that Kinko's and the video store."

"You gentlemen want a sandwich?" James asked the agents in the car with a wide grin as he passed them. He let Laura go ahead of him and hung back as they wiped their palms down their faces in frustration.

"How do you deal with this all day everyday?" one agent said, shaking his head.

James shrugged and chuckled. "Guess I'm just used to her ways by now."

"Oh, James, sweetheart, can you get my phone out of my purse in case family calls? It's in the trunk," she yelled over her shoulder and then went into the deli.

"Sure, honey." James glanced over his shoulder, trying not to laugh. "I'll bring you guys a corned beef on rye."

He watched her pick at her food, stalling, every so often glancing down at her phone.

"Midday traffic is thick," he murmured and then noisily sipped his soda through a straw. Before she spoke, he motioned to the phone, giving her the nod to put it in a hip pocket and keep her voice extremely low, given the unit might have also been tampered with and turned into a bugging device.

"He works on *North Broad Street* at the newspaper," she hissed. "It shouldn't have taken that long to get uptown, pick up the key . . . if that little knucklehead in the store tried to steal the phone—"

"Relax. It's not the uptown drive; it's fighting Center City traffic close to midday. Then circling back up this way to Spring Garden."

Laura dropped her head into her hands and sighed. "I don't even know what's in that locker."

"Never stopped you before, has it."

She peered up at James and smiled. "I'm getting too old for this mess, sweetheart."

She became still as her phone vibrated in her pocket. Laura casually pulled it out, flipped it open, then closed her eyes as she slid it away again. Wrapping up the remains of her turkey club, she ditched it, and walked out the store toward the Jag with James on her heels, and then quickly spun. "Oh, shit. I need boxes for all that mess at my uncle's. Let me just run next door to Kinko's and pick up some for the trunk. OK, sweetheart?"

James let out a loud, theatrical sigh. "Oh, for crying out loud, honey, c'mon!"

She blew him a kiss, passed Rick like a stranger, and heard him say three. Cool. Self-service machine three. Peeping over her shoulder, she saw James engaging the agents, keeping them briefly distracted, long enough for her to pick up the copies that had been on the machine and slip them under her shirt. The bulge was enormous. Shit, she should have kept the sweat top. But she was too close to her goal of knowing to give up. Rather than do that, she wrapped her arms around her waist and leaned against the desk.

"Hi. Got any boxes?"

"Yeah. What size?"

"Oh, I don't know. What's the biggest you've got?"

The clerk rolled his eyes. "Wanna see?"

"If it's not too much trouble."

He pulled out an assortment, brandishing them for her to choose from. Laura pointed at three sizes, paid the clerk quickly, and pressed them to her belly to cover the papers.

"All set," she said.

James gave her a curious look. "You wanna put those in the trunk?"

Her eyes widened. "No! And crush my good suit? Are you crazy? We're just around the corner, sweetheart. Besides, I want to get in the house, make a cup of tea, chill out, catch up on some reading, sort the mail . . . look over old paperwork to see if there's anything that can help us that I might have left in the house."

"I understand," James said with a yawn. "Not that my nerves would allow it, but I for one could use a good nap."

When they pulled into her block, evidence of police incursion was clear. A white florist's van was parked half a block down the street. Her front door opened and a suited agent gave the

thumbs up, and then glanced at the rooftops, talking into the
wire in his ear. The neighbor's white poodle was barking furiously, and Laura wondered if the poor animal had been freaked
out all day.

James got out of the vehicle, rounded it to get their clothes out
of the trunk, and then traded her the bag to press against her
stomach for the boxes she'd been clutching.

"Why don't you go upstairs and drop that bag of clothes and
I'll bring you some tea up to your office while you go through
whatever docs you have in the house?"

"Thanks, James," she said, kissing him softly, and then went
into the house.

The trick was going to be getting past all the FBI agents crawl-
ing all over her house, picking up a file from her hallway secretary along the way, and then going to the bedroom to set down
the bag—while simultaneously, accidentally on purpose, dropping the old file and new papers in a heap at her feet. Not knowing where hidden cameras were posed a problem, so she had to
do a sleight of hand without being sure which way her audience
was facing or where any blind spots were in the room.

Yes, she knew that this was all a part of her and James's so-
called protection. Yes, she'd maneuvered the feds into allowing
her and James to be a part of the sting. Yes, she'd wanted to bait
the hit man to her, and had wanted to smoke out who'd ordered
the trigger man on so many people. Yes, she knew that all of this
was a necessary evil . . . but she didn't trust them, didn't want
them in her house, and had no way of ever being sure every bug
was gone, once this thing was put to rest.

Laura feigned tripping on the edge of her plush teal and ivory
Oriental carpet as she entered the bedroom, spilling the contents of the folder and bag she carried, along with the papers
from beneath her shirt. Quickly standing, she muttered a curse,
gathered the papers in one communal pile, and strode to her office down the hall, blotting nervous perspiration from her forehead with the back of her wrist.

She could do this, she could do this . . . had to do this and do it smooth. She sat down in the butter-soft, high-back leather chair that she'd abandoned for more than a year, and closed her eyes for a moment to steady herself against the wonderful, familiar sensation. She glimpsed out the window, noting the greenness of the trees and how beautiful the view of the Art Museum was at any time of the year.

The first thing she sorted out in the top page of Akhan's documents was a letter addressed to her.

> *Dear Laura,*
>
> *I trust that if you have this letter, then something has gone terribly awry. Haines and I go way back, as you know. There was a level of trust between us that cannot be defined on paper. Suffice to say that he and I silently partnered on helping people get mortgages during a time when banks weren't lending to us, especially in regions down South. It was his good show of faith and my good fortune, now yours to manage. X always marks the spot. I love you. Be well and be gentle with yourself and our people. Follow the Xavier Mortgage Company memos and juxtapose that to all you heard as a child. Remember, follow the money . . . always.*

Laura tried to calmly turn the pages of the one will she'd never fully seen, Akhan's. The addendum she was holding in her hands nearly drew an audible gasp.

She knew all about her uncle and Haines's early business; on the surface, he was Haines's manservant. A layer below that, he was an enforcer. That had all quietly come out in the wash and had been viscerally understood between them when Haines had been murdered by his own wife's lover. Yet, until now, Laura had to admit that she never quite understood the unlikely relationship between Akhan and Haines, or how they came to be so inextricably linked. Now she did as she read on.

Old family whispers and partial oral histories made a memory quilt told in grown-folks-business hushed tones over dozing children's heads . . . but every shut eye ain't asleep. Laura read the will, read between the lines, remembered the murmurs and rethreaded old mental needles, stitching until she put the entire patchwork together to follow the drinking gourd. None of that subtext was on paper; all of it was stored in painful cellular memory. The ancestors wept. Nothing in print would incriminate her uncle or the dearly departed, but, oh . . . did the snippits that were written all make so much sense.

Laura made a neat tent with her fingers before her mouth, tears rising as her eyes sought to escape through the window and inner vision.

Her uncle Akhan had been on the run from the South, having quietly righted the unspeakable wrong against her mother's dignity, his niece. A rape avenged . . . first by her mother's father, who went forth with hope to a young, Main-Line-bred, Northern attorney just out of law school, Haines . . . who was too overconfident and too eager to make a name for himself by lobbying the system via demanding justice from the law of Jim Crow.

But that young attorney, Haines, couldn't fathom the way of the world, then, and was bitterly aggrieved to learn that his client's father had paid for his naiveté and lack of experience in unspoken Southern politics by hanging at the end of a rope slung over the branch of a tree . . . for overspeaking and overstanding what he nor a black father could never understand or countenance, overstepping their bounds during a time when everyone was forced to stay within the narrow highway divide of white lines.

An unpardonable debt was levied; a rapist caught and lynched in eye-for-an-eye justice; the silent case was brought to the court of unspoken back wood appeals. A brother on a mission found that good ole boy from North Carolina, who wound up riding in a car trunk across many state lines, then wound up fed to gators in the Bayou, perhaps Lake Ponchatraine, Mississippi burning, sweet home Alabama, amid Louisiana Creole gumbo jazz. It was all in there, the history.

Uncle Xavier Hewitt, a.k.a. Uncle Akhan, her grandfather's younger brother, her mother's dearest hero uncle-turned-Northern-state-street-warrior by way of Philadelphia, ultimately becoming Donald Haines, Senior's living ghost of injustice, dealt a blow— haunting him with his own spiritual deflowering, stealing the young attorney's mental virginity, when Haines could no longer believe in the system he'd spent his life worshipping.

It was implicit in the will before her. The knowledge that justice wasn't always just bound two unlikely strangers . . . creating a slowly rising bile within them to play the roles defined by polite society, but to also always attempt to beat the system by any means necessary . . . and the strange alliance left them both laughing that they'd bested the Southern confederacy in white-face masks; Haines laughing the loudest by always helping a friend that he owed for not knowing what he should have been aware of while younger.

Now she understood.

An offshore mortgage company set up in the Grand Cayman's, before it was fashionable. No wonder the Russians knew where to look for her, digging for answers. Xavier Mortgage, funded by the one-two punch of Haines's white privilege and Xavier Hewitt's black power. Mortgages to disenfranchised people down in the French Quarter, the Ninth Ward, along the Gulf, Biloxi, Slidell, Port Arthur, Gullah country Geechie Islands, plus cheap land in Jamaica before tourism caught on . . . triple digit millions—it was too much land to eminently domain in the wide public eye, and much more land than anyone ever expected black hands to ever hold.

If people defaulted on their mortgages, Xavier Mortgage, a privately held concern, owned the properties and lots. But knowing Akhan, he'd never call in the markers, even if the insurance companies found a way to slide out of rebuilding people's homes in good faith. The insurance companies could renege all they wanted. He'd still own a good chunk of a port city that brought in one-fifth of the nation's crude oil, as well as twenty-percent of America's goods and services into the belly of the beast.

If Akhan offered amnesty like he would, he'd set a glaring example for other lenders, causing riot, and the poorest folks in the region could still have their land; while wealthier folks would be held hostage by their angry, bigger banks. Poetic justice. No wonder the feds were worried and wanted to find this critical document that allowed so much to hang in the balance. Akhan's brother, her grandfather, had been lynched years ago, but he was in an inarguable position to financially lynch a fair section of Dixie land.

Her uncle had said that X marked the spot. Xavier marked a very big spot in a place that was supposed to be washed away. Laura closed her eyes. They knew the levees were gonna break decades before they de-funded infrastructure building projects. They knew a category-three hurricane was coming and was only a matter of time.

Legislation maneuvers tracked like the pending level-five storm—relentless, unstoppable, and unforgiving. Bankruptcy laws had been amended at a time when the financial levees around small businesses and homeowners were crumbling, making it easier for banks to foreclose and snatch land. Mercenaries were keeping the peace—contractors in arms. The rebuilding was too sweet to leave to old local Italian families; this was an international Mardis Gras, so the Russians had been invited into the party.

Two old freedom fighters were in the mix, one dead and probably laughing his Main Line ass off, the other smiling contently in the U.S. Embassy in Jamaica, knowing that the third party on the company docs was already dead—Lillian Braithwaite, Brother B's sister, not wife. The woman in the pictures, gorgeous, smiling, with babies all around her . . . Akhan's second family, his home away from home in the Caribbean.

Oval-framed, yellow-edged photos from home abroad blazed a white poker of awareness into Laura's skull as she read. And all of the weight of Xavier Mortgage was left in the nimble control of his very educated, very shrew, financially deadly grand niece—her.

Yes, things had come full circle, now it made so much sense why Haines had always shielded her under his wing, and why her uncle insisted that she learn business and politics to the bone. She also now thoroughly understood why she had a target on her forehead.

She laughed and closed her eyes, allowing tears to stream down her cheeks in release. Back in the day, old Alan Moyer, while still friends with Haines, had even drawn up Akhan's will pro bono. It was so outrageous it was absurd. The fox guarding the hen house, but the chickens almost pecked the fox to death when they came home to roost. Had her uncle predeceased Donald Haines, she and Haines would have been business partners. In Haines's last, controversial will change, rather than have his portion go to his estate to be squabbled over by Elizabeth and his son, he'd remanded his interest in Xavier to any living members of the partnership? Deep.

Laura reread the documents, incredulous. Akhan had left his entire portfolio of Xavier in her hands, should he die, and gave her current power of attorney over the section that Donald had willed back to him, trusting that she'd know what to do with it.

But had Akhan's long-time common-law wife survived severe diabetes, she could have amended the partnership agreement so that her children in the islands would have inherited not only her small house in Kingston and the land Brother B claimed by family eminent domain, but half of the Gulf region, to be shared with Najira and Jamal upon the last surviving partner's demise.

The will was iron-clad. No surviving heirs could manage or run Xavier except the three original partners . . . the loophole was the section that Donald Haines, Sr., had ceded to Akhan and had given his sign-off on, while in his clear and present mind that, Laura could stand in his stead. Wild.

Laura's hands trembled as she flipped through the pages of dense legalese. That's what nearly put a bullet in both her and her uncle's skulls. That's what had legislators scrambling for defensive postures, in case word of this got out and unhinged all their side deals. That's what had developers protecting their turfs. This was all supposed to be an easy, clean sweep to get poor folks out of the way after the big storm so the fat cats could come back in, rebuild bigger and better, and re-gentrify without anything or anyone getting in the way of their redevelopment plans.

True, they'd been pissed off about the lost lands in urban Philly empowerment zones . . . but what they stood to lose control of in the French Quarter was the real showstopper. They'd literally pulled out the big guns. And yet, if it hadn't been for an act of God, pure mother nature rising up and blowing hard . . . all of this would have been moot. Business as usual would have gone on in the Bayou.

But the only one who knew for sure just how bad the situation was, also just so happened to be the man who'd drafted the will—Alan Moyer. He knew what was at stake, had a personal grudge about his son being imprisoned, which she'd personally confirmed. He had the contacts, the money, and Elizabeth Haines was just a pawn. Moreover, he wanted everything ceded away by Haines given back, worse than any of the others. It went beyond money; this was a power thing going on. It was in Moyer's eyes, and the moves she'd been tracking. Now the trick was going to be how to pin it on the rat bastard. She couldn't get them all, but she had to at least get the main one who'd probably sanctioned the hits.

"You want some tea?" James asked quietly, stepping into her office.

Startled, Laura placed her hand over her heart and stopped breathing for a moment. She looked up at him, too awed and overwhelmed to immediately speak. Finally, she nodded. "Sure, sweetheart. Thanks."

Chapter 20

Alan Moyer approached the condominium complex walkway, seething. How *dare* that spoiled, high-society whore bail on him. He straightened his crimson and navy rep tie, then brushed dandruff from the shoulders of his charcoal, Brooks Brothers suit as he entered the glass-enclosed lobby and waited for the doorman to call up to Elizabeth Haines's unit.

"Sir, you may go up. Mrs. Haines has opened the elevator from her side with the key, just press her floor. Have a nice visit," the doorman said calmly, and ushered Moyer with a mannerly wave toward the exclusive banks of elevators that opened directly into unit foyers.

Moyer stared at the numbers as they climbed, feeling his blood pressure spike ever higher with rage as he kept his line of vision trained on the moving lights. When he strode off the elevator, Elizabeth took one glance at his expression and gasped, and then stepped back from him.

"Alan, I don't want to fight or argue," she said, clasping and unclasping her pearls as she walked away from him.

"We are not going to fight," he said between his teeth, measuring his tone. "But we *are* going to have a conversation that will stop this bullshit once and for all."

"Must you be so vulgar?"

He just stared at her for a moment to stabilize his emotions. If she knew how hard it was for men like him to climb out of the gutter, to earn true respect, to shed the disgrace he'd grown up with as an immigrant to impoverished parents . . . she had no concept within her privileged, snide, self-possessed little world.

She smoothed her hands over her taupe-hued cardigan and he watched her go to the living room bar. "I wish you wouldn't have come, if you're going to be unpleasant."

He watched her take a painfully long time fixing herself a martini and then splashing Scotch on the rocks for him. Still as beautiful and as stupid as ever, he thought, appraising the way her taupe and herringbone tweed pants clung to her exquisite figure. Why she had chosen an idiot like Sutherland to be unfaithful with was still an enigma to him.

She pushed a short wisp of silky blond hair behind her ear and handed him a drink as a semi-contrite peace offering. He liked her hair better long, and wanted to throw the drink in her face, but sipped it instead. Unpleasant . . . she didn't know the half of what he could be.

"Under any circumstances, Liz, I deserved more than an e-mail telling me you've decided to decline taking the position as executive director of Micholi." He watched her move to the window and lean against it, coolly sipping her drink. "I have spent the *entire* day in damage control meetings. Now this?"

"To parrot your phraseology, *under the circumstances*, Alan, can you blame me? What did you expect?"

"Loyalty," he said, glaring at her and taking a deep swig of Scotch. "Let's start there. Let's go back to—"

"Oh, let's *not* go back to the beginning and the good old days. It's boring," she snapped, sloshing her drink. "Donald is dead. I served my sentence living with him for years."

"And I did my sentence with you both, always making sure you could plot against him without notice, and kept all your dirty little secrets, including the affair with Sutherland. Am I wrong?"

"For that, I thank you," she said, raising her martini glass to him from across the room.

"Elizabeth, we're in a very delicate transitional period. Right now—"

"People have died," she said, her tone becoming shrill. "Scott, his boy, and then Polanski, Devereaux, and *his wife*. Are you mad, Alan? I don't want to be a party to anyone's death. I don't wish to be associated—"

"You were a party to your own husband's death," he said evenly, swirling his drink around so the ice could further chill it. "You wished that, and Sutherland made it so. I think we're splitting hairs on morality and involvement."

She began to walk in a tight circle, sloshing her drink as she spoke and gesturing wildly. "But look at all the people who've died. For what? Money? Now George has gone missing for days, along with his wife and children." She stopped her frenetic circling and stared at Alan hard. "What if that man is in the bottom of a river somewhere with his family?" she whispered, her eyes wide with terror. "I don't understand why Micholi even had to be involved with these, these Russian mobsters—scum of the earth!"

"Are you finished?" he asked calmly and set down his drink on the heavy, antique teakwood and jade coffee table before him. "Need I remind you that two hundred *billion* dollars have gone into the restoration of the Gulf alone? That's a developer's wet dream. Our friends in the overseas construction trades, who, by the way, get us into every conceivable foreign job as sub-contractors that they can wrangle . . . so that we don't have to directly negotiate with tense governments in lands that have been torn apart down to the foundation by war or get into slow, bogged-down politics to win a bid offer distinct advantages. We are their friends, they get the prime contracts and we get to redevelop, design buildings, and put the planet back together one country at a time. All they asked for was the written-off sections of the cities we have influence in. Delivering on Philadelphia was becoming difficult, and they asked for—"

"I don't care what they asked for, or what they didn't get," Elizabeth said, placing the heel of her palm to her forehead and closing her eyes. "I don't want to know any more of this, Alan. I want to stay as far removed from that sordid business as possible."

"But you are already in it," he said, his voice escalating as he paced toward her and then stopped himself from crossing the room.

"No. I won't be involved any longer. It was bad enough that I accepted messages from my ex-lover via strange and creepy individuals calling from, of all places, a penitentiary." She walked closer to him, set her martini glass down on the table, and folded her arms to glare at him. "Me. Elizabeth Haines. Taking calls from a prison? Then, I accepted calls from your son, after what he did to my Donny . . . do you know what he did to him?"

"We both know what the two of them did together, and it drove Donald out of his mind. However—"

"Don't make light of this, and don't patronize me. Just like you were willing to do everything for your son, I'm willing to do everything for mine. And the best thing I can think to do before this, this, virus of activity spreads to my good name and hurts Donny Jr. in any way is to divest my affiliation with everyone involved."

"Too late, Liz. You already took the money, already benefited by positioning, and—"

"What?"

He held up his hand and pulled his vibrating cell phone off his belt. "Moyer here." He looked at her with a threat to remain silent. She narrowed her gaze, but complied.

"Alanir Moyirveschi. Long time. Family should stay in close contact during difficult times, no?"

Alan Moyer cringed, feeling his face flash hot as a shiver ran down his spine upon hearing his birth name. "Long time," he said quietly.

"I am concerned. Things I'm hearing are troubling to me. One family turned on another to gain your favor, and thus, a good man, Vladimir Chertoff, was lost. Then another good man was lost during a job for you in the Cayman Islands, because he got incorrect information from your people. Another good man is now in police custody."

"That wasn't my fault," Moyer shot back defensively.

"No, but it is getting gravely expensive to continue to keep all these men on the job, for something as minor as a small section of ghetto rebuilding in Philadelphia, and supposedly the poorer sections of New Orleans—which we are also hearing you do not control as we had supposed. Nasty rumor, I'm sure, but troubling, nonetheless. We thought we were talking about multimillion-dollar contracts for those two sites alone. But I am hearing things, Alanir. Bad things."

"Nasty rumors," Moyer said, picking up his drink with a trembling hand.

"See, this is what I told the families when we conferred. Things can easily get out of hand. Men should talk, share vodka, and then come away with an accord, no?"

"That is always best, to dispel rumors, and let cool heads prevail," Alan said nervously.

"See . . . even without vodka, we have agreement." There was a pause and a long breath before the caller spoke again. "We are realists, Alanir. We know that we cannot compete for contracts in the areas where there will be more rigorous enforcement, like our Italian comrades have mastered. We leave those jobs to them. It isn't cost effective for us to build to complete perfect specifications. So, a slip here, a slip there, keeps our operations profitable. Building codes in other countries that aren't quite up to speed yet accept these realities. Sometimes buildings collapse, sometimes they lean, but they get built. Everyone is happy. But the U.S. contracts pay the best . . . urban areas, otherwise known as your ghettos, do not enforce as heavily, and thus, we are again happy. Therefore, I must say that we are disappointed if these nasty lies and rumors are true."

"There is no need for disappointment," Moyer said, knocking back his drink and swallowing it with a wince. He set his glass down hard on the table and avoided Elizabeth's prying eyes.

"Correct this problem, is good advice from me, a good friend to you—who has always been a very good friend to me." Another long pause raised the hair on Moyer's neck.

"We'll handle it," Moyer assured him.

"But you see, somehow, the Italians took offense. This adds to our problem. They dispensed with one of your friends, a Doctor Sutherland. Then, as a good show of faith that we were not involved, the first family who had experienced the loss of Vladimir, explained by example that Polanski and Devereaux were sacrificial lambs. Those two should never have ordered a contractor to be removed from the job without a complete discussion first. As the one who is in charge, as the foreman, I bring this complaint to you. Therefore, we have an imbalance. Four men, plus one who may become nervous in custody, so we will have to address him—call it five. Oh, yes, and we began by showing our seriousness with our contract by taking care of a senator and his wayward son, both who had reneged on that which was due you."

Moyer swallowed hard but couldn't speak. Sudden terror thickened his tongue.

A long sigh ensued before the caller spoke again. "You see, friend, the difficulty is that, this job, like many construction jobs that are ill planned and ill budgeted, just keeps growing with no end in sight, and we are trying to accommodate you, our client. But we were initially only contracted to remove two problems, a man and a woman, for specific remuneration. Now even that is in question. Troubling. We have cancelled the contract on them as a family, because things have become too exposed and too public. No more jobs like that, until our imbalance is satisfied."

"*Why* do you keep saying that your forthcoming contract is in question?" Moyer's gaze tore around Elizabeth's condo for answers, her horrified gaze adding to his growing terror.

"Do you not watch the news?"

"The news?"

"Put on your television. It is past four o'clock. Then you can call me back and explain our arrangement to me more clearly."

The cell phone call went dead. Without looking at Elizabeth, Alan Moyer dashed to the flat-screen unit in her living room and began fumbling with the remote. "Put on the fucking television—how do you work this?"

"What happened?" she whispered, as though her voice was lodged in her throat.

"Put it on!" He yelled, throwing the remote at her.

She sidestepped the hurled electronic device that landed on the sofa and quickly punched the right button with a French-manicured nail. They both stood side by side, horrified, eyes wide. He turned to her and grabbed her by both arms.

"You, George, and I are all that's left in the inner circle! Don't you bail on me, Liz. You stay the course and this will blow over."

"I don't need any more money. Donald left me enough to get by, he left me well off—"

"He didn't leave *us* well off, didn't leave *us* enough, you selfish bitch!" Moyer shouted, his face contorted as he shook Elizabeth hard, yanking her back and forth as he stared up at her blinded by fury.

"Dear God, Alan, let go of me! I'm not involved in this any longer, I swear I won't—"

Before she could finish her sentence, he shoved her hard and she lost her balance, falling backward into the coffee table. A loud crack rent the room, and she rolled over into a crumpled heap on the floor.

"Oh, my God, Elizabeth," he whispered, staring at her glassy, dead blue eyes and the bloodied dent at her temple where the coffee table caught it.

Panicked, he rushed away from her body, and began pressing on the elevator call button like a madman. When the conveyance finally arrived, he dashed in, hit the lobby button and repeatedly pushed the CLOSE DOOR button, then ran deeper into the elevator, hid his face against the wall, and wept.

"Got it all on tape," one agent said, glancing at his colleague. "Think we shoulda gone up there?"

"Happened so fast, nobody can blame us. She would have been dead by the time we got to the lobby."

The first agent nodded. "Think they've got the cell-phone transmission to Moyer's phone?"

"Yep," the second agent said, pulling off his monitoring headset. "Good thing Townsend gave us the numbers. This might buy the poor bastard a little leniency."

"Either that or give him more shit to dig out from under. Man, this is convoluted!"

She'd been lying on the small loveseat in her office after letting James read the will for himself. Her eyes had begged him to let her explain later, and his told her that later would be a much better time than now. With him sitting beside her, the most natural thing for her sleep-deprived body to do was to slide against him as her lids slowly lowered on their own accord. There was so much to think about, to position, to get a handle on. But sudden yelling through the house, footfalls, and all-out panic put her and James both on their feet.

"Oh, shit, turn on the news, folks! We've got a media leak that's gonna blow this case to hell!"

Laura dashed down the hall behind James, who took the stairs down to the living room in double time.

Every agent and officer in the house stood with Laura and James, hang-jawed, as the television blared.

"Just in. Breaking News," the news anchor said. "Rick, tell us how you uncovered this groundbreaking evidence?"

Laura covered her mouth with both hands.

"I have State Department documents from undisclosed sources that clearly show the conflict of interest that Micholi Foundation had with regards to large land development contracts here in Philadelphia, and throughout the nation. Their General Counsel, Alan Moyer, Senior, seems to be the lynchpin in this entire travesty, as his dealings include several blind trusts and private investments in firms tied to the late Senator Scott, his son, Howard

Scott, Jr., and more recently, Michael Polanski, the slain executive director of Micholi Foundation, as well as the recently murdered James Devereaux, once treasurer of that ill-fated foundation.

"Moyer, born Alanir Moyirveschi, had access to know about a will that linked the late Donald Haines, Sr., to Xavier Mortgage, which is the only lender in the nation providing loan amnesty to victims of the Gulf. A philanthropist, extraordinaire, if I do say so, Connie." Rick beamed at the camera and then shook his head. "However, the most bizarre twist in this tale of extortion, corruption, and scandal is the link between the deaths of Senator Scott, his son, and key Micholi Foundation execs, and of all groups, the Russian mob—all over plush development contracts promised but not delivered against, for the redevelopment of targeted prime real estate. Now live from the Cayman Islands with the far-reaching, international aspect of this story, is Byron."

Laura and James looked at each other, but the badges and shields in the room sat forward or leaned in to hang on every word. Rick had gone from print to screen in a few hours? Whoa . . .

The foreign correspondent put the microphone in Detective Hayward's face. "Tell us in your own words, sir, how the good police work on Grand Cayman led to a break in the investigation, and how you now have an alleged Russian mob hit man in your custody giving a statement."

"Son of a bitch!" the lead FBI agent said, jettisoning himself up from Laura's sofa.

"Can you believe this shit?" Captain Bennett shouted.

The other agents hung their heads.

"It's now gonna become a political football as to who nailed the case, did the assist," James muttered.

"Damn!" the agent hollered again, beginning to pace. He pointed at the television. "D.C., Baltimore cops in this shit. Jamaican police linking it to a bombing of a house and the U.S. Embassy took in Americans behind the shit? That's now Interpol's province. We, gentlemen, are screwed."

"New legislation is being considered now, in light of this tragic series of events," a reporter said. "Now back to you in Philadelphia, Connie."

Right on cue the next reporter began culling her street team for reaction from politicians. Every politician that spoke took their fifteen seconds of photo-op to grandstand, reverse anything they'd said before—using the incident as a catalyst for their so-called new awareness, and said how they thought it was best that victims of Hurricane Katrina get amnesty from mortgage payments for at least a year. Even some who'd proposed the tightening of bankruptcy laws now made sweeping statements about easing bankruptcy legislation for those affected by disasters.

"What!" the FBI agent said, turning away from the droning television to speak into his cell phone. "Elizabeth Haines? When, for chrissakes? She's a material witness. Tell me she ain't dead. You sure? The coroner—oh fuck him, what does he know about a DOA?" The agent flung his phone down on the dining room table, raked his hair with his fingers and walked into the kitchen to cool down. Nervous glances passed around the room.

Laura and James's eyes locked as they mouthed a collective, "Oh, shit . . ."

"Lady, and gentlemen, we're outta here," the lead FBI agent announced to his team. "Stay close," he said to Laura and James as he collected his cell phone and strode back into the living room. "We'll need you for court at some point," he added in a weary tone. "All right everybody, show's over. Pack up your gear, sweep the house clean of any listening devices, and head downtown."

"Always interesting when you two are involved," Captain Bennett said on his way out the door with a sly wink. He shook James's hand. "Take care of yourself, Carter—as well as that pretty lady."

Laura stood still for a moment. Elizabeth Haines was dead? Laura quickly shook herself out of the stunned daze and kissed Bennett on the cheek, then mouthed the words *thank you*. He smiled wide and mouthed back the words, *thank you*.

"So, that's it?" Incredulous, James paced across the room behind Bennett. "What about the trigger man? We've still got the Russians on our asses, and haven't—"

"They're gonna pick up Moyer, now," one of the feds said. "Seems he pushed Liz Haines into a coffee table in a fit of rage during an argument. Homicide agents and our boys caught it on tape."

"What?" Laura gaped, her gaze going between the officers moving throughout her home, James, and Bennett. "He brutalized that woman in her own home? Alan Moyer? You have got to be kidding me."

"She was in it," another agent said, passing her with a large metal briefcase of equipment. "She was the courier pigeon for the messages coming in and out of the state pen from both Sutherland and Alan Jr. Crazy . . . all that money, and all of 'em still scrambling for more."

"Yo, Cap, I'm talking about police protection until all the loose ends are tied up," James hollered behind Bennett's retreating form.

Captain Bennett stopped and smiled. "You want us to stay and babysit you, we can. But you can probably move through the Caribbean as celebrities, now that you've put a feather in several local forces' caps. Bet it's already on the BBC."

"No, that's all right," Laura said, just glad the law enforcement home invasion was temporarily leaving. "You guys have a nice evening and a great life—bye!"

She walked over to the large bay window and leaned against the sill, watching the tide of varying law enforcement authorities recede. Her once quiet, serene, sand-hued home with gleaming, pristine oak hardwood floors and art seemed soiled from the multiple violations. She wanted to move, rebuild her life in a place that no longer had residue from any of this. Her home was going up for sale tomorrow. Time for new environs for both she and James, but where and in what corner of the globe could one escape the knowing, even if one moved?

Still, relief, sadness, joy, anger, outrage, fatigue, all of the competing emotions swirled through her at once, making her drop her head and say a little prayer. She was blessed, James was blessed, and her family had been blessed. Everything had indeed come full circle. She could only hope that, now that the main individuals involved were about to be arrested, charged, and indicted, the bounty that had been on her and Akhan's head would be lifted.

It was time to talk to Akhan. They had to decide what to do with Xavier and set up an ironclad will structure to keep something like this from ever happening again. She needed to set up something whereby, if they died from unnatural causes, it would go to legit, community-rebuilding efforts—like Habitat for Humanity . . . she wasn't even sure any longer.

She looked up and was transfixed at her window just as a big, blue BMW sedan careened into the street. Officers immediately scrambled and took defensive positions, shouting. A short, fat, elderly, wild-eyed man jumped out of the car wielding a revolver, screamed her name once, and pulled the trigger. Moyer. The window shattered in slow motion before she could scream. A bullet seared her skin and lodged in her chest. Pain. She heard James yelling her name, could taste blood in her mouth—couldn't breathe, felt herself going down as she heard gunfire report. Commotion, running, words, "Assailant down. We got him!" rang in her ears in the distance. Then everything went black.

"Hey, sleepyhead," a low, melodic voice murmured close to her face.

A warm, rough hand squeezed hers. Then a light brush of the gentlest kiss in the world touched her forehead. Something wet splashed her face in droplets. She opened her eyes to the saddest, most intense brown eyes she'd ever seen a man wear.

"James," she croaked around the tubes.

He pressed his forehead to hers and just wept.

Epilogue

Six months later on the Island of Maui.

"I'm getting a tattoo," Laura announced, looking at the small circle of scarring just above her right breast. She sat up on the chaise lounge and dug her toes in the volcanic, black sand. "My vanity will *not* allow this," she said, scowling and putting sun screen on the tiny raised scar. "Maybe a moon or a star, or *something*." She chuckled. "Yeah, at my age, forty-something, I'm trying something new."

"I like it," James said, leaning over to kiss the place that made her frown. "Every time I see it, it reminds me that you're still alive, it didn't get your heart or an artery, or bone, or a nerve, or your spinal cord . . . so that little prayer you said just before the bullet came through the window musta worked."

He sighed with contentment and then placed a more lingering kiss where the bullet had lodged in her chest and damaged a lung. He took her hand and put it on his thigh. "Besides, it matches mine—but mine got all zigzagged. Ain't as pretty as yours."

She stroked his leg and gave him a sexy pout, then looked down at his thigh and kissed it gently. "I like your scar," she murmured against his sunbaked skin.

"Oh, do you now?" he said, chuckling softly.

"Uhmmm, hmmm . . ." She said, licking up his thigh until she reached the edge of his trunks. "Especially on a private beach."

He laughed harder. "It's only private as long as family doesn't pop by unannounced, as they are wont to do."

"I told Najira that, uh, I'd be spending the day—alone—with my husband. I'm still recovering and have to make up for all that lost time in the hospital."

"Let me see that scar again," he said, flipping the front hook of her bright turquoise bikini top open. "Need to make sure it's properly healed," he said, kissing around the scar and capturing her nipple between his lips.

She pulled in a quiet hiss of air between her teeth as he brought his hand up to fondle her. She closed her eyes and let her head fall back, enjoying the heat of the sun on her face and the heat James was creating within her.

"Wait," she whispered. "Lemme see your scar again." She slid out of her bikini top and moved over to his chair, curling herself between his thighs to blow on his scar before kissing a slow trail up to his groin. "Are you sure some of it doesn't go up here?" she asked, peeking inside his trunks.

"I don't know," he said, laughing, and settling back against the chaise. "I never really looked at it good . . . let me know."

She slid his trunks over his hips. "It's hard to tell, there's so much in the way. Let me get a closer look."

He laughed. She made him stop smiling with her tongue as she shimmied her bikini bottoms down and off her.

In a hard roll he covered her and found her scar again to nuzzle. "I'm glad you're alive."

"I'm glad you are, too," she whispered into his hair and then kissed his temple.

"I love this family we've got . . . and this life, Laura." He kissed her long, and hard, and deep, and moved against her like the slow, thundering tide.

She arched and took his earlobe into her mouth, slowly wrapping her legs around his waist. "I wouldn't have it any other way, James Carter."

The doorbell rang in the distance, and she could hear Najira's car stereo blaring. Laura laughed, popped her head up, and quickly grabbed the towel from her chair to wrap them in it.

"Oh, no!" She giggled and hid her face against his shoulder.

"Did I also tell you how much this family gets on my nerves sometimes, Laura?"

"Yeah, but you know we wouldn't have it any other way."

SHATTERED TRUST

LESLIE ESDAILE BANKS

ABOUT THIS GUIDE

The suggested questions are intended to
enhance your group's reading of
this book.

DISCUSSION QUESTIONS

1. What do you think about the way each character has evolved from their earlier personalities in the beginning of the series (*Betrayal of the Trust* and *Blind Trust*)?

2. What do you think about Najira and Steve's relationship, in context with her father, Brother Akhan?

3. Do you think situations like the Micholi Foundation conflict of interest could actually occur?

4. Do you feel that Laura and James would have been a good match if they'd met each other earlier in life—or do you think it was the mellowing of their personas through experience that makes them better as a more mature couple?

5. Do you like stories with older heroes/heroines, or do you prefer younger couples just starting out their life experiences?

6. Did you like going to different places within the Caribbean, or would you prefer story based in one locale better?

7. What did you think about the legacy left by Donald Haines? (Do you think that it's plausible for a man to feel so much guilt, and then have that grow into respect, that he could befriend a family in the way he did Akhan's?)